Spitting

Distance

Spitting

Distance

Jon Wright

An *Abacus* Book

First published in Great Britain in 1997 by Abacus

A CIP catalogue record for this book is available from the British Library.

ISBN 0 349 10888 9

Typeset in Palatino by M Rules
Printed and bound in Great Britain by
Clays Ltd, St Ives plc

Abacus
A Division of
Little, Brown and Company (UK)
Brettenham House
Lancaster Place
London WC2E 7EN

For the very wonderful
Tracy Ellington

One

If it hadn't been for Pablo Picasso I might have done something with my life. But there I was, William Wrose, dull,
dangerously close to my fortieth birthday and exhibiting all
the classic symptoms of the male menopause. I was
obsessed with finding someone who I could blame for my
life of mediocrity. Anyone would do as long as the finger of
suspicion didn't point at me. I was following the Picasso
line of inquiry while doing the weekly shopping at the
supermarket, an activity I enjoyed for two reasons. The first
was the sense of being a part of the global village, where the
best (and sometimes worst) of the world's produce was laid
out to tantalise your tastebuds and flatter your own sense of
sophistication. The second reason was more primal.

'Evening, sir.' The attractive young woman at the customer service kiosk wore a badge which introduced her as
Khalida and proclaimed that she was happy to serve me. I
returned her smile, unable to stop myself giving it an extra
spin of lust.

'Evening,' I said, looking at her badge and sighing wist-
fully. Supermarket girls in their acrylic uniforms and

corporate colours were one of the few pleasures left in the modern world. They were eternally welcoming and unceasingly friendly, and their whole purpose in life was to ensure that the customer was completely satisfied. They were like geisha girls, only with bigger feet. I wished I could have a couple of them by my side to sort out the difficult bits of my life. Of course that would mean they'd need to be on call twenty-four hours a day. Happy to serve me? How I wished.

The thought of being forty scared me shitless. It forced me to examine every failure and defeat of my life in the unforgiving light of hindsight. It was like seeing an unattractive neighbour's underwear hanging on the washing line, disturbing yet compulsive viewing. Forty. Only men like my dad reached forty. Only men who wore trousers which had an unhealthy percentage of polyester in the weave reached forty. I looked at my clothes and was horrified to see the aurora borealis of man-made fibres in friction shimmering from the cheap grey suit. Jesus, I thought, I look like a headmaster.

When looking for the worst insult I always turned to the teaching profession for inspiration. I remembered my school-days with a mixture of horror and, well, more horror really. It's funny how the past, when viewed from the perspective of middle age, always seemed a warm and cosy place, with the exception of school. Even now, twenty years after the experience had ended, the memories still haunted me. Psychopathic bullies at every turn, looking for any opportunity to violate the weak and vulnerable.

'And that was just the teachers,' I said, music-hall style, to a largely unresponsive audience of dairy products in the chiller cabinet.

I had left school in 1976, an event that still seemed like yesterday, or at least no further away than a week last Wednesday. I had broken free from the shackles of education only to find myself completely unequipped for life. I knew that the sine equalled the opposite over hypotenuse but did not realise that making your way in life equalled sucking up to every slimeball who held any authority over you. I was to find that, in my case, that was quite a lot of people. I never forgave my educators for this lack of knowledge, and paid them back with insults every chance I got. At school I had pushed back the boundaries like any self-respecting adolescent. It was the tail end of the hippie era, where protest was endemic to anyone under twenty-five who could work a badge pin. I had been excluded from school for refusing to get my hair cut, and then for adopting the skinhead look. I wore flares when everyone else was in straights, straights when everyone had got into flares. I made a badge for the breast pocket of my blazer which announced, with some authority, that the Pope smoked dope. My sartorial creativity ensured I was off school more often than on it, which was the general idea.

I showed little aptitude for anything at school, other than art. My drawings, which sometimes looked like their subject but more often looked like mashed potato, were the closest I came to showing potential. I came into contact with literature on art and artists which I pretended to read in order to impress girls and possibly even convince them to have sex with me. The theory was that if they thought I was an intellectual then a relationship with me would seem to offer complete fulfilment of both mind and body. I didn't allow for the fact that I was shallower than the Leeds–Liverpool canal. One book that I did read was a biography of Picasso. The man inspired me, partly because he remained a creative force to a great age, but mostly because he got to shag hundreds of women, lots of them gorgeous nude models. My teenage dreams had nothing to do with passing exams, following a glittering career or great personal achievement; all I wanted was to have sex. Lots of sex if possible, but some sex would do for starters. In this aim young men the world over are destined to fail but they continue to try because teenage man views the world not from an analytical perspective which recognises failure, rejection and humiliation, but from a penis perspective, which sees only opportunity.

But a young man's thoughts can be turned to more noble aspirations even when looking at life from behind a penis. Which is how Picasso indirectly ignited a fire in me. That fire was a desire to create, to be creative, and once lit it could not be doused. I set off to fulfil my destiny. From that moment on I was lost. Ambitions were stirred that could never be achieved and a chain of unhappy events were unleashed that led me to where I was today, shopping in a shiny suit on the way home from my shitty job to my patient wife, screaming child and heart-stopping mortgage repayments. As I dwelt on the reality of the situation, I felt the familiar shooting pain of heartburn that had become such an integral part of my job it should have been included in the job description, along with the long hours, crap pension and a boss who was as reasonable as a manic depressive with an out-of-date lithium prescription. And I hadn't got to shag any gorgeous nude models on the way. I clutched a frozen chicken (free-range, corn-fed) to my chest in search of relief from the discomfort. That was when I saw the face of the devil smiling at me from forty-eight boxes of bran flakes.

I abandoned the trolley and walked towards the vision from hell, caught in its spell. Forty-eight smug gits smiled at me and I wanted to kick each one in the teeth. The cartoon bubble coming out of the forty-eight devils' lips mocked me and everything about my life. The face was one I knew only too well, the sardonic smile, the perfectly spiked dark hair, the blue eyes given a Caribbean look with specially tinted contact lenses, the artificially lean features which had been well honed on a ridiculously expensive personal health regime supplied by a trendy health club. 'Bran is fun!' it claimed. 'Kirk St John's Top Ten Tasty Bran Recipes make you want to po-go all day', it sniggered and continued, in letters small enough to be read by the average high-powered telescope, 'Further purchases necessary.'

I was lost at sea. A tide of shoppers flowed past like a supermarket Gulf Stream and took me on a world tour. I passed Jerusalem artichokes (from Sri Lanka), lamb Madras (from Canada) and pizzas (from County Durham), I passed the checkouts where the store's in-house magazine, *Aisles of Smiles*, was displayed. On the front cover was a bowl of brown mush that looked like dogshit. Nicely presented dogshit, with a hint of mint and coriander, but dogshit nonetheless. The headline said 'Kirk St John's Bran-tastic New Way to Health'. This latest blow left me rudderless and completely unable to resist the ebb and flow of the crowd.

I looked around and noticed for the first time that there were more people than usual in the store. They weren't harassed mums publicly flaying their children, so it couldn't be half-term, nor were they the herds of elderly people that normally indicated an orange-label day, when goods were reduced for a quick sale before the onset of maggots. These people moved with purpose, they were there for a reason. Then I saw what that reason was. It was on a sign, printed on glossy cardboard in the store's corporate colours of brown and green, and it said 'This Way to William Wrose's Personal Nemesis'. What it actually said was 'Here Today, TV's Punk Chef: Kirk St John', but it meant much the same. Underneath it stated that copies of Kirk St John's fantastic (or should that be bran-tastic?) new book and video *Can't Cook, Won't Cook – Anarchy in the W.O.K.* would be on sale and available for him to sign between six and eight. The devil's triumvirate was complete. My fate was sealed. He had come for me.

The crowds parted before me, as if I were a doctor arriving upon the scene of a particularly horrific road accident. Kirk St John was sitting at a table, borrowed from the quaintly named 'Friar's Refectory and Diner' next door, with piles of books on one side and videos on the other. A notice announcing each would cost £9.99 had been placed upside down. It now read '666'. When Kirk looked up I saw the familiar cleft chin that had figured in so many of my nightmares over the years and I wanted to drive a great big heavy axe between its cleavage. That would take the annoying self-satisfied smirk off his face. If I was looking for someone to blame for my life, Kirk would do nicely.

'Book, video or both?' Kirk said briskly, without looking up at me. After all, TV personality or not, time was money. But I had lost all power of speech and my chest was going numb. I struggled for breath. Kirk assumed this was a yes and took a copy from each of the piles.

'What shall I write?'

'Meringue.' My body was in spasm, so from a vocabulary of over ten thousand words, including a smattering of Spanish and French phrases picked up on foreign holidays, the only word I could spit at the smug bastard was 'meringue'.

'Meringue?' he asked, as if seeking confirmation of the spelling. But I couldn't spell it. I was too busy having a heart attack and dying. The spotless marble floor that was cleaned twice daily in line with European environmental health directives came up to greet me and I swear that I saw my reflection in it just before it slapped hard into my face. I made a mental note to mention the high standard of cleanliness to the store manager at the next opportunity. In view of my current state of health that might not be until the Day of Judgment but I felt that it really ought to be taken into account as part of the final reckoning. Then my heart stopped. The remote control of life turned down the volume and prepared to switch off the set. I just caught Kirk's next sentence, as he looked over my prone body to the expectant face of the adoring fan who was next in line and said, briskly, 'Book, video or both?' Then everything went black.

Two

In order to understand my hatred for Kirk St John, entre-
preneur, successful chef, and ubiquitous TV personality, it is
necessary to go back to a time before our paths crossed, 1976
to be exact, to Wednesday 18th August, just after seven a.m.

The daily allocation meeting in the mess room started at
seven a.m. sharp. Unfortunately that was far too sharp for
me, I didn't sharpen up until well into mid-morning.
Before that I was as blunt as fuck. Seven a.m. was a stupid
time to begin work, especially when you're nineteen, and
find the prospect of work about as exciting as the Moscow
phone book, and didn't get to bed until past three, and
then lay awake until dawn while the drugs buzzed around
your brain. This meant that the unmistakable sound of my
banana-yellow moped was not heard approaching the park
gates until the allocation meeting was almost halfway
through the agenda. When at last it could be heard, screaming like a calf separated from its mum and destined for an
upsetting fate in a foreign crate, George Tong, Head
Gardener for Bradworth Parks and Gardens Department
and keen advocate of the 'Do it or else' management style,

looked up from his official clipboard and stopped speaking.

The rest of the twenty-five men who made up the park labour force quietly sipped tea from dirty mugs and smoked smelly cigarettes that had a tar content to rival the M62. They followed my progress as if it was a play on the radio. I rode around to the side of the building, cut the engine and put the moped on its stand. There was a crash, followed by the grating tear of metal on brick.

'Fuck it,' I said in what I thought was a whisper but which actually made twenty-five sets of ear-drums vibrate like badly played bongos. I tried several times to set the moped on its stand, even though I was fully aware of the stand's many design faults, the main one being that it didn't work. After a decisive sounding crash which prompted me to kick the machine and say 'Fuck you then, you bastard', the moped was still. If Buddha had ridden around on this model of moped the result would have been the same. He would have seen that there was a natural sense of order in the moped finding rest at the foot of the wall, that the stand was content with its level of functioning, that this was the way things were meant to be. At which point he would have kicked it and said 'Fuck you then, you bastard'.

I searched for the sandwiches that my mum made up a week in advance and kept frozen until required and which I had loaded on the moped the night before. An international drug runner with a condom full of heroin, a jar of Vaseline and a recent history of extensive colonic irrigation couldn't have hidden them better. I eventually located them under the seat, next to the fuel tank. Petrol had leaked over them. I greeted this latest twist in the plot with my usual phlegm. Twenty-five pairs of ear-drums bongoed away to a stream of invective. I kicked the moped again and split several toe-nails.

Stupid-fucking-yellow-bastard-machine safely parked and lunch found, I paused to roll a cigarette. The men in the mess room could only imagine the dance I was performing as I tried to extinguish the flames that roared up my forearm, egged on by my Zippo lighter. The only clue as to what was happening was the smell of singed hair and toasted sandwich that wafted in through the open window. When the fire was safely under control I marched to the mess-room door, the gravel path providing the perfect clichéd sound effect. This was better than a real radio play. Some of the men wanted to applaud, it was so realistic. I then spent a minute spiking up my badly cut hair using the reflection in the Gent's toilet window.

'Jesus, but you're gorgeous,' I said, intending to be ironic, but generally satisfied that I had retrieved it from the worst effects of the crash helmet. I then burst in through the mess-room door, faking an exhausted run.

'Sorry I'm late, problems with the bike. I've had to push the bastard from the war memorial.' Twenty-five sets of disbelieving eyes focused on me and forced me to seek an anonymous seat in the middle of the group. I stared at the floor to avoid attracting any more attention.

The Head Gardener cleared his throat as if he was about to spit in my direction and then continued with the allocation process. Item twelve related to the bowling green. George ordered Balance and Stuart to fill in the holes with as little fuss as possible. He looked at me with his poisonous green eyes. The rest of George Tong's face looked like it had spent too long on a Spanish beach after a night on the duty free. His features had been darkened and mummified by years of exposure to the elements, in his single-minded pursuit of an index-linked pension.

'I've already had a formal complaint from the Veterans, Mr Wrose.'

I imagined a group of world-weary mercenaries in combat gear carrying not Kalashnikov rifles but brown, leatherette bowling bags and tubes of Grippo. If I hadn't been so tired I'd have probably risked a laugh.

'I shall have to deal with it under section three, subsection two, paragraph D of the Complaints Procedure,' George said, as if tasting a dish that was an old and delicious favourite.

On the front row Roger Odsal's hand shot up like a distress flare. Like me, he'd left school two months before, unlike me he was finding the discipline a hard habit to break.

'Mr Odsal?' Despite the formal address, when George Tong used the term 'Mr' it only ever conveyed utter scorn and derision.

'Sir . . .' This was another leftover from Roger's schooldays, but it went down well with dictators like the Head Gardener.

'Without wanting to minimise the anger of the erstwhile mentioned bowlers, can I just explain my part in the incident?' Roger's part in the incident was that he had been receiving personal instruction on hoeing techniques from the Assistant Head Gardener, 'Nine' Bob Hamilton, at the time that I, stoned as usual, had been inadvertently digging out the putting green holes on the championship bowling green. I had claimed in my defence that 'it was flat and green, who could tell the difference?' Roger was what most mothers would call a well-turned-out young man. A spotlessly neat teenager who had literally no spots, and never had a hair out of place because he also had no hair. His mum regularly cropped it in a crew-cut style that was closer than any crew member I'd ever seen, and it wasn't just his head that was lacking hair, he didn't have any body hair at all. Witnesses from the changing-room showers at school alleged that his testicles were so smooth they reflected light better than the Goodwin Sands lighthouse. He was a self-important, self-centred prig, so it was no surprise that he try to clear his name, particularly if in doing so he condemned me. I was a small sacrifice for a big sneak. As usual George Tong was in no mood to listen to explanations. Complaints from the Veterans were taken seriously, but complaints from members of staff were dismissed with all the contempt he could muster, which was quite a lot.

'No you can't, Mr Odsal.' He didn't look up from his clipboard. 'Item thirteen, tidying the blind garden. Mr Odsal and . . .' he paused to moisten his lips with fresh bile, '. . . Mr Wrose. I don't think even you can ruin scent.' He smirked at the joke. There were a few polite chuckles from those in the room who wanted to remain in his good books.

Around item twenty-six – newly adopted procedure for the correct disposal of pruning waste: see section 2.5(c) – the toasted cheese, pickle, green slime defrosted lettuce and petrol sandwiches fell off my lap as I slept. They hit the floor with a slap that brought proceedings to a sudden halt. I sat up and found once more that every face was turned towards me and I mentally processed the varied list of excuses that I kept for just such an occasion. It was difficult to come up with a fresh one, but I was young and inventive.

'Sorry, epilepsy. Drop fits. Takes me like that. Boom. Don't worry though,' I added to forestall any rush of support, 'I'll be all right.' The twenty-five faces didn't look unduly worried. Nor did they rush to my support. They had a rough idea that the main reason for these drop fits was that I had spent much of the previous night under the influence of a couple of grams of amphetamines (purchased from someone with minimal personal hygiene who kept his supplies down the front of his underpants for security reasons). The night had finally ended in the kitchen of my parents' house where I had given myself a savage hair cut with the bacon scissors in order to declare to the world that I was a Punk.

The park had been given to the people of Bradworth in 1896 by Sir Joshua Kindside, a man who had single-handedly created the textile industry in the city. Single-handedly if you discount the thousands of souls who once toiled in his mill which stood opposite the park gates, a permanent memorial which, in its current derelict state, mocked his self-importance. Kindside had intended to use the land for a nice big house for his family (they desperately needed a bigger billiard room) but, after a near fatal illness, he decided to give paternalism a whirl in a desperate attempt to ensure redemption. He gave the land to the people of Bradworth and created a park. He allowed his workers the freedom to enjoy its amenities, out of work hours, as long as they didn't get up to anything immoral in the rhododendrons.

I would have loved to have got up to something immoral in the rhododendrons but if I had I'd have been on my own. It was a shame because that was the only thing about rhododendrons that even vaguely interested me. I was in an unfortunate dilemma. I was a gardener who hated everything about gardening. It was probably my dad's fault. He was a mad, sad obsessive gardener. He was a mad, sad obsessive man. He used a cut-throat razor on his lawn in order to perfect the candy-striped effect. 'It's just like Wembley,' he would say to anyone stupid enough to listen, except that, unlike Wembley, running, walking or even tiptoeing on the grass was forbidden in case it suffered terminal bruising and went out of shape. Playing on it was completely out of the question. 'Playing excites children and that's when they go out of control. Children should sit quietly in their rooms and count their blessings.' By the time I was fourteen I could count my blessings, get out of the bedroom window, shin down the drain-pipe and be smoking Player's Weights with my mate, Dougie, outside Bradworth Youth Club within four minutes.

So I had no expectation that the role of Assistant Gardener (temp) would blossom into a career. I'd taken the job because school had ended before I had begun to think about what I wanted to do with my life. The job was offered by the Employment Exchange and I agreed without a moment's thought. Roger Odsal had given the job years of thought. It was all he had ever wanted to do. He was an Assistant

Gardener (perm) and earned fifty pence a week less than me. I assume he made it up in later years. Roger had a sense of vocation about gardening. It was about the only sense he did have. He saw beauty in creating order from chaos, of taming nature's excesses, of taking petty orders and obeying them unflinchingly. For him the park was like an extension of school, except that it didn't smell of piss. Roger was duller than ditchwater – he was like someone who has made an in-depth study of railway timetables and wants to share the experience. He embraced traditional values without embarrassment and viewed imagination as a threat to law and order. At school his social circle had centred around the Trampoline Club, where even a limited personality like his took on a certain lustre against the backdrop of sweaty groins and knee bandages.

I had moved in different circles at school. I was a known face among the alternative crowd. We were the ones who weren't hard enough to be genuinely cool, so we concentrated on appearing to be cool. We read obscure books by forgotten writers, listened to music no one else had heard of, and behaved as strangely as we dared, with the result that everyone kept out of our way and even the hard bastards left us alone. We worked tirelessly at being unpredictable. We were always at the forefront of protest (we saw regular bathing as a compromise of the human spirit), wore a lot of black and were never afraid to invest in stupid hair-styles. Most of our activities were either illegal, immoral or incomprehensible, and preferably all three. Nobody understood us, probably because we didn't understand ourselves. That didn't stop us expecting great things of each other, with everyone expecting the greatest things of me. Not least myself. The only thing anyone expected of the resolutely un-hirsute Roger Odsal was to have a sordid fetish exposed in the Sunday papers.

We had both left school, never expecting to meet again, only to meet three days later at Kindside Park where, to our mutual horror, we were paired together as workmates. I hated Bradworth Parks and Gardens Department almost but not quite as much as I hated Bradworth Grammar School for Boys. Both were relics of ancient ceremony and tradition where life was governed by procedure. Enlightened thought remained outside the gates, patiently waiting for the end of the day when it could once more enter your life.

Forced together in unholy wedlock Roger and I realised just how much we had in common. Nothing. He liked to work hard, I didn't like to work at all. He would have died for Bradworth Parks and Gardens Department, whereas I knew that getting sacked was about as likely as being thanked, it was unknown in living memory. The only thing I liked about the job, apart from the fact that it paid for my beer and fags, was that it got me out of the house. Even then I wasn't safe as my mum had a habit of ringing up and leaving messages with George Tong, who delivered them with relish in front of the other men. They ranged from 'Can you make sure he eats all his haslet at lunch' to 'He hasn't left any dirty pants in the wash, he's not still wearing the orange pair, is he?'

'You really enjoy all this shit, don't you, Scrote?' I asked, using the term of endearment that anyone who knew Roger knew was a perfect description. He stood in a bed of dazzling red dahlias using a hoeing technique created by the Assistant Head Gardener for the inter-horticultural college Olympics of 1962.

'I might enjoy it more if I had some assistance.'

'Fag break.' I took the rusty tobacco tin out of my top pocket and began the slow and deliberate task of rolling a cigarette. I was sitting cross-legged in the sunshine while on the radio Elton John and Kiki Dee were singing 'Don't Go Breaking My Heart' for the eight hundredth time that summer.

'You might enjoy it if you had a go,' he said in an attempt at encouragement.

'I couldn't if I tried.' I sang along to the record. He grumpily returned to denuding the border of any unwanted greenery with the hoe, using 'Nine' Bob's specialist pattern that produced a perfect blend of efficiency and effectiveness, and just the right amount of muscle tension.

Roger weeded all the borders in the garden for the blind, cut the grass and removed the litter. I took full responsibility for controlling the volume of the radio. If it was a record Roger liked, such as Abba, who he said always paid close attention to the melody, then I turned it down. If it was one I liked then I turned it up. It wasn't an easy job as there weren't many records I liked, although the lame, giggling DJ, who sounded vaguely American but actually came from Dorset, did play a song from the new Ramones album. I was excited and turned it up to full volume. A distorted buzz not entirely dissimilar to my moped engine at full throttle filled the garden. The white noise evolved, just, into a fuzz box chord change.

'The radio needs retuning.'

'Fuck off, Scrote. Don't you know anything? This is Punk. It's the future of music, of fashion, it's . . .' my pomposity was rising to a critical level, '. . . the future of everything.'

Roger's blank look thrilled me. It was the thrill of being in on the secret of the Next Big Thing and people like Roger were completely oblivious to it. I had bought the Ramones album on American import two months previously for three times the recommended retail price. I was a part of a select, exclusive and separate subculture. I belonged. The only thing wankers like Roger belonged to was the Tufty Club. I tried to do the pogo dance I'd spent weeks practising in the privacy of my bedroom and fell head first into the dahlia beds, rolling through them and destroying Roger's work.

'Sorry,' I said and laughed.

'You will be.'

I was late back after lunch, which as an event wasn't something that caused Roger to anxiously check his watch and consider raising the alarm with the emergency services, but did seriously contravene the terms and conditions of my employment. I left the mess room and headed for the nursery area, sneaking into the shed at the back. I sat down and brushed the fine brown dust off the metal staging and took out several well-used Rizla packets. I then took out my tobacco tin and a plastic money bag that had once done sterling service for Barclays but now contained dried, crushed leaves. I ripped the last remaining bit of cardboard from a Rizla packet, which amazingly didn't collapse, and rolled the roach. As I did so I heard the door creak open. Hiding all the paraphernalia for making a joint in my lap, I turned around.

'Who's there?'

'All right, Billy?' It was Balance. He was in the merchant navy and bore the nickname because he had size twelve feet and, allegedly, a penis to match. The rest of him was also big, in an International Shipping Lane sort of way. On his meat plate of a face were two vast grey eyes, a nose that crossed several lines of longitude and commodious grey lips that could have doubled as a reasonably comfy sofa. His shoulders were so expansive they made even the heaviest of burdens look light and flimsy. His clothes must have been made by a marquee manufacturer and he always wore an enormous black donkey jacket whatever the weather. He was working in the park while between ships, or so he claimed, but as he'd been there for seven years I wasn't so sure. He smiled.

'Is that blow?'

'Is George Tong a wanker?'

'Is "Nine" Bob bent?' He laughed and motioned to someone behind him. Stuart's face appeared in the gap.

'What the fuck?' I tried to protest.

Balance apologised. 'Sorry, Billy, but Stu's never tried it. I said you wouldn't mind.' I lit the joint as they made themselves comfortable on the sacks of compost that lay around the shed floor. Stuart looked worried.

'Will it make me want to fly?'

'If it does I can give you the name of a good travel agent.'

Stuart was thirty-seven and claimed to have worked in the park since he was thirteen. He'd probably lied about his mental age. He had ridiculously golden hair that glowed in the sunshine and wore a permanent look of wounded innocence. Balance inhaled like a professional and passed the joint to Stuart. He sucked apprehensively and then coughed a cough that was a first cousin to throwing up.

'Take it easy.' Balance bashed him on the back, harder than was necessary.

'Just breathe in deeply, don't overdo it or you'll suck your pants up your arse.'

He took my advice, nearly choked again, but to everyone's surprise, carried on inhaling. He passed it back to Balance and grinned even more vacantly than usual.

'Can you really suck your pants up your arse?'

'Ask Balance. He'll show you the skid marks.' Balance gave me a warning look.

The door creaked again and I hid the joint while Balance waved the air in a poor attempt to disperse the sickly sweet smell. The newcomer was Colin Barnes, also known as Colin the Crab.

'All right, Crabby?' Balance asked, trying not to sound stoned and failing miserably.

'You blokes got any dope left?' Colin requested politely.

I looked at Balance who shrugged. 'I only mentioned it in passing.'

'Is it right you're growing it in Tong's greenhouse?'

'For fuck's sake, why don't you get it on to the allocation meeting agenda?'

'Wouldn't matter if I did, you always miss it.'

I didn't really mind them knowing as it gave me a certain credibility and that was important when you're an Assistant Gardener (temp), a rank that, in the park hierarchy, was somewhere below that of a slug pellet. It meant that I wasn't singled out for special attention when they wanted a ritual sacrifice when things were a bit slow, which was about every two hours. The drugs were a risk but the consequences of being caught were far less worrying than having your penis coated in rooting powder, which is what they did to Roger.

The four of us sat in stoned silence and listened to the compost decomposing. I couldn't resist asking Colin why he was known as 'the Crab'. He was in his forties, looked ten years older and was more wiry than a Ministry of Defence perimeter fence, a fact which didn't affect his inability to ever move anywhere very fast, sideways or not. Balance interrupted Colin in the middle of inhaling.

'He's the king of the sideways move. It doesn't matter how crap you are, the Corporation won't get rid of you. What they do instead is give you a reference that glows like nuclear waste, recommend a transfer, and off you go to your next unsuspecting department. That's right, isn't it, Crabby?'

From somewhere behind a cloud of noxious smoke Colin was nodding in agreement.

Stuart suddenly came out of his trance.

'What is this place?'

'Kindside Park,' I answered. His eyes were blank, recognition was not at home.

'How about Bradworth? Or Yorkshire?' offered Balance.

'No, what's this place?'

We all thought about it and then, one by one, realisation dawned and as it did so we began to snigger, and then giggle and then laugh.

'The potting shed,' Colin shouted, 'we're smoking pot in the fucking potting shed.'

We were still laughing about it forty-five minutes later when an unnatural desire for chocolate cake forced us out of our hiding place.

We were smiling when George Tong saw the four of us leaving the nursery area. Stuart had his arms outstretched and was making aeroplane noises, Colin was taking little side-ways steps and Balance was doing an impressive impersonation of an aircraft carrier. I tried to distance myself from this vignette, but George was too long a Corporation man to be fooled. He knew I had been up to something, he didn't know what but he was determined to find out. Despite the fact that he didn't like me he had to admit I was good for morale; whenever I was around, the men had smiles on their faces.

Even with the effects of the home-grown grass in my bloodstream, I didn't find the prospect of an afternoon with Roger and Radio One very appealing. I decided to spend the time in serious contemplation of my future. The job in the park was crap, not only that but it was temporary crap. So far I hadn't been given a date to finish but it was only a matter of time. Equipped with two A levels (D in Pottery, E in Communication Studies, 'Show me a vase and I could get it talking'), my best bet was to go to art college. Unfortunately the only firm offer I'd received was for the Foundation Course at Clitheroe College of Art, which was the art student's equivalent of a leper colony. Worse than that, it was in Lancashire.

Unable to do anything else I had submitted a portfolio to several colleges, confident of a place at the Slade, or the Glasgow School. One by one the colleges I had selected chose not to reciprocate my feelings. With the exception of Clitheroe. Clitheroe College of Art had accepted me, per-haps because the admissions tutor was in the middle of a messy relationship with a first-year student half his age. He had left his wife just in time for the student to realise what a fat, boring old git she had been saddled with. Otherwise engaged, he hadn't given my application a second glance, except to tick the 'firm offer' box, and ruefully wish that the same were true for him.

With this in mind I headed for the bandstand, intent on reviewing my life options in the peace and tranquillity of the storeroom. I passed the giant figure of Balance going in the opposite direction carrying a large jar of rooting powder and making submarine noises. Three teenage girls hung around near the bandstand. They were in the park most days hoping for a sight of a workman's chest so that they could nudge each other suggestively and swap dirty sniggers that they thought made them seem worldly. The one with chocolate-brown eyes snorted as I passed. 'Bloody kids,' I said out loud, with the air of one who knew. What I didn't know at the time was that she had recently returned from a kibbutz in the Gaza Strip after having run away with an unemployed actor. He had once played the role of Third Roman Guard in the touring production of 'Godspell' and claimed to have David Essex's phone number. Their relationship had soured when she had found out that he also had a wife in Southampton and a daughter who was two years older than she was. She had returned home from Israel to worried parents, contrite but considerably more experienced in the ways of the world, a fact that they desperately tried to hide from the neighbours. She was now on the pill and happy to share her knowledge with anyone smart enough to ask. She was the only seventeen-year-old in the district who knew not to chew when giving a blow job. She could have made all my dreams come true, instead of which, thanks to my gauche attempt at aloofness, she was to be another missed opportunity in a long, long list of missed opportunities.

There was a strong smell of rotten wood and creosote in the bandstand storeroom which for some reason I found sexually arousing. Outside on the bowling green I could hear Colin and Stuart laughing violently, obviously having abandoned their work tasks for a bit of serious larking about.

I took a deckchair from the back of the room and, with a minor struggle that was reminiscent of Norman Wisdom at his best, set it up and settled down to the task in hand.

Getting stoned affected me in one of two ways, it either made me hungry or horny. I'd eaten my sandwiches so, putting my future plans on ice, I wiped the dust off the men's magazine that had been left in the storeroom several ice ages ago, and tried to switch on my hazy imagination. The magazine was so old the women in it looked like respectable schoolmistresses accidentally snapped while changing. They were a picture of innocence as they blushed from behind strategically placed objects. It was difficult to get turned on when given only the merest suggestion of a nipple but it didn't stop me from trying. When I was stoned I could wank over anything: girls in bubble bath, girls in fishermen's waders, girls in iron lungs. Afterwards I read an article on sports cars that the magazine always included to give it an air of respectability. Sexually fulfilled and fully conversant with the torque ratios of a particular Italian roadster, I zipped up my jeans and settled down as far as the deckchair canvas would allow.

It was just after four, only a few minutes short of knocking-off time, when I woke up. Immediately I knew that there was something different about the surroundings. The smell of wood and creosote had been joined by something more subtle yet, in its own way, just as pungent. It was John Innes compost. I couldn't be sure but I thought it might be number 3. Roger would have been able to be more specific as he had studied the variations under the firm tutelage of 'Nine' Bob Hamilton. I opened my eyes and standing out against the dark background was the even darker and unmistakable shape of George Tong.

I didn't know what to do, whether to feign illness (another drop fit?), try an explanation so bizarre it may be believed ('There was this flying saucer and a green woman with three breasts who wanted my love seed. I tried to invoke the policy on harassment at work, section nine, subsection six, paragraph A, but she was insistent . . .') or go on the attack ('You can stick your job, fuck face . . .'). George Tong's well-prepared statement saved me from making a decision.

'Mr Wrose.' The formal title sounded like a death sentence, which it was.

'I saw Mr Odsal in the Gents. He was scrubbing his privates again. He said I might find you here. I've come to inform you that your transfer has come through.'

'Transfer, Mr Tong? I didn't request a transfer.'

'No, you didn't. But it's good news.' His oak-aged skin cracked under the pressure of the smile.

'It's not, I like it here,' I said, waving my arms around to indicate 'here' and realising too late that 'here' was a hideaway, a dirty book, a deckchair with a dodgy stain, and me.

'When I say it's good news, I mean, of course, good news for me.' George Tong gave a crafty-old-sod smile that he reserved for moments of great personal satisfaction. Forty years of implementing Corporation policies and procedures meant that the expression got little use.

'Both you and Mr Barnes are leaving us. You will be going to the weed-removal team.' He paused after the phrase 'weed-removal team' and an orchestra should have played a 'haunted-house theme'. It was clear that I was being sent to the Parks and Gardens Department's equivalent of a harsh, inhuman gulag from which few returned.

'The weed-removal team disbands at the end of August, and that will be when your contract with the Department expires. I shall complete the necessary paperwork.'

'Thank you,' I said. I wanted to be more combative and say something like 'We'll see what my union has to say about this', but as the only union I belonged to was the National Union of Students (Bradworth Branch) and only then with a forged membership card, he was unlikely to feel threatened by that approach. Instead I was resigned to my fate. It was the usual story, George Tongs were always there ready to interfere in my life. The bastard gave me no option but to make a decision.

So I made a decision. I would leave Bradworth Parks and

Gardens Department. I would embark on the Foundation Course at Clitheroe College of Art and I would leave all this crap behind for ever. Success was calling me forward and I was running to meet it. I stepped past him and out into the sunlight.

'One other thing,' he said. 'Your mum rang, it's cottage pie for tea so don't be late.' Having solved one problem I was immediately presented with another, and this was even more complex. How was I going to tell Mum and Dad that I was leaving home?

Three

Living at home is never easy when you're a penis-driven nineteen-year-old, and it was no different in the Wrose household. In my family home communication was about as common as a tasteful china ornament on the dresser. One look at Mum's precious collection of smiling tramps with loyal puppies showed that this was a home where talk, rather than being cheap, was subject to hyper-inflation. Speaking to one another, as in one party talking and the other party listening, was the equivalent of farting in public – it was only done by accident or in cases of dire need, such as after one of my mum's legendary sprout casseroles.

Dad hadn't spoken to me since my eighth birthday, on which fateful day I had ridden my new Raleigh (without stabilisers) over his recently laid front lawn, an action he claimed had ruined the nap for ever. He had always looked and behaved like a man old before his time. His hair had lost its lustre for life and settled for dullness well before he was twenty, and the rest of him had followed suit shortly afterwards. His face was so lined it looked like a recently ploughed field and his eyes had the distant, all-hope-is-lost look of a man of eighty. His body and soul had been prematurely aged by the problems of keeping his lawn neat. In the early days his behaviour was viewed as quaint eccentricity, nothing more than a lovable family trait, and so his decision to stop speaking to me didn't arouse much comment. It was only when he locked himself in the shed for three days and nights that anyone began to worry, and even then Mum was more concerned that he had enough to eat and drink. We discovered later that he had laid in enough supplies of bottled water, fresh fruit and vegetables to last a fortnight.

After a few years of acting daft he was re-diagnosed by professionals as a burned-out schizophrenic and allocated a psychiatric nurse, who was supposed to visit once a month but only came when, coincidentally, there was a sale on at the Mill shop down the street. Meanwhile Dad's behaviour became so bizarre that it was increasingly difficult to ignore. He refused to use his legs under a Labour government, tried to mow the living-room carpet, and on Monday mornings had to be persuaded to go in to work on account of the Russians bugging his office (there was a microphone in the light bulb). He also grew a moustache which he treated in the same way as his garden. He had a bathroom full of oils and soaps and scents to dress it, as well as fourteen different pairs of scissors to trim it to perfection. It was like Charlie Chaplin's, only with a touch of the fanatical, more like Hitler's maybe. Worried though we were, nobody did anything, because the peculiar, if repeated often enough, becomes the ordinary. To neighbours and friends the sight of Dad digging tiger traps in the back garden to halt the advance of the red tide was commonplace.

Like a devout trappist he stood by his vow of silence against me. Instead he developed a new vocabulary of grunts as a means of communication. If I asked a direct question he would fiddle with his moustache and tailor the grunt accordingly: 'Hammp' meant yes, 'Hummp' no, and 'Hemmp' maybe. If he was absolutely required to say more he would address his comments to an invisible third party. 'Nice day,' he'd say, 'anyone fancy going out for a drive?' I was the anyone he was referring to; I had to be, I was the only other person in the room.

Talking to Dad was a bit like talking to a stranger at a party, it was more of a duty than a pleasure. I could ask him about his work, his holiday plans, or his tip for the cup final, but the conversation would be all one way. I didn't know anything about this man who claimed to be my father. I gathered from eavesdropping on his conversations with others that he did something called 'middle management' but I didn't know whose middle he managed. He only broke his silence once, when I was fourteen, and he burst into my bedroom at six o'clock in the morning, thrust a cup of tea at me triumphantly, and announced that Ted Heath was the new Prime Minister and 'now we'd see'. As father and son bonding goes it wasn't a particularly warm moment. It was easy to see that he preferred his lawn (and his moustache) over me, probably because it was tidier and didn't answer back, although a feature of his condition was that he occasionally heard voices – usually from the Kremlin – so it's possible that the lawn gave him a hard time about his staunch support for the Conservative Party.

Mum was short and fat in the way Antarctica was cold and empty. In other words, very. She had thinning blue hair which I always suspected might be her natural colour, and fair skin which hung from her cheeks and neck and arms like clean sheets on a washing line. She insisted on wearing clothes that were identical to much more expensive outfits, apart from two small details: they lacked any recognisable shape and had no discernible quality whatsoever. At least Mum spoke to me. In fact she never stopped speaking to me, on and on all the time. She was such a wall of sound she would have felt at home on Phil Spector's Christmas Album.

Unfortunately she never said anything that was remotely worth listening to. She talked about washing ('Had I got any?'), she talked about food ('Have you eaten?', 'Would you like to?'), she talked about my existential lifestyle ('You shouldn't waste your life, not with all these foreigners about'). These were the three passions of her life: laundry, food, and the hatred of all things foreign. She subscribed to the views that cleanliness was next to Godliness, an army marched on its stomach and everyone who wasn't British (and by that she didn't include the sly Welsh, rude Scots and traitorous Irish) was equally awful and not to be trusted. She warned me that if I didn't apply myself, all the foreigners would get the good jobs, the darkies would get the rest and I'd end up cleaning toilets if I was lucky. She was driven by the desire to be middle class and had chosen the fast route of intolerance. To further this cause she collected milk-bottle tops to 'buy a guide dog for a nice blind Englishman', and made sure we only ever had BBC2 on when visitors called.

If I needed to communicate with these monsters who called themselves my parents, like when I wanted to borrow the car, I had to wait until they were a captive audience. This was only possible at mealtimes when the three of us, like moths to a flame, sought our final destruction at the table. Then Mum would put down her knife and fork, eye my grubby shirt collar and tell me not to talk at the table. 'We might be in Europe but that's no reason to behave like the French.' To Dad the idea of allowing me to drive his car would mean unleashing a force of Oedipal proportions, which would ultimately undermine his position as head of the family and result in his son having a sexual relationship with the love of his life, the Atco lawn-mower. He would look out of the window as if giving my proposal considera-tion while actually eyeing a suspiciously unsymmetrical stripe on the grass, which may have been the distant remains of a young boy's bicycle ride, and eventually say, to no one in particular, 'If people acted more responsibly they might be able to go out gallivanting in their own car.'

The problem wasn't that Mum and Dad would be upset about me leaving home, far from it, I was sure the unanimous response would be something along the lines of 'good riddance to bad rubbish'. The problem was going to be telling them.

A few days after my 'transfer' to the weed-removal team I came home from a hard day at work – surviving Paraquat in my tea and Agent Orange on my sandwiches, both occupational hazards of denuding the Bradworth streets of weeds, border plants and stray pets – determined to tell Mum and Dad of my plans. Dad was individually checking each raspberry for, he claimed, maggots, but was actually looking for Russian tapping devices. He tutted his 'it's my wayward son who's been such a terrible disappointment to me' tut as I let the yellow moped fall onto the freshly raked pebble path, which he had just checked with a spirit level. I waited, in vain, to see if he would say hello. Eventually I said it in my best 'fuck you' tone. He wasn't the only one with a secret vocabulary.

I hadn't resolved the problem of how to tell them that I was leaving the comfort of the family nest to fly to the squalid world of poor-quality housing, all-night parties and endless, carefree sex. I hoped the idea of going to college, even one as crap as Clitheroe College of Art, would appeal to Mum's bourgeois pretensions. This was despite the fact that she wanted me to stay on with the Parks and Gardens Department because a job with the Corporation was a job for life, and that would probably mean one less foreigner in the country. I knew Dad did have hopes of me going to college, only he wanted it to be Cambridge to study medicine. This was because he wanted a doctor in the family so that he wouldn't have to use our family GP, who kept insisting Dad was as mad as a hatter and ought to go for a long lie down at the local mental hospital.

I tried to break the news to them over tea but Dad kept on about how the Communists were using psychic rays to inhibit his carrot yield. Mum spent the meal trying to find out my laundry plans for the next month so that she could buy the correct amount of soap powder. I gave up. This went on for weeks until, one Sunday afternoon during the traditional roast dinner, which we had whatever the time of year because 'we're English' and which on this occasion had been served on the hottest day of the hottest summer for years, I couldn't wait any more.

'Dad,' I said, scaring him half to death with such a direct approach, 'can you give me a lift to Clitheroe.' He choked, blushed and began to sweat profusely. He searched through his vocabulary for something that would be appropriately impersonal.

'I might have a run out Clitheroe way, sometime. When though?' he asked rhetorically.

'Today, this afternoon. I'm off to college and I've got to book into the hall of residence by five o'clock.'

He looked out of the window to see if any more errant leaves had dared fall on to the patio. Mum put down the willow pattern gravy boat and looked at me from behind the Himalayan pile of mash on her plate. I could see the pain of separation welling up in her eyes. Her only child was leaving home. 'Your pants are still damp, I'll put them on the radiator.'

That was it. Dad took me to Clitheroe while Mum watched *Reach for the Stars* on BBC2. She gave me five pounds for emergencies – 'In case you run out of Omo' – and went back to mending Dad's gardening socks. Dad said nothing on the way except 'Aarm?' ('So you're going to college?') and 'Yimm' ('Art? Waste of taxpayers' money, you'd be better off getting a real profession, like doctoring'). He dropped me off at the hall of residence. I was wearing my 'Picasso was a Square Bastard' T-shirt and I stood in a car park full of sobbing parents and embarrassed offspring. All

I had in the world was a carrier bag full of crisp clean clothes and a box of obscure punk records that Dad couldn't disguise his glee at seeing the back of. He looked around at the other partings in the car park, sniffed haughtily and said (though not to me): 'Well, I don't know, it looks a right bloody awful place to me. And those flower borders aren't straight. Very shoddy.' Then he left. At last I was on my own. I was a grown-up.

When it came to parental advice my dad was no Citizens' Advice Bureau, he wasn't even a small serving suggestion on the back of a tin of pilchards, but his words of farewell proved astonishingly accurate. Clitheroe College of Art was a right bloody awful place, although I wouldn't consider myself experienced enough to comment on the layout of the gardens. Within four hours of arriving I was in despair and almost rang home to beg for a return journey in the scintillating company of my Dad. But that blessed mixture of fear, loneliness and exhilaration that leaving home produces kept me there. There was one other thing that kept me there. That was meeting someone who was exciting, thrilling and dangerous and who had me spellbound from our first encounter. That someone was Kirk St John.

Four

Life at college was a bit like life at home, except my clothes weren't as clean, I was always hungry and people spoke to me, sometimes. It was mostly dull and aimless with occasional frenetic moments of intense boredom to deepen the gloom. I spent a lot of time sitting in the canteen so that I might gain nourishment from the smell of the food and warmth from the free heat laid on by a benevolent college administration. I religiously avoided the big mistake that all new students make, that of making best friends with the first person you meet. Examples of these relationships could be seen in every corner of the canteen, the sad imploring eyes of people trapped for ever in the company of someone who had a hundred different stories about their weekend camp experiences in the Scouts, or blow-by-blow accounts of each gymkhana event they had taken part in since 1969. I pitied them but I also envied them, for I had no friends, not even boring ones.

The first person I had met was my flatmate, Dave Souter, a nineteen-year-old with advanced Asperger Syndrome and a head so square he always looked like a television. His black hair was plastered to the flat surface of his head by a combination of grease, sweat and Brylcreem, of which he was the only person under seventy who still used it. He was impossible to make friends with, partly because he hated the human race and partly because he was a fully matured git. Not for him the warmth of friendship or close relationships, all he wanted was isolation and alienation. His personality guaranteed that he got it. He was a sociology student who had no intention of interacting with the world around him. He never left the flat in the halls of residence, not even to attend lectures. He preferred to spend all day in front of the television in case it brought some meaning into his life by broadcasting a snooker tournament. He picked his flat nose all the time and wore a succession of sweatshirts with statements printed on them that he had made to order to reflect his view of the world. His favourite read 'I don't go to the University of Life'. He never made any eye contact, conversation or effort. His ambition was to be Clint Eastwood and blow people away. He was the flatmate from hell. Spending all day in the canteen was infinitely preferable to spending half an hour with Dave Souter.

Two weeks into the course I had become as pretentious as a discretionary grant would allow. Thirty per cent of my income was supposed to be made up by parental contributions, but all I ever saw were parcels containing clean pants and fresh packets of Persil. Despite this shortfall I managed to re-invent myself, something which every other student seemed to have done as well. Clitheroe was like Hollywood, dreams came true there. My dream was to look like an enigmatic artist whose every action was part of the creative process called life. This meant that I wore black nail varnish and had my ear pierced. I thought I was pretty great and was sure my fellow students thought so too.

One person who didn't think I was great was Mike Gummerson, my tutor. He was thirty, wore shirts open at the neck, looked like Ruskin (a comparison he worked hard at, pretension not being the exclusive preserve of students), quoted Lenin and Duchamp in tutorials and drove a blue Triumph Vitesse. He was a child of the sixties and claimed to have been a regular on the drop-out and love-in scene. Basically this meant he let us call him Mike, and he particularly encouraged informality amongst those students who were female, pretty, under twenty and would do anything for straight As. The odds were stacked against me from the start.

Mike Gummerson's biggest joy in life was bringing about the abject humiliation of those students who weren't female, pretty, under twenty and willing to do anything for good grades. He achieved this through his 'Art Crit' sessions. These were a bit like a public hanging, except that, as the rope was placed around the victim's neck, the executioner brought out examples of the victim's dirty underwear, thus completing their degradation. In Art Crit sessions each student was expected to play the role of both executioner and executed. We took it in turns to display our latest work and listen in silence as the rest of the group were made to criticise it. Nice comments were not allowed, Mike Gummerson found them offensive, reactionary and bourgeois. My early attempts to get off with Fran Butcher, who wore tight sweaters that rose up and exposed her navel at every opportunity, were destroyed by this process. Not allowed to feign delight at her weak attempts to imitate Cubism, I had to tell the truth. I told her as nicely as I could that they were pathetic copies which, if described as childish daubs, would be insulting to the child. She gave me a withering look and crossed her legs. They made a sound like heavy double doors being locked shut for ever.

The Art Crit sessions were bloodbaths and we became ever more competitive in our attempts to destroy one another and so win the approval of our tutor. The more extrovert of the group adopted braying laughter that conveyed sarcasm and disdain without any further comment being necessary. The more literate read up on articles by professional critics and made intelligent observations about the use of light being rather obvious, or poor brush technique. Those of a thespian disposition feigned camp anger at the effrontery of a piece of work, screaming that they'd seen gift-wrap that had more to say.

I was unable to keep up with the pace of vitriolic analysis. I'd worked my way through the thesaurus and had already used worthless, deplorable, lamentable, pitiful, vulgar, lousy, loathsome, crude, beastly and abominable. I had nothing left to say. So I committed the fatal error, I began to repeat myself. I lost my edge. I became fair game for the hunting pack and as the weeks went by the comments made against me became more personal and less grounded in fact. I was now the weak link in the group, a reactionary quisling of the art establishment.

'Take a tip from the Dada revolution, Wrose. The world doesn't owe you a living,' Gummerson said, feeding the frenzy of the student mob. 'You've got to earn it, and the sweat on the artist's brow is talent.' The sweat on my brow was fear.

If I'd been asked at that moment to name the person most likely to fuck up my life, I'd have chosen Mike Gummerson without hesitation. But then I met Kirk St John. I was hiding in the canteen, having skived off from that week's Art Crit on account of not having done the homework (an abstract on the title 'Life Must be Revolution'). I was eating lunch, a bag of peanuts, when I saw Kirk for the first time. He was wearing a white jacket and black-and-white checked trousers, which were the uniform of the canteen kitchen where he worked as a 'commie commis chef', as he put it. He had dark spiky hair and was carrying a bundle of leaflets. His fingers were blue with printers' ink. He was in his mid-twenties and it showed. Confidence oozed from every pore as he moved, in sharp contrast with the nervous, homesick teenagers that crowded the canteen in search of security and succour. A pretty girl, who was either in love with him or in awe of him, or both, followed him loyally. I caught his eye and he immediately took this as an invitation.

He marched assertively over and thrust a leaflet in my face. The girl bobbed along behind him like a dinghy in the wake of an ocean-going liner.

'Hi. My name's Kirk St John, and this is Debbie.'

'Deidre,' she politely contradicted, full of admiration for the man who couldn't remember her name.

'Debbie, Deidre, whatever. We've come to interfere in your life.'

I took the leaflet and read it. 'Smash the Nasis?'

'Yeah, there was no Z in the print shop. They ran out doing the "Fuck the Fuzz" posters for the end-of-term demo. Am I right in thinking you're also a punk?' I felt good being recognised as a fellow traveller.

'Dee's got a cousin on the *NME*.'

The girl was chewing gum and looking out of the window, captivated by the sight of the car park. She managed to break off from counting cars and looked at me as if I was a slow-drying variety of magnolia emulsion.

'He's a freelance smudge.'

'Smudge?' I asked.

She smirked at Kirk who smirked back. It was the first, but by no means the last time I saw him do that. 'Photographer,' she said wearily. 'He did the cover on the Hotrods first single.'

There was something about me and girls like Deidre, well all girls really. When they found me boring it made me want to prove what a cool guy I actually was. I began to gabble in Art Crit mode. 'Hey yeah, I saw that, great use of light . . . and grainy,' I added desperately.

'You need some excitement in your life,' Kirk said in a pitying tone.

The leaflet insisted that I march to the town hall the following Sunday morning at a time that even Bradworth Parks and Gardens Department would have found obscene. Once there I was to lobby against the 'Nasis'. It didn't say who I was to lobby. 'It's a bit early,' I whinged.

'This is the 1970s, Nazis have alarm clocks now. This is your chance to get into some real anarchy, direct action. Infiltrate and obliterate, together we can be great.' He said this last bit in a bad imitation of a Rastafarian accent.

Until that moment my political credo was about as well developed as Deidre's cousin's crap black-and-white photos. Like every punk I thought of myself as an anarchist but if asked to define what that was I was buggered. As far as I was concerned it had a lot to do with staying in bed while everyone else got on and did the work. I was now in the presence of someone who seemed to know the ins and outs of the philosophy and it was imperative that I appear aware and committed.

'There won't be any trouble, will there?'

'Anarchy is trouble. In three months the two sevens clash and you know what that means?'

I didn't, but I pretended I did.

'Crisis time when Babylon fall.' I found his terrible Jamaican slang hard to follow but I could see from the look on her face that it was turning Deidre on. That was what decided me.

'Right, I'll be there. Count me in. Mighty.'

I didn't ask what it was anarchists actually did for fear of looking foolish in front of Deidre. I prayed that all the commune stuff was a thing of the past as I had no intention of sharing my record collection with anyone, although I would have been into sharing money, as I had none, and women, as I had even less of them. We talked for a few minutes about punk until he spotted another lonely face in a crowd of lonely faces and went off in pursuit of their support for the revolution.

That Sunday I was up early, dressed in my best Italian Army combat trousers and 'Punk is Coming' T shirt, and headed for the town hall. I had tried to convince Dave to come with me but it was sweatshirt wash-day and so I left him alone in the flat, as usual. I waited for two hours on the town hall steps. I read the *Observer* from cover to cover, including the financial pages, and then did the same with the *News of the World*, particularly the sex scandal bits. I saw no demonstrators, no anarchists, no revolution. And no Kirk. There weren't even any Nazis. I should have known from that moment on not to invest any faith in him, but it was 1976, I was fresh and innocent and Kirk was wild and anarchic. He was cool and chic and if you couldn't be cool and chic yourself, you hung around with someone who was.

I didn't see him for a couple of weeks after the town hall fiasco. I'd just been called a 'cancer in the body of true expressionism' by Kate Simpkin, a quiet girl who'd arrived at the start of term with a reputation as someone who could draw kittens that looked real enough to stroke. Reeling from this body blow I went in search of solace in the canteen. Kirk was there, wearing a chef's hat this time. He was accompanied by a girl. It was not Deidre but she was just as pretty and just as besotted with him. She was also just as contemptuous of me.

'I like the "Fuck Pink Floyd" T-shirt,' he shouted across the crowded canteen. He came over. 'I want your advice. What do you think about a punk night this Halloween? I'm thinking top bands, free bar, cheap tickets.'

'Pardon?' I asked. He handed me a leaflet, in green this time, which matched his fingers. It read:

VOTE
Kirk St John
Entertainments Officer
(Independent Conservative)

'What happened to anarchy? Has the print shop run out of Ys now?' I said as ironically as I dare, which wasn't very much.

He looked at me and recognition dawned across his face.

'It's you, Barry . . .' he read my lips '. . . Billy. Of course, the
town hall demo. I was otherwise engaged.' He looked at the
girl, then back to me and winked. 'How was it, anarchy now?'

'Or never.'

'The world's not ready.' He didn't sound too impatient.

'Clitheroe certainly isn't. So is that why you've sold out
and gone Tory?'

'Shit no. I've switched sides to get elected. That's what
anarchy's all about. Plus as an employee of the college I'd
get time off for fulfilling my duties as Ent's Officer. Beats
working.'

'How about this for an idea then? For your punk night, I
mean. Hire loads of instruments, p.a. and stuff, pile them on
stage and just let everyone have a go. That would be pretty
anarchic.'

'That's not a bad idea, I can work that up into something.
Make a note,' he said to the girl. 'Jean here is my campaign
manager.'

'Gina.' She didn't smile as she corrected him.

'Jean, Gina, whatever. Her dad's a Conservative council-
lor; he's been very useful. Remember, we must use the
enemy.'

Gina stopped giving me a look of total abhorrence. She
had hair so mousy it reminded me of a Tom and Jerry cartoon, and she looked permanently glum. The edges of her
mouth were clearly feeling the full effects of gravity and
were pointing to the floor. The rest of her body was well
hidden in black, but my groin was the Sherlock Holmes of
groins and quickly spotted a body to fuel a thousand fantasies. Suddenly she made a fist in the air. I thought she was
going to hit me. 'Black and white unite and fight. Man and
woman liberate the human.' I noticed she was speaking in a
bad Rastafarian accent.

Kirk gave her a 'right on!' smile and turned back to me,
pulling a 'who the fuck *is* she?' face.

'Fancy coming to a club tonight?' He was irresistible. I'd

never met anyone quite like him. He flitted around from idea to idea like a butterfly on speed. One minute he was giving you his undivided attention, the next he had discarded you like a used rag. He made me laugh because he didn't take anything seriously and the lack of a single moral thought in his head would have made me angry if I hadn't been so completely devoid of morals myself. I agreed to meet him at the club, inside, so that if he didn't turn up at least I'd be warm.

The Squat was the coldest nightclub I'd ever been in. It was in a cellar that was below a basement. Water lay around in great oily puddles on the stone floor. A ramshackle bar stood in one corner and sold only beer, in cans, at twice the recommended retail price. The sound system was a Fidelity stereo, five watts per channel if the wind was in the right direction. The light show was a spotlight stolen off a fire engine. As nightclubs go it was empty, stark and soulless. I loved it. As did all the other punks in Clitheroe, all forty-two of them. Like some secret meeting place for transvestites, they came from all over the area and gathered there to display all. Girls arrived in taxis looking ordinary apart from the black bin-liner they carried. Round the back they quickly changed into fishnet and leather and topped it all off by wearing the bin-liner. Boys wore tight trousers with bondage straps and badges that said things like 'Star Killer' and 'Death to Music'. The atmosphere felt wild and dangerous while actually being as safe as houses.

I bought a beer with what was left of my overdraft and waited for Kirk. While I waited a band came on to the stage, which was actually a bundle of pallets tied together with nylon twine. The band was called 'Shite' and proudly lived up to their name. I risked a pogo and found I had a real talent for crashing into people. A girl aged about eighteen and wearing black eye-shadow and little else slammed into me and gave a friendly smile as I rubbed my bruised arm.

The band were well into their fourth number, 'Bomb Habitat', when I noticed the bass player. He was wearing a pink mohair sweater under which could be glimpsed a T-shirt that said 'Fuck Art Let's Dance'. It was Kirk.

When the band finished the crowd drenched them in enough snot to keep a Hepatitis B clinic in business for a month. Kirk jumped off the stage and came over to me. Several of the audience shouted things like 'You were shit' and 'Stop acting St John' as he passed and he thanked them as though he meant it. A beautiful Chinese girl stepped out of the crowd and took up the usual position of adoring acolyte at his shoulder. He introduced her, wrongly, as Kim, then went on to tell me how she could suck stuff out of his fingernails that, if she French kissed it back to him, helped him keep it up all night.

'Her grandma taught her how to do it apparently. She keeps Grandma's skull in the wardrobe now. Spends all Sunday polishing her.' She heard all this but didn't seem angry or embarrassed at his indiscretion.

'I didn't know you were in a band,' I said, trying without success to keep the admiration out of my voice.

'These dead beats aren't a band, they have no vision.'

I gave a 'that was my perception' kind of nod.

'Was that your perception?' he asked.

'I thought you were great,' I fawned shamelessly.

'Ta. Do you play?'

I shook my head. 'I'm an artist,' I said without realising how pompous it sounded.

'This can be art. Punk, I mean. The way we play it isn't, some of us still want to be Led Zeppelin.' He smirked over to the bar where the rest of the band were standing. 'But it could be.' The expensive beer was playing havoc with my sensibilities which was probably why I tried to impress him.

'I play guitar.'

'What sort of guitar'

'Rhythm.'

'No, what make, I mean.'

'I'm not sure,' I said embarrassed. But I was sure, I was certain. I just didn't want to admit it. My guitar was a Woolworth's Winfield Telecaster (copy), on which I had developed a working knowledge of two chords, A minor and E major. In 1976 the Winfield Telecaster (copy) was the best electric guitar in the world. It was constructed from the finest, seasoned, South American chipboard, lovingly covered in a teak veneer that never quite laid flat, and had strings made from industrial strength cheese wire. The strings hung so high above the fretboard that even a dedicated Buddhist who had achieved a state of nirvana would have found it difficult to hold down an A7 chord for longer than ten seconds without passing out from the pain and loss of blood. It was uglier than the Austin Allegro and had been subjected to similar quality-control standards. It was such a dog it could scare burglars. It did have one redeeming feature. At £19.99 it was the cheapest electric guitar in the world. It had been made in a region of the world where the concept of an economic miracle was to get the goods on to the boat bound for Europe before the glue dried and bits fell off.

Kirk was impressed. 'Brilliant. You should have a word with Dim.' He changed down to a whisper that was the same volume as his shout. 'He's a Fender bender, really booooring maan.' Kirk waved his long arms towards the guitarist who was still at the bar, guitar slung around his back, drinking from two cans of lager.

'Dim, over here.' Kirk turned back to me 'Dimitri really is an anarchist. He blows people up. It's a kind of hobby.'

He welcomed Dimitri over and sent the Chinese girl off for more drinks. Something in my subconscious made me start biting my fingernails as I watched her short rubber skirt disappear into the crowd.

'Dim, this is Billy. Dimitri's a Greek philosopher. His philosophy is "bomb the fuckers!" I can't tell you his surname; he's fleeing deportation, so it's not safe.'

'He can't freaking pronounce it is what he means,' Dimitri said, without any sign of having a sense of humour, let alone a surname. He was short and dark and hairier than a barber's floor at five o'clock. The space between his throat and chest sprouted what looked like a whole family of swarthy gonks.

'Billy here is also an anarchist,' said Kirk, dropping me right in it.

Dimitri gave me a look from red eyes that could only be described as dangerous. 'What faction?'

I resisted the urge to give him a flippant answer when again I saw the bloodshot madness in his eyes. 'I tend to gravitate towards direct action,' I bullshitted.

'So you're a situationist?'

'I'm more of a situationist vacant.' The alcohol in my brain encouraged me to make one quick stab at political satire. He wasn't impressed.

'Don't mock the power of a single event. History can turn on it.'

'That's for sure,' Kirk agreed with a wink towards the Chinese girl as she returned with several cans of lager.

Dimitri had a vocation. His every waking moment was spent in the pursuit of a new world order where everyone was free. He was barking mad of course and anyone who got involved with his demented schemes would have been equally insane.

'We should do something together,' Kirk suggested, as if he was organising a boys' night out, which in a way he was.

'Great,' I said with less enthusiasm than an agoraphobic agreeing to a weekend of outdoor pursuits in the Arctic wastes. Dimitri took out a chewed Biro. I just managed to stop myself from saying something trivial about the pen being mightier than the sword.

'Give me address. When I get target I let you know.' I considered giving a false address, like my parents' or George Tong's, but that would have meant losing face in front of

Kirk who knew where I lived. I relented and gave the number of the payphone at the hall of residence.

'Come on, Dim, destiny is calling us,' Kirk said, noticing that an expectant hush had fallen across the crowd and everyone was looking in our direction. It was time for Shite's second set, which was exactly the same as the first only played much faster. Dimitri walked toward the stage, looking every inch the aloof rock star. Kirk sighed and whispered to me in his ninety-seven decibel whisper.

'He's so progressive rock, wanking guitar solos and pelvic thrusts. You and me, we'd be different.' He winked and trotted off, detuning his bass guitar as he went in order to introduce an extra element of chaos into their sound. I felt the warm blush of excitement spread across the back of my neck. Did he want to form a band with me? I tried to engage the Chinese girl in conversation, asking after her grandma, but she wanted to listen to the band, not to some sex-obsessed adolescent. I shut up and concentrated on getting even more pissed.

A few days later I was in the weekly Art Crit session, trying to defend my painting of a waterfall against the charge that it was a chocolate-box picture of immense tweeness. I claimed that it was instead an ironic indictment of the evils of consumerism. This was a difficult task as I had copied the picture off a box of chocolates that Dave Souter had bought for his mum's birthday. At the end of the session Mike Gummerson asked me to stay behind. When the last of the group had left, making cut-throat signs to me as they did so, he motioned me to follow him into his study. He called it his 'Chagall Room' because there were several prints by the artist on the wall which created a restful mood of blue hues. His students called it the 'Shag-all Room' because it was there, according to popular rumour, that he seduced his victims. I hadn't been called in for seduction, I was there to be bollocked. The room was small and filled with cans of powder paint and quality art paper. Gummerson's desk was immaculately tidy with his pencils lined up exactly and his books organised according to size and the colour of the spines.

'I don't like you, Wrose.' When Gummerson had dirty work to do he didn't piss about.

'No, Mr Gummerson?' I knew my refusal to use his first name irritated him. Unfortunately it was the only weapon in my armoury.

'No. But it's nothing personal,' he said, as if that made it all right. 'I just can't stand people who have no convictions.'

An old joke flitted into my mind, but I rejected it. This was serious stuff.

'I hate people who have no talent. You have less than no talent. You don't even have a set of brushes.' I was getting the general gist of what he was saying, but I wasn't sure where it was going. I was probably better off not knowing, but I had to ask.

'So, what are you saying? Should I concentrate on pottery?'

'I think you should concentrate on finding a job for when you leave the course at the end of term.'

'Leave the course?'

'Leave, as in "fuck off and stop wasting my time". And your time, and everyone else's time for that matter. Understand?'

There wasn't much more to say. Mike Gummerson had been unusually pithy. I was to be chucked out just as soon as he could arrange it. My artistic ambitions were finished. I tried smiling, to show that I didn't care whether I was on his poxy course or not, but the effort made my eyes fill up. I noticed a jumbo box of man-size tissues on top of the filing cabinet and almost took one but remembered just in time that, if the rumours were true, he probably used them to wipe his cock on.

When I got back Dave Souter was watching television and picking his nose, in that order. The television programme was a soap opera set in Scotland where the breathtaking views of mountains wobbled dangerously whenever the cast moved about too quickly. As well as the dried contents of his nose, Dave was eating a giant bag of pop corn while he flicked through a movie magazine dedicated to Clint Eastwood. He pointed a two-fingered snotty gun at me while looking out of the window to avoid eye contact.

'Go ahead, punk, make my day.'

'I'll be leaving at the end of term, will that do?'

His smile showed that it would do for starters. He blew on his fingers, giving them a surreptitious lick before putting them back into their imaginary holster. Some gun, he thought.

'You had a caller,' he said, still avoiding eye contact.

'Who?'

'Didn't say.' Which meant Dave hadn't asked. 'He said that discretion was the foundation of the revolution. He'll meet you at eight in the Crown and you should take matches because it's going to be explosive. I think he was foreign.'

I groaned, things couldn't get any worse. I decided to cop out and not go. The revolution would have to manage without me, besides which my life had been revolting enough for one day. There was a knock on the door. It was Catriona from down the hall. She was six foot two, the majority of which was made up by her legs, had long blonde hair and a gentle tan that caressed her luminous skin. Her looks were such a cliché she should have had staples across her middle. She was gorgeous and to many of the male students, including me, she was the Patron Saint of Self Abuse. I'd been looking for an opportunity to speak to her since the beginning of term.

'Phone for you.'

I threw every ounce of charm I had at her. 'Thanks, Cat . . .'

'And you can answer the bloody thing yourself next time, some of us are trying to work.' She turned away, her body language indicating that this was our last conversation, ever.

'Hi,' said Kirk. 'I'm just checking you'll be there and not thinking of turning chicken.' I laughed at the suggestion, aware that my forced jocularity had the ring of a Rhode Island Red about it. 'Cluck cluck cluck,' it went, the sound of my laugh echoing around the phone booth and out into the hall.

'I'll be there,' I said firmly and hung up. I went back into the flat, switched off the television, took Dave's magazine off his lap and threw it out of the window. He squirmed away from my presence and went to watch his magazine float down five floors and come to rest in the middle of the warden's ornamental carp pond. Clint Eastwood could just be seen, mouthing up at me, asking if I felt lucky.

I didn't go straight to the Crown. I went to five or six pubs on the way. This was to get as drunk as I could before the fateful meeting with Dimitri and hopefully increase the chances of falling over and never actually getting there. I was so scared I was shaking. I left the last pub a bit happier, a lot pissed and completely numb. But I didn't fall over. There was no sign of Dimitri in the Crown and my spirits rose. It was a quiet night and the only other customer was a woman who was probably in her eighties. She had a worn and wrinkled face that after eight pints of lager drunk very quickly, looked interesting. She turned to me as I ordered another beer and double whisky chaser.

'I was in the First World War, you know,' she said. 'I was a nurse. I was on the Somme. Terrible, terrible.' She sipped her sherry and described the horrific scenes she had witnessed. She told her stories and I listened. I felt I owed it to her to do so. After ten minutes or so she knocked off the last drop of Harvey's, wiped her pale thin lips, grabbed my bollocks with her right hand and whispered enticingly in my ear, 'If I were twenty years younger, I'd fuck the arse off you.' With that she put on her coat and left, shouting farewell to the landlord who didn't bother to look up from doing his monthly accounts. I felt a bit ashamed. I was so pissed and scared that I'd have happily dropped Dimitri and his mad scheme to fuck the arse off her if she was only *ten* years younger. Or possibly even five.

The door opened and Dimitri came in, managing to look even hairier than usual. There was a suspicious bulge under his leather bomber jacket. I remembered what Dave had said about matches and wondered if the choice of jacket was significant. My heart thumped so loudly I thought someone had put on the jukebox. I begged the landlord for more drink, causing him to lose his place in the mess of forged double-entry book keeping. Dimitri turned down my offer of a drink.

'We gotta go, we gotta go,' he said, panic in his tone. This drained away my last few drops of confidence.

'What about Kirk?' I pleaded, hoping the stupid plan would have to be abandoned if we weren't quorate, as if such regulations were laid down somewhere in an anarchist rule book.

'He meet us there. Come on,' he urged, using his dangerous tone. Obeying, I took the glass of whisky with me. The landlord didn't seem to mind, he was too busy trying to explain a rogue invoice.

We walked quickly to the college car park without any attempt at disguise or discretion. Outside the front doors of the college Dimitri stopped and took out a petrol can from inside his jacket. The sloshing sound told me that it wasn't empty.

'What the fuck are you doing? There're people in there . . .' I said, pointing to the lights inside the college where several hundred people were engaged in something called 'adult education'. 'We can't burn them . . .'

'Shut up. We freaking do this.' He pointed to the left. 'This' was a big black BMW. It was the Principal's car. It was parked in a single bay marked with yellow stripes and a number plate on the wall which read 'PRI'. To which some wag had added 'CK'. Even in my pissed state I despaired at the standard of Clitheroe College student humour. So we were to blow up the Principal's car. What was this meant to achieve? I didn't know, and I didn't care. All I knew was that I was dealing with madness and so there was no point trying to reason with it. Dimitri's actions made my dad's attempt to build a full-scale model of the Panama Canal in the back garden look eminently sensible. I wanted to have as little to do with this craziness as possible.

'Let's wait for Kirk,' I suggested. Dimitri gunned me down with a threatening look. Bullied into submission I shrugged and awaited my orders. He gave me a crowbar which he had kept hidden in his jeans.

'And I thought you were pleased to see me.' If ever there was a time for humour, this wasn't it.

'Get petrol cap off,' he ordered.

I tried to gently prise the cap off without scratching the paintwork, which, as an artist, I could see was beautifully applied. Dimitri watched me for an impatient moment.

'For freak's sake give it to me.' He shoved me aside, wrenched the cap off in one move, jammed some rags into the hole, poured petrol from the can over it, and then stepped back to admire his handy work. That was when I saw it. Beyond Dimitri, beyond the Principal's BMW was a greater sight. It was the holy grail. It was bluer than the Danube, and had a white stripe down its side like tooth-paste squeezed from a tube. It was a blue Triumph Vitesse, circa 1967. To be more precise it was Mike Gummerson's blue Triumph Vitesse, circa 1967. It was my turn to give the orders.

'Out of my way,' I said, pushing Dimitri. 'Give me that.' I grabbed the crowbar back. There was a new enthusiasm in me that hadn't been there before. I took the rusty chrome petrol cap off like a knife taking the top off a boiled egg, deliberately scratching and denting the wing as I did so. I stuffed the hole with wadding and poured petrol over it and the soft top for good measure. It was Dimitri's turn to be horrified.

'No. That's Gummerson's. He's socialist worker.'

'He's a wanker.' The drink was talking and what it was saying was 'don't try and stop me, you mad Greek bastard, this is my fucking party now'. I took out my Zippo and lit the fuse. Dimitri swore at me in Greek.

'The SWP will freaking kill us.' And with that he ran off, screaming like a lamb in a mint sauce factory, completely forgetting the Principal's car in his panic. The spark from my lighter rushed along the floor, a blue ball in search of its blue source. The Triumph Vitesse was embraced by flame, like a timid child in the arms of a fat aunt. Then big yellow tongues of fire licked up into the night sky. Just before the big bang that blew the Triumph Vitesse into smithereens I saw a flash of light that was nothing to do with the flames. It was whiter than the light of any fire and came from behind me, sending my shadow scurrying across the car park into infinity. It was accompanied by a whirring noise.

I turned round. It was a powerful flash gun on a very good camera. Behind the camera stood a cameraman. Behind the cameraman, directing operations, stood Kirk.

'Great stuff, Billy. Try to look really angry. Pose it, man.' The camera flashed and whirred again and again. It was Deidre's cousin from the *NME* (or was that *Debbie's* cousin from the *NME*?). Kirk giggled and clapped his hands like an excited child. He shouted out directions to the cameraman and then to me, so that every possible angle on the blaze and my part in it could be captured. He was in his element, the choreographer of chaos.

'This is anarchy man. This will put us on the map. Are you listening record companies? Get your fucking cheque books out. We're going to be big, Big, BIG.'

Five

The record companies didn't get their fucking chequebooks out when it came to paying my fine, they paid cash. Monty Gliver, owner of Tonic Bender Records, Bradworth's premier (indeed only) record company, took out a bundle of ten-pound notes that he'd earlier carefully counted and arrogantly tossed it to the chief cashier of Clitheroe Magistrates' Court.

'Keep the change, you capitalist lackey,' he said, loud enough for Lacy Tasker to hear. Lacy scribbled the quote into her notebook. The chief cashier wrote a receipt but refused Monty's request to make it out to 'Billy Petrol' on the grounds that no such person existed. Monty and Kirk pointed out that he did exist because that was my stage name and she'd better get used to it because I was going to be bigger than the bastard Beatles. Monty was in his fifties but had never lost touch with his youth. He had a perm that would have made Kevin Keegan blush, and wore teenage fashions that he had to have specially made to fit his portly frame. His chubby face never stopped beaming, even when he was asleep. This was probably because he was dreaming about his profits. All in all he worked hard to maintain his credibility as a young-at-heart streetwise hipster. All in all he was a big, fat, embarrassing wanker, but he was able to make decisions about me and my name because he was also a successful impresario. He owned both a recording studio and an independent record label, and managed several minor celebrities who made a living playing the tatty night-clubs in the area. It was Monty who had masterminded the 1972 top ten smash 'If You Could See What I Can See When I'm Reading Meters' by Bradworth's own whistling gas man, Tommy Trout. As potential financial backer of my new musical career he could call me anything he wanted, as long as he called me. The chief cashier remained unimpressed while Lacy followed the argument closely, scribbling the finer points of the debate in her book.

Lacy Tasker was seventeen years old and her pencil was more venomous than an Australian brown tree snake. She wrote for *Suck Up*, a local fanzine that had played a major part in fuelling the punk movement. Its photocopied and stapled sheets appeared 'every now and then' and man-aged a circulation which caused editors of the more staid mainstream music press considerable concern. The latest edition had me on the cover. I was walking away from a burning car in the company of two policemen; in the back-ground Kirk could be seen laughing. He was laughing because he was the one who had called them. The headline underneath, originally written in blue felt tip, read 'burn it down Billy uses petrol to flame the fans'. This had inspired Monty and Kirk to give me the name to go with my new image. Lacy was thinner than a bread stick and her pallor suggested she hadn't been outdoors for several years, which she probably hadn't. I would have described her as pretty if she'd put on a few dozen pounds, took fewer drugs and washed her turd-brown hair at least once a year. Lacy had assigned herself to following my career, sensing a scoop that would rival that of the Sex Pistols, who had recently

gone on tea-time television to tell Bill Grundy he was a dirty
fucker and who were now starring in the tabloids (and the
long-term plans of several major record companies) as a
result. A break like that would confirm Lacy's reputation
and give her the bargaining power to join one of the staid
mainstream music papers on her terms, which, unlike her
Suck Up activities, would involve regular payment. With
her eyes on the prize Lacy was giving the 'Billy Petrol
Affair' the full treatment .

As Monty led the party out of the court building, like
everyone's favourite, if slightly psychopathic uncle, she fell
in beside me.

'So, how does it feel to be a star?'

'Star?'

'Sure, that's what you are. "Star" means all sorts of stuff
these days. Meinhoff, Manson, Nixon. Nobody wants heroes
any more, criminals are the new stars.'

'Thanks. That makes me feel a lot better.'

'Trust me, you've got what it takes. That's why I'm investing so much in you.'

Down in my groin area there began a little dance, a
primeval urge jiggling to an ancient jungle rhythm, given life
by her suggestive comment. It was funny how I didn't fancy
her until there was a slight chance that she might fancy me,
and then she became the object of my desire. Unfortunately I
was badly out of touch with my primeval self.

'So tell me about Kirk,' she asked with more than a trace
of interest, 'is he shagging anyone?'

Outside, the group of unfamiliar faces who had gathered
to support me and be a part of what Lacy called 'the event'
were getting into their cars. By the time I got there all the
cars were full and the last available place on Kirk's knee
was gratefully grabbed by Lacy, her fragile form dropping
into his lap like a red admiral on to a sweet pea. She gave me
a snotty look before slamming the door in my face. I heard a
familiar voice behind me.

'Need a lift?' It was a voice I knew but which was some-how different. I turned and saw Gina, one time consort of Kirk. I hadn't seen her in the court but then I'd hardly taken my eyes off the magistrates as I concentrated on not shitting myself and ruining my only suit. Kirk had been accompa-nied by the Chinese girl, so I was sure Gina wasn't with him. She smiled. That was what was different about her, she was being nice to me. The groin dance began again.

'A lift would be . . . nice.' Bugger my vocabulary.

Gina had only two speeds, stop and ninety-nine miles per hour. In the face of this onslaught the car slipped and slid all over the road, so that Gina could never quite gain control. Not that she didn't do her best. She oversteered and under-steered and when that didn't work she didn't steer at all. Two cars moved on to the pavement rather than risk con-frontation and the one-way system immediately ground to a standstill.

'Is this car yours?' I asked, more to take my mind off the oncoming lorry, the driver of which was mouthing 'Holy Mother of Jesus', than for confirmation of ownership.

'Sort of,' she said, meaning that it was sort of hers in the sense that it was completely her father's.

We headed for the motorway. The Pennines parted like the thighs of a favourite centrefold and welcomed me in. I may have had my day in court, mocking the ridiculous ritual of it all in the full glare of the press, or at least the Lacy Tasker version of the press that used a photocopier rather than hot metal, but the bastards had still had the last laugh. As a condition of the probation order I had to reside some-where where I would be out of harm's way and where temptation would not find me. The magistrates had decided this should be my mum and dad's address. It was ironic as this was the one place where temptation would be all around me, given my lack of empathy with Mum and Dad. What the magistrates hadn't considered was that this solu-tion might tempt me to use Dad's collection of scythe blades for a more nefarious purpose. The promiscuous Pennines sucked me towards Bradworth. I'm not sure if it was the thought of home or Gina's terrible driving, but I suddenly felt very sick.

We were the first to arrive at Mum and Dad's despite being the last to leave the court. Mum was expecting us and stood at the front door offering a plate of chilled ham. Out of an upstairs bedroom window she had hung a sheet, freshly laundered, with the phrase 'Billy Wrose is Innocent' neatly written on it in red ink. She had, as usual, got it wrong but it was the thought that counted, which in her case didn't count for very much. Dad gave us a look that was even colder than the ham. Nothing had changed in the three months since I'd left, except that they'd stripped and redecorated my bedroom, removed any hint of my occupancy and turned it into a brushed-nylon haven for the guests they never had.

'At least the Russians will be comfy if they invade, Dad,' I said, but he chose not to hear.

Mum greeted Gina like she was a red-hot certainty for the daughter-in-law steeplechase.

'Not for me, Phyllis, I'm a veggie.' In seven brief words Gina had committed a joyous double blasphemy. Firstly, she had turned down Mum's offer of food and secondly she'd called her by her first name. I regretted that my frankness during the long terrifying journey had let out so many family secrets. Mum insisted on being called Felicia as it had a ring of the well-to-do about it that the name Phyllis could never aspire to, being too close as it was to 'syphilis'.

'Vegetarian?' Mum still couldn't grasp the principle even after I'd explained it to her. 'Are you a Catholic?' In Mum's world weirdos were usually Catholics, and as Catholics had an inherent loyalty to Rome, this also made them foreigners. She said that Gina was a pretty name, insinuating that it actually sounded like a dirty Eye-tie sort of name. I was relieved when Gina shut up, which was probably the one and only time she showed any tact. Then Kirk, Monty, Lacy and the rest of the hangers-on arrived and took Mum away on stuffed pork-roll duties.

We were all mesmerised by Monty's outrageous entrance – a Royal Command performance, involving several low bows and even some crocodile tears at the spontaneous ripple of applause his arrival caused. Then Kirk emptied amphetamines into the bowl of fruit punch and Monty's bonhomie subsided for a moment as we all sipped our lethal cocktails in silence. Dad was outside on the patio using a camel-hair brush to paint the hibernating roses with some concoction that would keep them clear of black spot the next summer. Unhappy that his delinquent son was being fêted for breaking the law, he was refusing to join the party. As far as Dad was concerned hanging would have been too good for me, in fact hanging baskets would have been too good for me. Monty nodded to Kirk. The two of them went off into a huddle in the glazed lean-to on the side of the house, which Mum and Dad pompously called the gazebo.

I chatted to Gina for a while, trying to hit a peak of wit that never even reached the foothills. Feeling awkward I grabbed a tray of potted-meat sandwiches and went over to pester Kirk and Monty. Monty gave me a smile as fake as his perm.

'My boy, come and join us,' he said, 'we're plotting the downfall of western capitalism.'

'Great spread, Billy, it's like a frigging funeral,' Kirk chuckled.

'It is a frigging funeral. It's the ham tea at the wake for Billy Wrose.'

'He's not dead,' Mum shouted at Monty, 'although he could do with a good square meal in him.' She took several empty glasses into the kitchen to give them the benefit of her special wash and wipe technique.

'Billy Wrose is dead, long live Billy Petrol,' Monty toasted.

'And I saw Warsaw,' Kirk said, raising his punch cup by the ridiculous tiny handle from which his little finger was elevated, like a polite Nazi salute.

'Who the fuck is Eyesore Walsall?' I asked, momentarily overwhelmed as the speed gatecrashed the party in my brain.

'I saw Warsaw. It's the new name of the band.'

'Very iron curtain, don't you think?' Monty chipped in quickly.

'I thought we were going to be called The Shit Shovellers,' I said, punch drunk and unable to remember what we decided, or what day it was, or who I was. Who was I?

'Too punk, it'll limit future appeal,' said Monty, as if mentally calculating distant profits.

'Monty's getting us a decent bassist and drummer.'

I tried to focus on Kirk. In the kitchen, over the splashing sounds of soapy water, I could hear Mum talking at two hundred words per minute, with no gaps or opportunity for intervention, on the subject of fabric conditioner and how a properly aired washroom could well do away with the need for it.

'Aren't you the bassist?' I said, stabbing a finger in what I thought was the direction of Kirk but which was actually towards the ceiling. Kirk and Monty both looked up to where I was pointing, as if I was showing them the way to true enlightenment. Above could be seen the dozens of identical swirling circular patterns of Artex that had taken Dad six months to perfect.

Monty said: 'You're needed for the overview, to give some sense of . . .'

'Yeah, that. I'm going to be the singer and writer too,' Kirk said.

'I thought I was going to do that . . . those.'

'You will. Well, you'll write the music and I'll do the words. Roll over Lennon and McCartney, eh, Billy?'

'Roll over Beethoven,' added Monty.

'Ahhm,' was all I could say. The effects of the drugs were making me hungry and horny but they were also reducing my vocabulary down to the level of my dad's. I resisted the hunger pangs despite the brief attraction of Mum's cheese straws, which were so good they not only looked like straw, they also tasted like it, and instead tried to concentrate on Gina's legs which I could see across the room.

'How many songs have you actually got?' Monty asked.

'I've got loads,' Kirk lied. He smiled at me.

'Hinng,' I said. Kirk wisely changed the subject.

'I'm going to call myself "Don One" from now on, what do you think?' But all I could think about was the fact that we had only one song, and I wrote that, and it was crap. It was a turgid number about unrequited love (Claire Heaton from the lower sixth), a society that oppresses lovers from different backgrounds (her mum hated the sight of me), and the eventual failure of love in the face of an unfriendly world (I threw up over Claire's Dansette and ruined her copy of 'Ziggy Stardust'). It was my first attempt at song writing and the best that could be said about it was that things could only get better. Whatever the truth, Monty was impressed, or just so stoned he didn't give a fuck.

'Excellent. We'll need a demo of course, and then gigs. Maybe even a trip to America?' Monty looked like a cartoon crook accidentally given the keys to a bank vault. He had pound-note signs in his eyes.

'Not before you've thought about an advance,' said Kirk, adding assertively, 'and then doubled it.'

Monty looked at me a little impatiently. He laughed a laugh that was so fraudulant the ink was still wet, put his arm around Kirk, and said, 'Not in front of the children, dear.' He led him to the table in the corner of the gazebo where Dad liked to read the *Daily Mail* and perfect his outbursts of right-wing indignation. Kirk gave me a 'let me handle this, I know what I'm doing' wink.

I went off in search of the woman I was prepared to fall in love with, especially if it meant having lots of dirty sex that thoroughly debased the both of us. The drugs were making me even more irrational than usual, because I actually believed both of these things would happen. Dad was buzzing around the living room as Lacy had enticed him indoors and given him a glass of punch. He was now talking to everyone, like a chipmunk on helium. Everyone apart from me. It was medical proof that, despite the views of many experts, even mind-bending drugs can't undo years of social conditioning. Mum was busy flirting with every man in the room, and by the look of her wobbly mouth and wet lips she had seen more of the punch than Sonny Liston. It was horrible. Watching your parents get stoned is even worse than watching them have sex.

The whole thing was unreal. Everywhere dozens of people who I had never seen before hung around in small groups, laughing, talking, shouting, drinking, smoking and speeding. It was Dante's inferno with Twiglets and warm Liebfraumilch. I sat on the bottom stair and waited for something to happen, hopefully something dropped by the Enola Gay, that would end this horror. My head was down so I only saw the gorgeously familiar legs as they slowly and sexily appeared in my field of vision.

'Show me around?' It was Gina but it wasn't her voice. It was a voice from an old science fiction film and it was giving heavy hints of things to come. I stood up, obeying the demands of my rushing brain, which wanted to party for at least half a century. This keenness to get on and get down made me grab for her arm, which she interpreted as affection. Maybe things weren't so bad after all. Confidence growing at the same rate as my erection, I decided to start showing her around upstairs, preferably beginning with a room that had a lock on the inside of the door. Romantic bastard that I was I chose the bathroom. Dad's freshly washed pants hung like the sails of a becalmed tea clipper over the bath.

'Isn't it funny that as men get older their pants get bigger?' Gina said, perceptively. I nodded in agreement as I hastily took them off the shower rail and threw them out of the open window. I couldn't risk her thinking that the offending acreage of white cotton belonged to me. She laughed and I pushed the bolt across, locking us in. The smell of damp towels and Dad's Old Spice provided an erotic backdrop as we began a bout of sexual wrestling, three rounds, two falls, total submission. We took it in turns to avoid touching the plastic shower curtain with our bare skin. As I released the tension on Gina's bra strap it twanged like a Duane Eddy solo. The hook caught in my earring and then, like a mugger dragging his victim into the bushes, pulled the lobe around the back of my head.

'Jesus,' I screamed, as politely as I could.

'Is that nice?' she asked, referring to the tips of her fingers as they said farewell to the last-chance saloon of my belt and moved south. The pain in my ear wasn't nice, in fact it was awful. But as her fingers found my fly buttons, pain was suddenly a distant memory.

'Oh God,' I moaned, the way I'd seen people in racy movies moan.

'Billy?' There was an urgent knocking on the bathroom door.

'Oh God,' I moaned, the way I did when Mum fucked up my life. Gina started to snort with laughter and expertly put her beautiful breasts away into the beautiful black bra and then replaced her beautifully tight sweater over the lot. Shit.

'Coming, Mum,' I said. Gina gave me a 'You wish . . .' look. I tried not to think about my erection in the hope that it would go down. This made it worse. It now took on the proportions of Cleopatra's Needle, threatening to tear my trousers asunder, burst out and shout, 'Look, Ma, top of the world!' Mum wasn't bothered or suspicious at the two flustered people who came guiltily out of her bathroom adjusting their clothes, probably because she was too busy pushing past and throwing up in the sink.

'What a swell party this is,' I said, trying to sound ironic while privately wishing that Mum would disappear down the plug hole along with her vomit.

Across the landing I saw the guest-room door closing. Through the narrowing gap I could make out Kirk and Lacy, reading Lacy's notebook and laughing. Gina saw them too.

'Bastard.'

'Does it bother you?' I asked, hoping she would say no.

'No,' she said. It was funny how, now she had said it, it didn't make me feel any better.

'You and him . . . have you . . . are you?' I couldn't bring myself to finish the one question I wanted to finish.

'God no. No. No,' she said firmly. I sighed with relief.

'Good.'

'No, not recently.' Her indecision was helping my erection collapse so fast it was inverting into my groin.

Downstairs someone had put 'Anarchy In The UK' on Dad's old radiogram and turned the volume up to 10. The ancient needle was clearly enjoying having a run through fresh vinyl, rather than the well-worn paths of Reg Dixon's organ favourites that it was used to. Dad came panting upstairs, announcing his arrival with a variety of 'Hurrums' and 'Harraps' as he did so. Chatting to the Chinese girl about the art of bonsai, he had absent-mindedly polished off several more cups of punch, and this had not only spaced out his mad mind even further but had also filled his minuscule bladder and turned him into the incredible leaking man. He begged Gina's pardon as he passed, calling her 'dear' as if she were a well-established member of the family, ignored Mum as she wailed 'Oh my Christ' down the plug hole, and happily pissed in open view of all of us.

'Lummd,' he said, which roughly translated as 'Better out than in'.

'Billy, what's happened to you?' Gina was suddenly looking at me with renewed interest, only this time it was ghoulish rather than sexual.

'What? What do you mean?' It was clear from her concern that there was something seriously wrong with my face.

'Where's the nearest mirror?' she asked, hinting heavily

that I should go to it, without passing Go or collecting two
hundred pounds.

The nearest mirror was in my old bedroom, the one I had
just seen Kirk and Lacy enter, and even the huge quantities
of speed in my bloodstream couldn't convince me to break
in on them. Instead I ran downstairs to the hall where there
was a full-length, gold-plated mirror with little silver swal-
lows cut into the glass (Mum had chosen it). A small group
of hangers-on watched me descend the stairs and began
applauding. The reflection that greeted me was one of total
carnage. There was blood everywhere, pouring initially
from my ripped ear and then spreading far and wide,
helped on its way by the recent frenzied grope with Gina. It
was on my face, my hands and my clothes, and, I discovered
much later, Gina's breasts. I was awash with the stuff. Monty
cut through the crowd like a scythe.

'Dear boy, you have the gift. An outrage for every occasion. I love you.' To prove it he kissed me on my bloodied
cheek. Lacy leaned over the stair rail, smugly dishevelled.

'Nice touch. Cool cat calmly coagulates. Very sexy,' she
shouted, before going back into the bedroom where she had
left her notebook.

Six

I didn't meet Chopper and Churchill until February 1977 at
I saw Warsaw's first rehearsal. Chopper's real name was
Blackburn, but that wasn't punk enough so Kirk changed it.
I never found out Churchill's real name; all I knew was that
he was called Churchill because he was a football hooligan
who, during the closed season, went to the nearest seaside
town and fought on the beaches. Churchill was a drummer,
Chopper played bass. Chopper was a serious player, a real
musician, and Monty had chosen him to give my songs
'feel'.

'One word, Billy boy, "longevity". If you want longevity
your songs must have feel.' I think what he meant was that
they should have a melody, structure, and preferably be in
the right key. Chopper was a boring prat who thought he
was the best musician in the band. This arrogance was
fuelled by the fact that he was the best musician in the band.
Of course it wasn't a difficult achievement as he was also the
only musician in the band. If Chopper was a proper musician, I was, in comparison to Churchill, Mozart, with several
knobs on. He thrashed the drums as if they were a sworn
enemy, such as a Leeds United fan, and he didn't give a shit

about rhythm or beat as long as it was bloody loud and pissed off the neighbours. Monty had chosen Churchill to give the band an anarchic edge. The one word you wouldn't use when describing Churchill's lifestyle was longevity.

'Your image is about pretending to take risks, Billy. But Churchill really takes them. He'll be good for headlines.' Monty was working on his image as Media Manipulator on account that it made him seem interesting. Punk was freeing him in the same way that it had freed me. People who had a bit of capital and an entrepreneurial spirit could harness the forces that were at large and make a name for themselves. They could also make huge amounts of money. Three grand, a cash-in-hand deal with a pressing plant, and five grams of coke in your back pocket and you could become a fully fledged His Master's Voice in miniature. Monty had all the required attributes bar one, he was boring. His fondness for slacks, his morbid fear of being caught not wearing an expansively flared rayon tie, his psychological need to be within reach of his cardboard briefcase at all times, combined with his forty-something age and fifty-something white hair, which gave him the air of a seedy, slightly over-the-hill string mop, helped undermine his claim to be 'Punk's cool banker'.

'Punk's total wanker,' Churchill dubbed him, rather predictably.

Kirk, on the other hand, had no need to enhance his personality. It was already reaching the gigantic proportions of a paranoid monster. He was throwing all his energies into plotting the band's tactics, developing a 'master plan' that he wouldn't share with anyone, least of all me. In fact he didn't share anything with me. I had now written three songs, both words and music. Kirk had looked at them and listened as I played and sang them. He'd said he'd give them some more thought before tidying them up a bit. We were well into rehearsals and they were still as untidy as when I had written them.

At the fifth rehearsal we took the unusual step of actually practising. We decided to forgo the usual snort of white powder or two, which inevitably led to everyone lying around trying to remember how to plug the instruments in. After half an hour of free-form rehearsing Chopper broke off from his favourite and interminable Miles Davis jazz riff.

'I like that one about the policewoman. It's got an ingenuous sense of whimsy,' he said in his usual smart arse tone.

We went through it again:

> Oh, I love police woman
> I wish she were my police mate
> If I were only three inches taller
> We'd live together in a police state.

'I fucking hate that song,' Kirk spat angrily. 'What is it saying? "I like women in uniform"? It's so juvenile. It's wasting our time.'

It was difficult to cope with Kirk when he was in this kind of mood and he usually was in this kind of mood when Lacy was present, her notebook perpetually open at a fresh page ready to record every gory detail of the band's birth pains. If I had been a bit more cynical I might have suspected that when Kirk was acting-up in front of her, he was doing just that, acting.

'He's trying to impress her so he can knob her,' was Churchill's observation.

'It's about policewomen and, you know, the fascist state,' I explained, trying to play down the ingenuous whimsy. 'It's like, uniforms can cause sexual, as well as political, oppression,' I said, mainly for Lacy's benefit.

'What fucking shite. The Pistols sing about anarchy, The Clash about white riots and we sing about emotionally stunted gits with a fascistic fetish for women in stockings.' It was Kirk's lips that were moving but I was sure it was Lacy's words that were coming out.

'The Damned are covering Beatles numbers. It's about fun as much as class war. I like it, it's very British. Reminds me of The Kinks.' Chopper had to mention The Kinks, and he'd been doing so well, the boring bastard.

On cue, Kirk reacted, kicking a speaker cabinet over and throwing a glass ashtray in Chopper's general direction. Boring bastard though he surely was, Chopper ducked like a member of an élite squad in the armed forces

'The Kinks? How many times do I have to tell you, you muso scumbag, the 60s are dead. D.E.A.D.' Kirk spelled it out just in case we missed the subtleties of his argument.

'For fuck's sake.' He took Lacy's hand and dragged her out of the 1st Bradworth Scouts and Guides HQ which had been hired for the purpose of band practice. It was the second time that day and the fifth time that week he had walked out after one of us had committed some indefinable error. If it wasn't admitting to the wrong set of musical influences, as Chopper frequently did, it was me writing stupid lyrics or Churchill's Neanderthal behaviour. I rolled another joint, Chopper disappeared to the toilet for an hour and Churchill returned to carving his initials on the sadly empty 'Roll of Honour' notice-board.

'Told you,' he said, mid-whittle.

'Told me what?'

'He's probably knobbing her right now, the sly bastard.'

We had chosen to make our base in Bradworth partly to satisfy the requirements of my probation order and partly because it suited the band's image. I had been dubbed 'The Bradworth Bomber' and this provincial authenticity gave us real credibility. The 'Hicksville USA Factor', as Lacy called it, was central to punk. The thing had been born in London and most of the big name bands came from there, but this was a movement that allowed anyone to get up and do it, even in dull backwaters like Bradworth, which, surprised at suddenly becoming cool, began producing home-grown talent from under every damp stone. The fact that it was also Monty's home town meant that he could round up all the usual contacts and give us a head start.

'And anyway,' he said when we jealously eyed the London scene from the squalor of our scout hut, with its distinctive aroma of uncontrolled pubescent urges and stale biscuits, 'once we've cracked it we'll all bugger off to the smoke and make the big money.' I laughed, sure he was joking, because the point of punk was that it couldn't be bought and that was why everyone was so scared of it. I must have looked like an apple from Marks and Spencer, it was so obvious that I was fresh off the tree

Bradworth was also handy for Kirk, who was still living and working in Clitheroe. The pittance he earned from his job as a chef kept us in guitar strings and lager. None of the rest of us worked, which probably didn't help Kirk's temper. Instead we relied on unemployment benefit and Monty's less than generous handouts to fund our substantial narcotic appetites. He wasn't rich but he was a lot richer than any of us and clearly intended to stay that way.

Being based in Bradworth also meant I was within easy reach of Gina although I hadn't taken advantage of this nearness as yet, unlike Kirk and Lacy who took every advantage of theirs. Lacy was now unofficial press officer for the band, a post created by Kirk while we were all down the pub one night. They were now rarely apart, although both claimed it was a purely professional relationship. I wished I could be having a similar professional relationship with Gina. We hadn't seen one another since my coming-out party. I had her home phone number but I hadn't dared ring it for three reasons. Firstly I kidded myself that I didn't want to hurt Kirk's feelings, which was daft because he didn't have any that I could see. Secondly, I was sure she'd tell me to drop dead. The last thing she'd said as she left the party, driving over Dad's crocus bed, was that I shouldn't assume I owned her. She was a woman and that gave her rights. I nodded, pretending I understood what she meant, and jumped back from the car's spinning wheels just in time to avoid having my legs torn off. Another reason was because I had a sneaking suspicion that if I said the wrong thing she was capable of ripping off other bits of my body.

During the spring of 1977 punk was seeping out everywhere, like a bad head wound into a clean white bandage. Everyone under twenty was in a band. Everyone in our local pub was in a band. Everyone we knew was in a band. Some of these bands actually existed and others were mere names scrawled on the cover of someone's school exercise book. There were the Dead Bastards, Yummy Treats and The Cock Suckers, all of whom were formed over someone's mum's kitchen table at lunchtime and disbanded before last orders on the same day. Others, like Dub Certainty, Warmed Up Stiff Bodies, and Fucking Rubbish made it to rehearsals but no further. We were different. We were going to make records, we were going to tour, we were going to be massive. We were sure of this because we had Monty, who, while definitely dodgy, at least had proven form. He kept making noises about 'American dates' that he was negotiating with his 'Stateside contact'. This was another affectation of Monty's, he talked in quotation marks. He talked about our 'major potential', he told Lacy that I had 'an aura', and that Kirk was 'central to the whole blag'. None of us knew what he was on about but we liked it because it flattered us, which was why he did it.

Lacy also believed the band had major potential. She'd managed to get a couple of pieces into the wider music press, in which she described us as both etiolated and plangent, as well as verging on the prescient. The headline had read 'Punk Pirates Shiver Me Timbres'. If Monty talked in quotation marks Lacy talked like a dictionary. Lacy spent days finding the exact word to describe something. She preferred words that no one had ever heard before and then tossed them in as if they were part of everyday usage, challenging the reader to admit their ignorance. Churchill laughed when he read her assertion in *Melody Maker* that we were eclectic.

'Course we're electric, stupid tart. Is she thick or what?'

'That's eclectic, Churchill,' Chopper pointed out in an unwisely patronising tone. 'It means we draw our influence from a wide variety of sources.' I heard the smack in the next room as his nose felt the shattering influence of Churchill's forehead, very hard.

The *NME* carried spotty new faces and shaky new ideas on its front cover every week. We read it avidly and either loudly dismissed them, which meant we wished we'd thought of it first, or laughingly mocked them, which meant we wished we'd thought of it first. Lacy was working hard to help us achieve a similar status. The piece she wrote for *Sounds* was a bogus review of our first gig which had yet to happen. She raved about our genius, which we liked, and our Rabelaisian disinterring of the realities of the 70s' zeitgeist, which we didn't understand enough to have an opinion on.

In the national press Punk was a major talking point along the lines of 'this evil is poisoning our kids' minds and turning them against us'. I read this in Mum and Dad's newspaper and could only disagree. 'Too fucking late,' I thought, 'that happened years ago.'

I spent little time at home, preferring to hang around the rehearsal room, Monty's flat, or the pub. I only went home to be present at the monthly visit from the probation officer, a ragged little man who was more burned out than Mike Gummerson's car. Mum enjoyed his visits though, and always baked a tray of cakes specially. The probation officer, who was divorced, due mostly to his total lack of social, emotional and practical skills, started to bring his dirty laundry along and he and Mum happily discussed the complexity of immigration regulations while waiting for it to complete its wash spin cycle. The reason why he was there in the first place, me, was completely overlooked. Freed from the torture of answering questions like 'How did that make you feel?', I was able to go upstairs and practise my stage presence in the bedroom mirror.

Kirk and Lacy were now in charge of strategy. They'd discuss it late into the night, locked in the spare bedroom of Monty's flat, where they spent much of their time. Churchill nudged me hard in the ribs.

'He'd poke anything, wouldn't he? She so skinny I'm surprised she don't break in two.' I wasn't sure if he was poking her even though they spent hours locked in the bedroom together. Most of the time they only seemed to be talking, although there were occasional short bursts of grunts and giggles. I wanted to appear as a man of the world who knew about such things and yet the uncomfortable feeling was starting to grow in my mind that I knew very little. I didn't know what to say to Gina, I didn't know how to play guitar (even though I now had a lovely cherry red Gibson SG which Monty had 'loaned' me the money for, insisting that decent instruments, while having less street cred, sounded better) and I didn't know how to write songs. If Kirk was right and 'Police Woman' was a pile of shit, quirky and British maybe, but still shit, then perhaps I knew fuck all about anything. Unusually for a moronic, vicious, uncaring bastard, Churchill came to my aid.

We were at Monty's flat and had been drinking vodka with slimline tonic and then, when that ran out, cough mixture with slimline tonic. We spent all our spare time at Monty's flat because he was always out 'doing deals' and didn't care what we did so long as we remembered to feed his cats. It was somewhere in the middle of the night, or possibly the middle of the day; it was hard to tell after the third bottle of Benylin. We were out of fags and had begun rolling up the dog-ends from the ashtray. I was about to start rolling up from the dog-ends of the already rolled up dog-ends when Churchill, who I'd thought was asleep but was actually trying to out-stare the ceiling tiles, suddenly reared up from Monty's sofa like a monster from the deep, grabbed the phone and hit me on the head with the receiver.

'Twat. Ring her.'

'Who?' I asked, rubbing my eye, wondering if the blurred and double vision was a result of the blow, the vodka, the cough mixture or the third-hand, third-lunged tobacco.

'Her, the bag. Gina. She's your only fucking hope.'

'But I don't know anything about her. I don't know if we've got anything in common. I don't know if she feels about me the way I feel about her.' I was giving him all the arguments I had been rehearsing in my head every night for the last two months. I waited for him to give me back the line I had deliberately fed him. The one about 'Well you won't know unless you ask her, will you'.

'Fuck all that crap. Get her over, shag her, then chuck her. At least you'll have something to think about while you're doing all that wanking.' He held the phone menacingly, as I cursed the lack of privacy available in Monty's toilet. 'Hey, you could even write songs about it,' he added enthusiastically. I thought about it, it wasn't a bad idea. I rolled us both a recycled ash cigarette to celebrate.

'It'd be like using my dick to write songs, wouldn't it?'

'Would it? Ouch,' he replied, unable to grasp this delicate use of symbolism.

As a rule Punk songs were two minutes, thirty seconds long. Which by a happy coincidence was about the average duration of my sexual performance including foreplay. In fact it was the foreplay that managed to push it over the two-minute mark. The medium was made for me. All I needed was the experience to write about. I rang her. Her dad answered. He pointed out, clearly and concisely, that it was three-thirty a. bastard m. He had every right to be angry but, to his credit, at least he passed on my message. The next morning she rang me back.

'Listen, I'm sorry,' she said.

'That's OK. I was about to get up and have breakfast.' I looked at the clock, it was nearly eleven.

'No, I mean about us.'

'Us?' I didn't like the sound of 'us', it sounded too close to 'I wouldn't go out with you if I was a raving nymphomaniac and you were the last man on earth'.

'Me and you, it wouldn't be right.' Oh bollocks, I thought, here it comes.

'No?' I said, trying not to sound like I was begging even though I was.

'Me, you, the bathroom thing. It was on the rebound. I was on the rebound. From Kirk. I'm sorry. I really like you,' she said, meaning that I was a pathetic squirt.

'Thanks for being honest, I really appreciate that,' I replied, a pathetic squirt who was a red-hot tip for the pathetic squirt of the year award.

She said she would come to our first gig and we promised to stay friends. I put down the phone and twenty-two minutes later had written 'Probably The Last Song I'll Ever Write About Gina', which was actually the first of thirty-eight songs I wrote about her, all of them seeking bitter vengeance.

> You dream of another's jeans
> I'm spitting in my sleep
> You contaminate these feelings
> Love's a whore and you're just cheap.

'That's better,' Kirk said and beamed the first time I sang it for him. He took the scraps of paper that I had written it on and went off to 'just smooth off one or two rough edges'. Monty said he thought 'the Americans' would love it and immediately booked us into his Tonic Bender Studio to record it. The studio was a poky room he rented over a sewing-machine shop and in which he'd installed an ancient eight track to produce low-quality demo tapes for the highest possible hourly rate.

We were all fighting less now. Even at rehearsals, and despite a feigned indifference to the task, we were actually working harder on our music than on our image. We still started every day with a chemical breakfast but had now cut the barley wines down to one or two social bottles. We were becoming the 'I saw Warsaw, electric noise for acoustic ears', that Monty was promoting heavily. He had even arranged our first gig, hyping us up on the back of Lacy's unfathomable reviews in order to sell more tickets and generate interest amongst 'the business'.

A week before the gig, we were recording what would eventually form the basis of our first album. I had given it the working title of 'That was Zen, but this is Nous'. We'd taken a break while the engineer put ear drops in to ease the pain. Kirk took me on one side.

'When we finish here, I want you to load the gear into Churchill's van.'

'It's all right, Mont says we can store it here.'

'No, I'd rather we took it away, it's the gig next week and I want us to remain . . . flexible.' Kirk was implying something was up but I couldn't tell what. I figured it was best to go along with him, as to disagree would inevitably spark one of his Lacy-led tantrums.

We finished the third take of 'Sulphate Sex' (written about a wet dream in which I'd had an erotic encounter with Gina and I'd composed while the sheets were still damp) when Kirk took Mice, the almost deafened studio engineer, out back for a celebratory spliff. As he did so he waved his arms behind his back to indicate we should start loading up, quietly. We dutifully put everything into Churchill's transit and waited for him. After about ten minutes the front door to the sewing-machine shop opened and Kirk came running across the road towards us.

'Get the fucker started,' he yelled. We stared at him, bemused, and did nothing.

'Get bastard going for bastard's sake.' I looked at Chopper who looked at Churchill, who started the engine without a word.

Kirk leaped from the pavement about seventy feet away and landed inside the back of the van. I grabbed his arm to secure him against the G-force acceleration of Churchill's knackered transit. In his hand was something familiar.

'It's the tape,' I said, matter-of-factly.

'I know,' he said, equally matter-of-factly. Behind us the shop door was thrown open for a second time and the twenty-two stone figure of Mice filled its frame.

'Come back here, you thieving bastards,' he shouted, a death threat in every decibel.

'Go, Church, go,' Kirk yelled. 'If he catches us we're dead.'

I wanted to query Kirk's use of 'us' and 'we're' as I wasn't aware the rest of us had done anything to incur the wrath of Mice, who, apart from being a brilliant sound recordist, was also the man Monty employed to frighten off his business rivals.

'We've got to have the tape,' Kirk tried to explain.

'Why?'

'It's ours. Possession is nine tenths of the law. These are my songs . . .'

'Our songs,' I corrected, still being over generous as they were really my songs.

'Our songs. And we deserve a good deal on them. Fuck Monty, he's treating us like small fry. He needs a reminder of our potential.' Judging by the look on Mice's fast disappearing face the only potential we'd have if he caught up with us would be as fish bait.

We avoided Monty for the next few days. Word was out he was looking for us but we politely refused to return his calls, instead we went into hiding at Kirk's place. I returned home on the day of our first gig, unsure if it would still be on. Mum gave me seventeen phone messages from Monty that ranged from 'Let's talk' to 'Tell him he's fast becoming an endangered species'. Mum thought the last one was sweet, assuming Monty was merely affirming that mine was a rare talent. I set off for the club leaving Mum and Dad to watch *Top of the Pops*. Mary McGregor was claiming to be 'Torn Between Two Lovers' and not sounding too unhappy about it, probably because she was also torn between great piles of cash. The message of the song made me think about Gina, the bloody cow. Dad threw a comment into the ether that it was 'a proper song, not like some rubbish I could mention' as I stuffed my guitar into its case and prepared to catch the bus into town. I felt like I was setting out on a great adventure that could lead anywhere. The first place it led to was the dressing room at Stabbers, which was not a particularly salubrious start. I was wearing ripped jeans, ripped T-shirt and ripped school tie; I looked the antithesis of a million dollars. 'I Don't Care' was scratched across the front of my expensive guitar. I was hip, happening and ready to go.

Churchill was drinking lager with an aftershave top and was also ready to go. He was persuading Chopper to shave off his moustache so that he would also be properly attired for our big moment. Persuasion was something Churchill was very good at.

'Shave the fucker off, you frigging, hippie, jazzy, bastard, or I'll bottle your ugly face. Seen?' Chopper saw and quickly shaved in the dirty sink provided by an ever generous club management. His lip bled for hours from the excesses of the blunt razor but Churchill wouldn't let him clean it off, because it looked 'fucking A1'.

Kirk arrived late with the sheaf of papers on which I had written the fruit of my labours. He had yet to make a single change to any of them.

'Are we shit hot or what?' he asked. We nodded to

indicate the former. Monty followed Kirk in through the door, which was actually an ancient red velvet curtain. Monty looked like an evil assassin swathed in the blood-red cloak. I was glad to see that he hadn't brought Mice with him.

'Boys,' he said, doing an unconvincing imitation of someone being apologetic. 'Things have been said that shouldn't have been said.' He looked at Kirk, as if he hoped it was for the last time, 'And things have been done that shouldn't have been done.'

'If you want the tape you've got to be prepared to deal.' Kirk didn't look up from reading the pile of song lyrics as he spoke.

'I think when you hear about the American dates, which as we speak are in the final stages of being firmed up for finalisation, you will return the tape to your old mate Monty, probably wrapped in a pink bow.'

A voice from the other side of the curtain told us to get on stage or we'd not be paid.

'It's a bit early,' I said, looking at the broken clock on the wall.

'It's never too early to change the world,' Monty enthused, 'trust me.'

It was too early for the audience at Stabbers nightclub. There were only twenty or so people waiting for us as we went on stage with our expensive instruments carefully camouflaged to look crap. I struck the first chord of 'Looking for the Perfect Haircut'. Kirk unleashed his well-rehearsed stage persona, which consisted mainly of pointing at the crowd and calling them wankers. Churchill set off on an uncompromising abuse of his drum kit which bore no resemblance to the songs we had rehearsed. Chopper was the only one concentrating on the music. His fluid bass lines kept our fractured and fragmented sound together, just. It was great, I felt alive, as if the electricity feeding the Simms Watts' amps was also flowing through me. We played for thirty minutes on full throttle. The crowd liked us but even their enthusiasm couldn't make up for the fact that hardly anyone was there. We tried to compensate by banging out an extra twenty thousand watts of impure sound that would have made Mice's ears bleed again, had he been there.

But he wasn't there, he was across town, providing security at another gig promoted by Monty. The other gig was packed with our potential audience, who were watching a band called Jason's Magic Fleece. This wasn't their real name, their real name was The Sex Pistols. They were doing a low-key tour, a necessity forced on them by media pressure which had ensured they were banned everywhere. Monty had been contacted by the band's management as the major, indeed only, local impresario who could set up such a concert. Given the choice between our ungrateful behaviour and the opportunity to swim in the big pool of concert promotion, he'd made the only decision he could. He'd chosen the money. It was my first experience of watching the old guard reorganise, infiltrate and eventually take over and exploit the forces of revolution. As far as Monty was concerned Punk was going to be popular and what was popular made him rich, and why care if it did give him a headache. Mice had come up with the name Jason's Magic Fleece in order to convince the club owners that it was just a bunch of safe drippy hippies. Monty then put the whisper around and word of mouth had sold out the gig within five days. If we hadn't been hiding in Kirk's horrible little flat in Clitheroe we might have heard something, instead of which we were exposed as the stupid idiots that we undoubtedly were. We had missed the opportunity to play in front of hundreds of punk hungry fans, journalists and record company executives.

'What a cheat,' Kirk said, disguising his own hypocrisy with well-practised verve.

'Sorry, boys, but that, as you will one day learn, is

business,' Monty said, unable or unwilling to hide his victorious tone. 'I think this experience will make us stronger.'

'Us?' Chopper asked.

'Us, you, the band.'

'Oh,' Chopper, Churchill and I said in unison.

Despite Monty's machinations the gig had given us a buzz that was better, and, as it turned out, more addictive, than any of the drugs we took to give us courage to get on stage in the first place. I was still high from both when Gina came into the dressing room. I thought she looked like a princess swathed in the red velvet curtain, but then I was out of my head. Kirk winked at her and raised a bottle of beer in an ironic fashion.

'Hi, Toots'

'Drop dead,' she said. Encouraging start I thought. Lacy and Kirk sniggered quietly together and returned to their usual private whispers. Lacy laughed out loud and said that the opprobrium of a woman wronged was a terrible thing to witness. While Kirk giggled she wrote it down in her notebook. Out in the hall Churchill was throwing up and Chopper was hiding in a toilet somewhere, so things were pretty much as usual.

'You were good,' Gina said.

'Thanks, we tried our best.'

'No, the band were shit. Kirk can't sing to save his life, anyone would think he'd never read the lyrics before. But you were good.'

'Thanks,' I said, trying to ignore the jungle rhythm that had started up once more down below in the dark depths of my jeans.

'Do you want to go somewhere?'

I wasn't sure if she was talking about my career, or me and her. She ignored this hesitation.

'Can we go somewhere, now?' Never known for her patience, she didn't wait for an answer; instead she grabbed my hands and pulled me out of the ancient soiled armchair, led me through the thick velvet curtain, and into the hell that is an incompatible relationship.

We walked back to Monty's flat via the corporation playing fields, where I noticed the football pitches had almost recovered from my efforts with the weedkiller the previous summer. As we crossed the centre circle Gina paused. She stood absolutely still and took a deep breath. She was moving her lips as if arguing out the pros and cons of what she was about to do. Then, as if she had decided the terrible thing must be done even though she might regret it, she relaxed. I watched her, confused. Like a rabbit on the motorway at night. That was when she leaped. She wrestled me to the ground and rolled on top of me. She was wriggling and struggling with something that she eventually worked free with a grunt. It was her top, which she threw away into the darkness and the general direction of the corner flag. She rolled over, forcing me into a position on top of her. She handled me roughly and with urgency, as if hurrying before something made her change her mind. She undid the buttons on my jeans and slid them down expertly using her legs as levers. The narrow drainpipe bottoms got stuck over my motorcycle boots, which I hurriedly kicked off breaking the ankle zips without a care. We rolled over again, and again, continuing this roly-poly role reversal as we shed our clothes alternately, until we were both naked. I finished up on top, Gina lay below me in the wet, cold mud of the Bradworth Juniors practice pitch.

I employed every technique I had read about in various men's magazines to try and fully satisfy her, before embarking on the brief and inevitably disappointing act of full penetration. She encouraged me with 'yes's' and 'ohs' that I tried hard to ignore so that I didn't get over excited. We were both covered in a thick film of mud by the time she gave up trying to find fulfilment and instead violently pulled me into her to get it over with. I focused on a distressing scene from my childhood memories, of which I had plenty to choose from, in order to try and prolong my sexual stamina, as I began the rhythmic thrust that I had spent a lot of time practising. Alone. She began massaging my buttocks, roughly, giving them something that was between a fondle and a slap.

'Kinky,' I said, feeling a dangerous flush of excitement in my loins. I reduced my thrusts down to three per minute.

'What?' she asked angrily, her concentration momentarily broken. I picked up the tempo and gave a couple more quick thrusts that took me closer to the edge of no return. I risked opening an eye and was gratified to see she had hers firmly shut. She was obviously thinking about something. I wondered if it was me. I threw what little caution remained to the wind. She moaned reassuringly, which didn't help. If Monty had been with us his advice would have been 'Longevity, dear boy, you need longevity'.

Her activities around my buttocks were increasing and it was turning me on like mad. It was like having them gently scrubbed with heavy, damp glass-paper. I wondered if the Chinese girl's grandmother had known about that one. Gina let out a sexy little scream that made ejaculation, already a probability, now an imminent inevitability. It would have taken two world wars to stop me now.

'K . . .' she started to shout, then bit her lip. In my jealous mind World War I had just begun.

'. . . Khrist,' she finished, unconvincingly. Suddenly something really weird happened to my arse. The glass paper was no longer just damp, it was wet, so wet it was almost tidal. How was she doing this? It was amazing. It was incredible. And now it was horrible. World War II had been declared. I was first to hear the snuffle. I turned around and saw the huge Labrador with its big black nose and even bigger pink tongue hovering over my backside.

'This is fun,' the look on its big soft face said, 'better than fetching sticks, and much, much tastier.' It licked its lips as

Gina dug her nails into my shoulders trying to force me to a climax. Instead I anti-climaxed. All I could think of was finishing the whole thing, getting dressed, killing the dog and running home for a long hot bath. Afterwards, as we continued our walk across the playing fields, Gina told me that it was normal for a man to fail on the big occasion in a tone which implied that it was also laughable and pathetic. As she went through the motions of appearing concerned, she insisted on playing with the dog, patting it, whispering in its ear and kissing its nose. As lovers went it was clear which one of us she preferred.

From nowhere the dog produced a ball.

'What a clever boy,' she said, picking it up and throwing it gladly.

'This evening should make for an interesting song,' I said to myself, as I followed her and the dog home.

Seven

The white cotton T-shirt hugged the man's muscular chest so tightly that the logo printed on the front followed the curving lines of well-toned muscle as closely as a child's finger follows a line in a story book. This made the logo wobble uncertainly in places although it never completely obscured its message. 'I was in 'Nam', it stated proudly.

Around the table there were another six of these shirts, all of them seemingly spray-painted across ridiculously manly torsos, subjecting the material to the severest of stretch tests. As well as bearing the same proud legend, the shirts contained a second, more subliminal message. It said that these men were as hard as nails that had just undergone basic training with the Nail Foreign Legion, Psychopathically Hard Brigade. There were dozens of these men in the Club House bar. Most of them were black, attracted to the venue by the prospect of sweet soulful entertainment guaranteed to soothe even the most savage breast. From the wooden ceiling above their uniformly short hair hung a flaccid banner that looked like it had been made out of an old sheet. Yellow stains spread out from the centre and it touchingly reminded me of my own bed at home. It said:

America Welcomes Isaac Walsall – British Funk at its Best –
Get Down Isaac!

If this was meant to feel welcoming it fell some distance
short of the mark. It merely reinforced the sense of dread
that all four of us felt. We were scared. If this was autumn in
New York you could keep it.

Except that it wasn't New York because it wasn't America,
it wasn't even autumn. On the reverse of the men's shirts
was another logo, a cartoon of a country yokel, with a compulsory piece of straw hanging from his dumb mouth and
cartoon bubble wafting above his head like a stray fart,
which announced that:

I was in 'Nam . . . Fakenham. 1313th USAF, Falconbury

This didn't make us feel any better. All around us in the
Club House were men who made brick-built shithouses look
as flimsy as papier mâché that hasn't set properly. They were
drinking Schlitz beer from easily crushable cans and smoking Pall Mall cigarettes, which Churchill pronounced as 'Porl
Morl'. The jukebox played a constant stream of records
chosen to remind them of home. Fleetwood Mac sang 'Don't
Stop' as in 'Don't stop buying all our records, don't stop
we'll soon be millionaires', and Peter Frampton sang 'I want
you to show me the way . . .' To the door, hopefully. The men
were chatting or playing cards or getting mindlessly out of
their heads, while they waited for Isaac Walsall ('Get Down
Isaac!') who they assumed was, at that moment, backstage
pulling on a spangled jacket and shoving a sock or seven
down his lurex trousers before bounding on stage to sing
about love and stuff, babeeee.

Except that he wasn't. They had no idea that the group of
bedraggled itinerants, that at least one person had slandered
in a loud whisper as 'faggots', were Isaac Walsall, British
Funk at its best! We were sitting in the furthest, darkest

corner of the Club House, making the most of Mess Sergeant Kosko's amiable 'Help yourself to beer, boys, it's free for the band.' We were getting pissed as quickly as humanly possible in order to blot out the horror of what that bastard Monty had got us into, while, as unobtrusively as possible, shitting ourselves.

'What about "Papa's Got a Brand New Bag"?' Chopper asked.

'What about it?' I snapped back.

'Well can't any of you play it? It's got a simple bass line, I could play it all night and we could jam.' Chopper was resorting to the unfathomable language of musicians again.

'Jam? We don't jam. Tossers with music degrees jam,' Kirk snorted with derision.

'We can't jam,' Churchill pointed out, with surprising astuteness.

'It'll be cool, we can show these Yank bastards,' Kirk said, a little too loudly for comfort.

Several suspicious faces turned in our direction and I felt the warmth of embarrassment that wearing bondage trousers and a shirt with 'WANK' scrawled across it can cause when surrounded by five hundred macho killing machines.

'I think we need another drink,' I said. 'My round.' I went to get another dozen cans of free Schlitz that Mess Sergeant Kosko would regret offering when he tallied up the bar tab at the end of the night.

As I walked towards the bar I heard the rest of the band start laughing. They were looking at me and nudging each other.

'Woof, woof,' barked Kirk.

'Bow, wow,' growled Churchill.

'How much is that doggie in the window?' Chopper sang, perfectly in key as usual.

I should never have mentioned the incident with Gina and the dog to Churchill; I should have known that his interpretation of my plea to 'keep it confidential' would be to take out full page adverts in the dailies. The loud mouthed, gobby sod. I was still waiting for the barman to serve every other person in the room, even those who didn't want a drink, before he would begrudgingly serve the scruffy weirdo in strappy trousers, when Kirk came up.

'I'm going to scout around, see if I can't make this fiasco worthwhile,' he said and winked. I immediately felt frightened, having visions of him stealing a Phantom jet or something. I urged him to be cautious even though I knew he would pay as much attention to me as he would to an ancient public information film warning of the dangers of double parking.

'Trust me, cautious is my middle name,' he assured me. Yes, and your first name is Not and your last name is At All, I thought.

'Hello.' Gina sounded pissed off, as if the phone had got her out of the bath.

'You don't sound too pleased to hear from me.'

'I was in the bloody bath,' she said.

'What I would do for a bath; I haven't had one since I was with you last week.'

'That was nearly ten days ago.'

'It's horrible out here, you know.'

'You're only in Norfolk.'

'It might as well be Siberia. Life in Churchill's van is a primeval swamp, only with fewer mod cons. And if there's no shower in the dressing room, which there never is, then there's no shower after the gig. We've all stopped moving around on stage so that we don't sweat too much. Except Churchill of course, I think he likes the smell. This life is shit.'

'And so say all of us. I thought we got this flat so that we could be together, but I never see you. And I don't know anyone in Bradworth apart from your mother, and she's like the angel of death only without the sense of humour.'

'And my dad. You know him.'

'Oh yes, my kind of man, the weak, silent type.'

'I'm sorry.'

'Don't. That's what your dad would say. If he could speak, that is.'

It was funny how now we were together my dad had also stopped speaking to Gina. He obviously saw us as a couple, which meant Gina was now included in the communications embargo. At least he acknowledged our status as a couple, which was more than Gina did.

'We're playing a US air base,' I said, hoping for sympathy.

'Another one?' she said, not giving it.

'I'm going to kill that fucker Monty if I ever get out of here alive.'

'I saw him yesterday. At Stabbers.'

'Did you ask about our money? You were at Stabbers? On your own?'

'He said he'd sent it on to you. Of course I was on my own; do you think I'd take your mother along?'

'Well, we haven't got it. Thank God everything is free here. I've had nine packets of pretzels for tea.'

'I hope you're not putting on weight.' I could tell she was pulling her 'prissy pissy missy' face, the one which could put lemons out of business. For a second I was pleased to be where I was, but then three bigger than average American airmen walked past the phone booth, looked at me and the one nearest the ceiling mouthed 'mother-fucking faggot' to the others. Unfortunately, military training had tended to concentrate on things like physical fitness and how to fire a gun, which was why the man hadn't really got to grips with the concept of silently conveying a message to his colleagues.

'Who said that?' Gina asked from two hundred miles away.

'Gotta go.' I hung up and jogged back to the relative safety of the bar, where at least there would be witnesses.

*

The tour had been a terrible experience, even by our unimpeachable standards of terrible experiences. We had set out with cheerful enough spirits at the beginning, back in May. It was nearly summer, it was sunny, we were young and the adventure was beginning. It had started in Cleethorpes, at the Winter Gardens, in front of fifteen uninterested people. We didn't know it at the time but that was actually the high point. The promised American dates had turned out to be dark and dangerous venues that never had more than a tenuous link with the New World. There had been Captain USA (the hamburger café in Newcastle), the California Social Club (a camp site in Norfolk), and of course the Kennedy Hotel in Boston (Lincolnshire). There had also been the various air bases across East Anglia where our presence had been as welcome as a Russian military attaché with a file on everyone's darkest sexual appetites, including pictures.

For three months we'd been on the road, living, sleeping, and eating in Churchill's van. We'd even done some shagging in it, or at least Kirk had. His relationship with Lacy apparently having faded, he threw himself into a successful one-man campaign to sleep with every woman within whistling distance of the A1. The close proximity in Churchill's van ensured we got to know one another very well indeed. That was when we discovered the true depths of our hatred for each other. It was deeper than Einstein's Theory of Relativity. The result was that other than on stage we never communicated, we lived separate lives in our own corners of the Ford transit. We shifted our own equipment, did our own sound checks, rehearsed our own parts. If we could have gone on stage and played separately we would have done. In fact this might have been the one thing that would have made us more popular with the audiences. It wasn't that the punk audience didn't like us, they never got to see us. Thanks to Monty's bizarre booking policy our audience consisted of families on camping holidays, or people eating greasy chicken in the basket who were expecting to see almost forgotten light entertainers backed by a troupe of overweight dancers in skimpy costumes.

Gina and I had moved into our flat together just before the tour started. I wasn't sure why. I was sure I loved her, because I told her I did whenever I wanted to have sex with her. And that was most of the time. I wasn't convinced that the feelings were mutual. She seemed to find life with me a bit of a chore and something to be endured rather than enjoyed. I think that was how she felt about sex with me, too. She hated my obsessions, such as washing up once a week, or putting the rubbish out when the bin was full. She preferred to live a more unstructured, artistic life, free of the usual bourgeois constraints. 'Pig in shit' was how I'd rather foolishly described it after the first week and during our nineteenth argument. We were not compatible, we both realised it, but it seemed silly to let such a petty thing like that come between us. I made sure I rang her at least once every day, so that we could either finish yesterday's row or start a fresh one.

The latest bone in a whole skeleton of contention was my lack of time spent at home. The funny thing was that this complaint was reversed when I did get back for a couple of days. 'I hate it when you're around all day, you really get under my feet,' she would say. I was surprised she noticed as it was mostly her partially empty Chinese take-away cartons that got under her feet. Returning home caused me mixed emotions. On the one hand I looked forward to the regular sex, even if with Gina it was somewhat cold and insincere, while on the other hand I dreaded the rubbish skip of a flat that would greet me. Her father's politics had rubbed off on Gina, in the sense that she was a traditionalist. She liked to conserve the past, such as last week's litter or the dust under the bed. Life with Churchill's feet was only slightly less preferable than life with Gina's idiosyncrasies.

The summer had gone on and the mood of the band became blacker. The gig at the Falconbury base was just another dark rain cloud on our gloomy horizon. If we were unable to get back to Bradworth, Monty would mail the next list of confirmed gigs to the nearest post office so that we could move remorselessly on. It would have helped if he'd mailed on some of the money we were owed, the bulk of which he cleverly made sure was paid by the local promoters direct to Tonic Bender's bank account. Instead we scraped by on his measly allowance, or 'disallowance' as we named it, as it was so little we couldn't afford to do anything with it. We had got to Falconbury early, knowing from past experience that food and drink were cheap and plentiful at the bases and this was a lifeline when we were still waiting for Monty to send last week's money. The gig list had kept coming, week after week, bang on time, without either a break or any semblance of sanity, insisting on the band playing in the North of England one night and Cornwall the next. If we didn't know better we'd have thought Monty was doing it on purpose. Which of course he was.

I went back to Churchill and Chopper. There was no sign of Kirk, who I imagined was out on the perimeter fence somewhere with a pair of wire cutters, working quietly under the shadow of a machine gun post, to steal an early warning satellite dish. Churchill was drunkenly sounding off about football.

'Put an average English football team and an American football team on the same park, and we'd thrash them. No problem. There's no skill in American football.'

'And we'd get lots of free kicks for all those hand-ball offences,' Chopper chipped in pedantically.

'Keep it down for Christ's sake. We're already getting screwed by half the bar.' I didn't need to add that the half who were staring at us malevolently were, coincidentally, the half who were over six foot six. I grabbed another squashable can of beer which practically imploded under my tense grip.

'The way I see it, we're probably going to die when we first set foot on stage and they see we're not soul brothers, so we may as well go out with a bang.' Churchill, cheered on by an afternoon of free beer, was in a carefree, football-hooligan mood.

There was a commotion from the other side of the room. In the doorway stood Kirk. At least I thought it was Kirk, all I could see was a high pile of beer cans and cartons of cigarettes.

'Look what I found.' It was Kirk's voice all right. The pile came tottering over to us, upsetting empty chairs and glasses of beer on the way. By the time it reached us there was a wake of extremely disgruntled drinkless people to mark his route.

The pile was rested on the table and Kirk's smiling face appeared around the side.

'I've discovered the PX store. It's amazing, everything is really cheap. The Yank government must subsidise it. Look at these fags, less than a third the normal price.' He was excited at the haul of goodies which he claimed were the fruits of a politically defiant act. We all agreed and generously helped ourselves to his fags and beer as a gesture of support for his action.

Mess Sergeant Kosko came over looking a worried man. He was a big Country and Western fan ('So he doesn't know much about music,' Kirk had sniggered), but he did know that, on the whole, funk, soul and disco tended to be played by a certain type of musician.

''Scuse me saying so boys, but you ain't black.'

'We ain't musicians neither,' Churchill whispered quietly enough for the mechanics in hangar one to hear.

'Blue-eyed soul, Serge,' Chopper reassured him. I think even Kirk was grateful for the boring bastard's obsessive knowledge of music at that moment. Mess Sergeant Kosko still looked a little nervous but, with a cursory glance at our clothes and a hushed reminder that we had got a changing room at the back of the stage, he went off relatively happy.

'What's the plan, Kirk?' I asked.

'Plan?'

'As in "the plan to avoid an early death"?'

'No problem, I've been giving it some thought.' For some reason this didn't instil me with a great deal of confidence.

'We'll go on and stay on until the bottles start flying. Then I'll run off and get the van started, while you lot keep the rhythm going. Give it a couple of minutes and then follow me. We'll come back for the gear in the morning when things are quieter. If there's any gear left, that is. Simple.'

'Simple as in safest option for you, you mean,' Churchill commented. But it was the only plan we had so we decided to go with it. There was a buzz of anticipation building up in the Club House that was becoming impossible to ignore, so we made our way to the privacy of the dressing room where we could concentrate on ignoring it more thoroughly.

'How long are we going to keep doing this?' I asked no one in particular.

'Wossup?' Churchill was the only one who seemed even vaguely interested in what I had to say.

'This. This stupid waste of our lives playing stupid gigs to stupid people who don't give a stupid fuck about our stupid music.'

'Are you trying to tell us something?' Kirk said dryly. Mess Sergeant Kosko's worried face appeared around the door. Six weeks as Mess Sergeant and he was feeling the pressure. He was already wondering if he should try something a little easier, like bringing about world peace or finding a cure for cancer.

'Are you ready, boys?' It was more of a plea for us to go on before the men started killing one another than a polite question as to our readiness. Everyone looked at each other to try and gauge if we were, indeed, ready. I kept my head down so that they wouldn't be able to see the defeat in my eyes. I knew I could go on stage, but I wasn't sure I would be able to do anything once I was out there. We ran up the short flight of stairs and out into the naked glare of the spotlights, on loan from Runway Three.

'Remember, when I go off, keep the rhythm up for a couple of minutes before you join me,' Kirk said quietly. Unfortunately he was too close to the mike and the whole of the restless audience of five hundred soul fans shared the information. I quickly punched the opening chords of 'Fascist Military Death Creeps'. This had started life as a jaunty number about the row I had with Gina, when she discovered the pile of men's magazines hidden at the bottom of my wardrobe. It had been intended as a musical dissection of the argument 'Is the erotic pornographic?' but Kirk had changed the title to give it a sharper edge. It worked too, as whenever we played it at venues like Falconbury we invariably felt things with sharper edges. He didn't change any of the original words, choosing instead to sing them in a way that no one could understand them. In this respect he was a consummate professional. The way he sang he could never be accused of clarity.

We got as far as verse two line three – 'She's the perfect partner for a single bed, I said' – before the first howl of outrage was directed at us. This response wasn't usually heard until at least verse five, and once it had begun it spread like hot gossip at a dull party, and we were immediately showered with anything heavy that wasn't screwed down or couldn't be released with the minimum force. Kirk looked back at us and winked his infamous wink. It was a signal that was too often a precursor to disaster.

'This isn't the end, it's only the beginning . . .' Kirk finished every gig with the same words, attempting to sound portentous and only ever sounding pretentious. He swept regally past me towards the back of the stage.

'This isn't the beginning, Kirk, it's the end,' I shouted at him, my mind made up under the influence of several flying chair legs. Just before he jumped into the darkness he turned back and smiled. For the first time in months he seemed to be agreeing with me.

We went into an instrumental version of 'Scratchy Old Shit', a homage to the Bob Dylan records that Chopper played whenever he was given the opportunity, which was never if we had a hammer handy. Chopper used the chance to develop the bass line from 'Papa's Got a Brand New Bag', which was completely at odds with the fast chainsaw-guitar rhythm that I was playing and the bull on acid in a cymbal shop that Churchill was managing to mimic with some style. The angry crowd didn't seem to notice. They were mad as hell and nothing was going to distract them from their chosen task, which was to get hold of us and rip us limb from limb. If the United States Air Force ever needed a motivating force for their servicemen they could have done worse than employ I saw Warsaw. We obviously had the knack of getting right under their skin and driving them on to acts of extreme violence. We began the second song but it was as clear as the chunk of bar top that flew past my right ear, flung by the barman himself, that we had to follow Kirk to the van as quickly as possible.

We unplugged our instruments and noticed that, such was the intensity of the mob's screams, it made no difference to the volume levels. We ran off with as much grace and style as we dared, which wasn't a lot given the proximity of the mob. Chopper led the way with me following closely. Some way down the corridor behind us we could hear Churchill yelling.

'Come on, you Yank bastards, I'm the last of the Mohicans.' You probably will be, I thought, before leaving him to his fate.

'Come on, Church, for Christ's sake,' I shouted, as we burst out the double doors into the cool evening air. The large car park had all sorts of vehicles in it. There were Chryslers and Buicks and Chevrolets and Corvettes. I could have written half a dozen songs about them. What I couldn't have written was a song about a 1972 Ford Transit 32 cwt van. Because nowhere in that Chuck Berry song of a car park was there one to be seen.

'Churchill, where's your fucking van?' I screamed, quaintly believing that although he was tied up re-enacting the American War of Independence, he may be able to shed some light on the mystery. As he caught up with us and saw the lack of an escape vehicle he suddenly lost his mask of bravado.

'Oh fuck, we're going to die. We're really going to die. I'll kill that bastard St John first. Where is the yellow shit bag?'

'Behind the steering wheel of your van?'

The double doors opened again and a small range of mountains came out.

'Looking for us?' I asked weakly, wishing I had a pair of glasses so I could claim diplomatic immunity as a sissy.

'What are we going to do, Chopper?' I whispered, turning to see him wearing a pair of round John Lennon glasses that I'd never seen before.

'Good luck Billy, and you, Churchill,' he said, just before running off towards the nearest dense undergrowth.

One of the mountains stepped forward. It wasn't quite Ben Nevis, but could easily have been Snowdon.

'I wanted to kill you when I first saw you. Give me one good reason why I shouldn't kill you now, you mother-fucking punk.'

At least the misunderstanding between funk and punk had finally been cleared up.

'Cigarette?' I pulled the pack I'd stolen off Kirk from my pocket and it came out accompanied by a lump of Lebanese Black that was the size of a small paving slab. I'd purchased it the night before to help blot out the memory of playing 'Kill the Old' to a group of horrified pensioners at the Over 60s Club in a village hall.

'Pall Mall?' he said, a softer, friendlier tone entering his voice.

'Don't smoke anything else, do we Billy?' said Churchill, sensing a wafer-thin chink of light in a black hole expanse of darkness.

'Look, guys, Pall Mall,' Snowdon said, winking to the rest of the range around him. They started to smile, nodded their snow-capped peaks and helped themselves to my dope, and, as an afterthought, Kirk's cigarettes.

Mess Sergeant Kosko was very understanding, particularly after we had blamed the whole affair on Monty and advised him not to pay any money into the Tonic Bender account.

'What happened to your friend?' It seemed an oddly out-of-date description of Kirk. 'He was in the PX earlier, spending all your dough on drink, cigarettes, electrical goods. Everything. He said he was investing his royalties.'

'His royalties? The thieving shit.'

'I helped him put all the stuff in the van, I hope that was OK? It was parked out back of the Club House.'

I looked at Churchill. I didn't say 'I quit', because it was obvious from the look on his face that he was intending to do exactly the same, and the thing about quitting a shit job is that it's only any fun if you tell someone who is staying put. Chopper was still at large somewhere on the air base, although the military police were hard on his trail. More so once I let slip the information that his dad regularly took his holidays in Albania. This was information that would have surprised Chopper's dad no end, as he'd never been further east than Cleethorpes. I wished Kirk was still there so that I could hand my resignation in to him in person. Preferably attached to a house brick.

'Shall we go?' Churchill asked me.

'Where?'

'Anywhere but here. Home?'

'This isn't the end, it's the beginning,' I said ironically.

'I fucking hope it's not,' Churchill replied, as pithy as ever.

Eight

I left the flat above the Bliss Bridal Wear shop, where Gina and I lived in ironic non-marital non-bliss, and gladly cycled away through the wintry cold and uncannily quiet early morning streets of Bradworth. I narrowly avoided a marmalade tom cat returning from a night on the tiles where it had successfully pulled a bird, and was now concentrating on ripping its wings off before taking it home to show its master. It was so early I hadn't even switched on my basic life signs. Instead I was being led by my nose, which could pick up and follow the scent of old people's piss even though it was two miles to where I worked at the Joshua Kindside Geriatric Rest Home. This olfactory automatic pilot was a natural gift that allowed me to finish off any particularly exciting or enticing dreams from the previous night's sleep, but it did mean the journey was often a risk to life and limb, sometimes even my own.

As I arrived outside the home the acrid smell of ammonia scorched the back of my throat and kicked me into consciousness. Stale urine was better than a double espresso. The time was still a couple of fags off seven o'clock but already Aggie was at her post just inside the doorway.

'Martha's got her chest back, you'll be laying her out by second tea break.'

'And good morning to you too, Aggie,' I said, wasting valuable sarcasm on her. Aggie was eighty-four and convinced she was still in the fourth form at the girl's grammar school, the one that had been destroyed in an air raid in 1943. I should have humoured her but it was too early to be sensitive. Ken Dubbin was in the staff room, changing out of his button-down nylon jacket with pale-blue epaulettes; he had ordered it from the nursing outfitters in the hope that it might give him an air of gravitas. As far as I could tell the only thing the grubby, stained garment gave him was an air of gravy. He had lank greasy hair and an even lanker greasier face, which was so long it seemed completely out of proportion with the rest of his body. Standing out from the layer of grease on his rubbery skin were the finest collection of spots and pustules this side of a small-pox epidemic.

'Have a good night, Ken?' I asked, with as little interest as I could.

'Two dead. Martha with her chest, and Sadie, that new woman who was an emergency admission yesterday. I laid them out in the day room. Oh and Maude decided to visit her son-in-law again; police found her hitching on the M62 at three o'clock in her mules and nightie. Silly cow. Otherwise pretty quiet.'

I gave Ken my 'I'm sorry, did you think I was paying attention?' look and went in search of something hot and brown that hopefully came from a cheap cash-and-carry tea bag rather than the sluice drain, although I had to admit it would have been difficult to tell the difference. I wasn't too concerned about Ken's tales of murder and mayhem. Everyone, even the most senile resident, knew he was a pathological liar and ignored his extravagant fantasies, even on the rare occasion when they sounded plausible. On this occasion they were more than plausible, they were true. The night-shift staff had even paler faces than usual as they wearily detailed the body count at the hand-over meeting. It was like the denouement of a low-budget slasher movie, only less realistic.

When I got to the dining room Churchill was already at work, cooking bacon and eggs for fifty and singing along with Spandau Ballet as he did so.

'Work till you're muscle-bound . . . Morning Bill. How many eggs, or has Gina still got you on that bran shit? . . . Don't lie down . . . Shame about Martha, eh? I reckon it's Ken, women would rather die than spend the night with him.' He laughed, until the fifty eggs spat an ocean of hot lard over his hand and sent him running to the enormous stainless steel sink to wash the wound.

'He shouldn't speak like that about the recently deceased.' Alf was sitting by the hatch licking his lips and waiting for the first serving, as he did every meal time. He was so old he looked like he was made out of ancient Egyptian parchment that had just been exposed to the modern world and was quickly deteriorating as a result. It was a matter of some debate amongst the care assistants of the Joshua Kindside Geriatric Rest Home as to exactly how long Alf had lived there. He'd certainly been there longer than me, but there was one school of thought which claimed he'd been there since the rest home opened in 1936, waiting at the hatch for the first meal to be served, and still moaning about the old days when he was treated properly with decent service and proper respect. It had even been suggested that Alf had supernatural powers, as if he was a sort of Flying Dutchman, destined forever to walk the polished corridors of the Joshua Kindside Geriatric Rest Home. Whatever the truth, I reckoned he must have gone to live there shortly after leaving school and just before the outbreak of the Boer War.

I felt I ought to defend Gina's holistic approach to our diet. She believed that treating the body with respect and only putting things into it that were pure and natural would make us healthy and whole. It was a philosophy that was completely at odds with her attitude to housework. I was about to challenge Churchill over his jibe but then the smell of his wonderful, if deadly, fry-up hit my nose and I resolved to say nothing. Who knows, maybe my telling silence would shame him into reconsidering his position.

'How is the old tart?' he asked with a wicked smile, using a term that, if Gina were present, would have resulted in yet another name being added to the morning's roll-call of death.

'OK,' I said, almost too casually. I saw Churchill narrow his eyes as if he was about to say 'Oh yes?' in a knowing way, and stopped him just in time.

'I mean yes. Yes. She's great.' Don't overdo it, Bill, I thought; even on her best days she's never great. 'She's going down to London today, for a conference.'

'Again? What is it this time, or will I regret asking?'

'"Wimmin in the 80s, from Sex Objects to Gender War Warriors."'

'Let me translate. A bunch of hairy old tarts who are so ugly they can only get sex through lesbo licking games, demand that all men should be forced to present their bollocks for gender reorientation on the nearest butcher's block.'

'Ouch,' said Alf, taking the top off the tomato ketchup bottle and licking it.

Churchill had little patience with Gina, never being afraid to express this frustration to her in person. I was somewhere in that uncomfortable no-person's-land (Gina's preferred terminology) between them. Gina was my girlfriend, or rather a partner in a relationship of equal rights and responsibilities that we had mutually agreed to inhabit, and Churchill, to my undying surprise, was now my best friend. I played a dangerous game of diplomacy to keep them both close, but not so close that they could inflict real harm on one another.

'I've got a soft spot for both of you,' I explained to Gina when she had challenged this unholy combination of my relationship with her and my friendship with Churchill.

'I know all about your soft spot for me, thank you,' she replied with enough sarcasm to strip several layers of Dulux off a pine door. She liked to blame my lack of sexual performance for our lack of a sex life. If I had been asked for my opinion, which I wasn't, I would have defined the problem as a complete lack of sexual attraction. Gina made the North Sea in January seem a warm and inviting prospect.

'Fancy coming to watch City on Saturday?' Churchill asked, taunting me with the prospect. Football. In our happy home it was the love that dared not speak its name. A game played by men. It was rough, dirty and competitive. It was gender fascism in a tasteless nylon claret and amber striped shirt and I loved it. Once upon a time I would have died for City, now I would die if I went near them.

'Can't, I've promised to help out on the *wimmin's* CND stall on the market. Gina says that doing stuff together helps us explore our relationship.'

'You'd be better off with a map and compass.' I threw a salt-pot in the general direction of Churchill's groin. As a gesture I felt it showed suitable support for my sisters in the struggle.

I swallowed a fried egg whole, in the manner of a delicious Scottish oyster and went upstairs to find an elderly gent to whom I could offer assistance. This would both enable the elderly gent to live a fulfilled and valued life, while enabling me to look busy and so keep out of the way of Attila the Hen, a.k.a. Henrietta Swallow, Officer in Charge, bossy bastard and general mad cow. Attila the Hen was a couple of years older than me, a couple of feet taller and liked to put her make-up on with a trowel. Her brittle hair had the broken, defeated look that only a lethal combination of home perms and natural henna colouring (which always came out as unnatural dayglo orange) could produce. She had tiny eyes that reminded me of a hooded cobra and breasts that reminded me of the Chiltern Hills. She also had a vision – she was going to be a senior manager before she was thirty. Some of us felt she had already been promoted to beyond her level of incompetence As a result of this she was having other, more worrying visions. She was having a super nova of a nervous breakdown which unfolded slowly in glorious Technicolor detail each day. Unexpected visitors to the main office might find her in a variety of moods, from examining the time sheets in obses-sional detail, and finding a one-second discrepancy that would be enough to summarily dismiss the member of staff responsible, to knocking back the old folks' Tamazepam in an attempt to stifle her uncontrollable tears. She was so unbalanced the key to her office door should have been left on the outside.

I helped Norman Thwaites to button his flies and Eileen Cox to shave her moustache before taking a three-day-old copy of the *Daily Mail* and hiding in the top-floor Gents' toilet. This was the only place in the building that was totally Attila the Hen proof as she had a morbid fear of the penis and all its workings.

I had been employed at the home for three years, thanks mainly to Churchill. After the band split he had gone there as a care assistant. He'd worked at the Joshua Kindside Geriatric Rest Home for three days before he understood what the term 'Geriatric' meant. He thought that it was really weird that only old people seemed to get it. When he discovered the truth, he realised it was an easy life as long as you could eat hot food stolen from the kitchen and didn't mind cleaning up sick and shit, often at the same time, and getting a miserly two hundred a month for the privilege. I was hungry, skint, and coming to realise that the national campaign for Billy Petrol to be signed up by a major record company and be paid in million-pound notes was probably postponed indefinitely. Wallowing in sick and shit seemed preferable to living off the wages of sin, which was one way of describing Gina's salary from her job as a clerical officer at the DHSS, working at the very same office where I signed on and made many dubious claims, such as the one about living alone.

Care assistant wasn't actually a bad job, and of course it was temporary. Three years on and I was still on a temporary contract and was as much a fixture in the home as the smell of piss. The residents knew I was a lazy sod and therefore willing and able to sit and listen to them all day. They clamoured for my attention, knowing that once they had it they would have someone to talk to for the best part of an afternoon. Attila the Hen (not a nickname that I dared use in Gina's presence) tolerated me as I was an example of 'Socialisation' she could use to impress the seriously grey-suited senior managers during their occasional visits. She might have been less tolerant had she been able to ever actually find me, but I made sure that shortly after the start of each shift I disappeared and didn't reappear until just before home time. I left plenty of clues to where I had been, old folks basking in the glow of having just spent an amiable twenty minutes chatting about the war, freshly made beds here and there, a newly mopped floor where ten minutes before had been a pool of something sticky from the bodily fluids range, but of me there would be no sign. I knew every short cut, hiding place and forgotten cupboard big enough to hold a man and a fully extended broadsheet newspaper. I was so good at avoiding detection the residents had nick-named me Lord Lucan.

The headline read 'From Saboteur to Sabatier' and it grabbed me the instant I saw it. I didn't know that Lacy Tasker had progressed from high priestess of Punk to a high-profile column in a daily newspaper. I wasn't surprised at this as I too had given up all interest in music around the end of 1978, when I'd noticed graffiti on railway bridges and motorway flyovers that claimed 'Punk's Not Dead'. I'd

taken this as a sure sign that it was as dead as Martha and
Sadie. My guitar now had a layer of dust on it thicker than
the one we'd have on the sideboard if Gina was left in
charge of the cleaning. It got less use than my prick, which
had an even thicker layer of metaphorical dust on it.

Lacy now wrote about something called 'lifestyles', which
seemed to consist of pretentious waffle about rich people
doing ridiculously expensive things. But it wasn't any of
these items that grabbed me. It was the short piece she had
written on a new restaurant. It was about Kirk. I hadn't seen
or heard from him since the band split up in the foreign fields
of Norfolk but Lacy was happy to fill in the gaps for me:

> From wild Punk singer to cordon bleu chef, Kirk St
> John continues to break the rules. His considerable tal-
> ents have led him back to his North Country roots and
> the setting up of 'Saint's' restaurant. 'There's a lot of the
> Punk in what I do,' he said over a fine Australian
> Chardonnay which perfectly complemented the
> *Esquinado à l'huile* and Yorkshire pudding. 'I'm the only
> one with any anarchy left. Don't come here expecting
> prawn cocktail and steak, because what you'll get is
> dangerous innovation.'

Lacy raved about his radical rethink of traditional favourites
like onion roll and sticky toffee pudding and the way he
combined them with Mediterranean cuisine, which was, she
gushed, pure genius. I wondered if they were still shagging.
From the lavish praise she was heaping on him I figured
they must be.

I checked the address, it was in Bronte Bridge, about five
miles out of Bradworth. I started thinking, always a dangerous thing to do when I was on the toilet. I could retrieve
the credit card from where I had hidden it in the Habitat
paper lampshade. I'd done this in an attempt to cut our
spending down, which had failed because whenever the

light was on, the shadow of the card reminded us of its whereabouts. There'd be enough left on it for a meal at Kirk's inflated prices, so long as we only had one bottle of house white, and it might be just the thing to put the spark back in our relationship. Although if I was honest with myself, which would have been a first, our relationship probably needed a spark that was akin to St Elmo's Fire. But it would be an opportunity to see Kirk. I couldn't wait to see his face.

'Smash the fucker's face in and get my eight hundred quid back,' Churchill said when I told him of my plan in the staff room later. He was clearly unfamiliar with the saying let bygones be bygones.

'And then ask the bastard what he did with my van.'

The flat was in darkness when I got home which was a good sign. Gina was still in London, which meant there wouldn't be a row and that meant I could get on with some dusting and hoovering. I nipped out to the chippy on the corner and bought fish, chips, chicken and mushroom pie, peas, gravy and curry sauce and ate them outside, staring in the window of the Bliss Bridal Wear shop for in-meal entertainment. The smell of unwholesome food would not be the best welcome for when Gina arrived home. I then boiled some lentils and put them in the fridge to create the image of something left over from a natural healthy meal. It was a low and deceitful trick but it was also a proven strategy for survival.

The phone rang about nine.

'Sorry, love,' Gina said, 'the conference has thrown up a number of issues I need to resolve.' I didn't completely catch her explanation as I was still puzzling over the word 'love'. It wasn't one that I'd heard her use before, I wasn't even aware it was in her vocabulary. In fact I didn't think I'd heard her say the word 'sorry' before either.

'I'm staying at Maxine's.'

'Maxine? The lesbian?'

'No, the woman who's my oldest friend. Sometimes your acceptance of patriarchal values is unbelievable.'

'I was only checking to see if it was the Maxine I thought it was.'

'I'll be home tomorrow lunchtime,' she said, ending the discussion.

I went to bed alone and had the best sex I'd had in a long time. It was probably because it was the first sex I'd had in a long time.

The next morning I rang 'Saint's', thankful that the voice that answered was not Kirk's. It was a woman's voice that for some reason drew my mind back to the lustful excesses of the previous night. I booked a table that was 'somewhere romantic'.

'Can't do that,' the voice said, in a matter-of-fact tone that had been sieved through twenty Woodbines a day to produce something that was more like distilled sex.

'Fully booked?' I asked.

'No, it's just not allowed.'

'What?'

'Mr St John won't allow it, he says that candle-lit segregation is the apartheid of the restaurant. You're sat where he puts you, I'm afraid,' she said, whispering the last two words apologetically.

I agreed to be put wherever Kirk wanted to put us but I gave false names so that he wouldn't be forewarned and put us in the car park.

'Is Mr St John there?'

'He's away on business but we are expecting him back for tonight.'

I thanked her for her help and said goodbye.

'See you tonight,' the voice signed off, as if genuinely excited by the prospect of our attendance.

Luckily Churchill didn't drop round, even though it was also his day off and he usually dumped himself on me and refused to leave until he had smoked all my cigarettes, eaten all my biscuits and picked a fight with Gina, so I was able to create a welcoming ambience for when Gina returned. She breezed in about four-thirty and kissed me on the cheek.

'Bought you a present,' she said, throwing a parcel at me. I couldn't remember the last time she'd bought me a present. It was a book.

'Great. *What's So Wrong With Castration?* Thanks, really thanks.' I sounded like someone with two weeks to live who's just been given a copy of *War and Peace*.

'Sheena Muller, she was one of the speakers, she was inspirational. She's twenty-two stone and unrepentant. It was a defining moment for the whole audience.'

'Does this mean we can start having fry-ups?'

I spent the next half an hour explaining that I had been joking and I was really very sorry for being so insensitive. Eventually she forgave me and carried on telling me about the conference. I picked up the crumpled list of speakers she had dropped on the bedroom floor.

'Hey, Dainty Evans was on in the afternoon. I saw her on telly last week she was quite good,' I said, trying to avoid sounding patronising and failing so badly I crossed myself and waited for the attack.

'Was she?' Gina asked from the bathroom where she was soaking in the last of the hot water. I picked up her clothes from the hall and living room where she had dropped them and popped them in the wash basket.

'Didn't you notice? She was on for two hours.'

'Oh yes, Dainty Evans, I remember,' she said, before turning on the radio and drowning out further conversation with Mahler's 5th.

'How do you fancy going out for a meal tonight?' I asked, trying to make it sound like a four-week holiday to the Bahamas.

'Oh, I don't know, I'm tired, yesterday was a long . . .'

'I promise you you'll love it. I've booked us in somewhere

really special. It'll be a fantastic surprise. Trust me. Go on, say yes.'

'Yes,' she said, meaning 'anything to shut you up and stop this irritating emotional blackmail'.

I put on my best shirt, the one which still had all the buttons in place, held there by a variety of different coloured cotton threads, and the pair of original American 501s that were my only happy memento of Falconbury air base and which were now a little too tight around the waist. Just in case Kirk had gone all Establishment on us I also wore my old school tie, putting a knot in it which was smaller than something found in a toddler's shoelace.

Gina wore a long flowery relic from Laura Ashley's 1976 collection, which was a sure sign she wasn't trying. When she went to her women-only do's she wore short black things that never saw the light of day when she was with a 'potential rapist' like me.

I got out of the taxi in the restaurant car park feeling quite nervous. Gina looked up at the sign which pretentiously announced itself as 'Saint's'. There was a germ of recognition in her eyes that made me excited about the surprise to come. Inside, was a young woman with coal-black hair, coffee-brown eyes and bent white teeth that looked like a row of attractive old marble headstones. Her smile took my breath away with its sincerity. Having taken my breath away she then took my torn and grubby denim jacket.

'Thank you, sir,' was all she said but it was enough to tell me that she was the Voice from the phone call. I watched her short black skirt slink away before remembering Gina was with me. I turned expecting a barrage of sexual harassment allegations, but was pleased to see that she was too busy examining the lush interior of the restaurant. I had to admit Kirk had done a nice job; 'French provincial' Lacy had called it and I was sure she was right, although never having been to France I couldn't swear to it. Some old 30s jazz played

softly in the background and the subdued lighting was provided by Art Deco table lamps. It was tastefully expensive.
I wondered how much of it had been paid for by my stolen
earnings and whether I could make a backdated claim.

'This way, sir.' It was the Voice, which I now knew also
had the Legs. Gina sniffed her 'never mind, *sir*, I'm an
equally valid part of this couple' sniff, but the Voice and the
Legs didn't seem to notice nor care. She led the way and I
followed, grateful for the unrestricted and breathtaking
view of her rear. When we arrived at the table I was sorry
the journey was over, but not as sorry as Gina.

'We're right by the bloody Gents. Do something.' Gina
loved to have a cause she could order me to fight for.

'I can't, it's all part of . . . the owner's plan,' I said.

'He's right, it's the rules,' the waitress said, coming to my
aid. Gina didn't look too impressed but accepted it with bad
grace after attempting to wither her with one of her looks,
but the Voice and the Legs had been a professional too long
and easily avoided a life as a stone statue by ignoring her
and going to fetch the menus. When she returned we were
none the wiser as the thin sheet of paper had only five words
typed on it.

'You'll Have What You're Given,' it ordered.

'We'll have that then,' I joked and was rewarded with a
gorgeously crooked smile from the Voice and the Legs. I half
expected a verbal attack from Gina on why flirting was a
betrayal of trust and how in the brave new wimmin's world
the offender's foreskin would be removed with a blunt and
rusty blade, but she seemed otherwise engaged with some
inner turmoil. I put it down to an unresolved issue from her
course the day before.

'It's nice, isn't it?' I was the king of small talk, and my
kingdom was the trivial and inane.

'It feels a little decadent, and that always weighs heavily
on my conscience.'

'A bit like using the Hoover,' I thought. I drank the

obligatory pint of lager as a stomach liner before diving into the carafe of house white, the price of which took my credit card to the very brink of bankruptcy. I was enjoying myself, not least because of the dangerous excitement of ogling the waitresses, all of whom had obviously been hand picked by Kirk for their oglability. I wondered when to unveil the surprise of Kirk, both of him on Gina and us on him. A delicious plan began to unfold in my mind.

We enjoyed the starter of fried *saucisses aux pistaches*.

'Black pudding that's won the pools,' I described it, determined not to be taken in by what I saw as the pretentiousness of the restaurant, before gasping as the wood pigeon *en papillotes* with Parfumé of Ceps arrived, looking like the Sydney Opera House as it sailed towards our table. I picked at the wrapping as if there was something in it that I didn't like. I called the Voice and the Legs over.

'What are you doing?' Gina snapped suspiciously. I waved her query away imperiously. Nothing was going to take away my enjoyment of this moment.

'Excuse me, I'd like to speak to the cook.'

'Pardon?' the Voice and the Legs asked. I could detect fear in her voice.

'The Cook. I want to see him. Here.' I pointed triumphantly at a spot just in front of our table.

The Voice and the Legs went off in the direction of the kitchen as if it were a path to the gallows. The swing doors swung closed ominously behind her. We heard a whisper, and then a thump, and then a scream. Kirk came through the swing doors as if he was rocket powered. He was carrying a great big cleaver and looking back into the kitchen where he was still directing his verbal assault at the waitress.

'Cook?' he was shouting, 'you dozy tart, you don't ever call me "cook", I am a chef.' He turned toward us. His mouth opened but nothing came out. He tried again, no success. And again, still nothing. Finally he summoned up with a great effort, 'You'.

I smiled at him, then at Gina, and then back at him. I looked back at Gina, who was looking a shade of white that my mum would have killed for on wash day. I wondered if she was ill. Probably the *saucisses aux pistaches*, I thought.

'Us,' I answered him, rather pleased with the response.

'Wow, mucho surprise. Much mucho.' He still hadn't recovered, I was enjoying this. Behind Kirk the swing door swung again. The Voice and the Legs stood proud and tall behind him.

'I may be dozy and I may be a tart, although I don't think I'm either, but at least I'm not a pompous stuck-up fraud who uses cheap margarine from the cash and carry claiming it's specially imported Normandy butter, and who makes a ridiculous profit margin on each meal. He . . .' she pointed at me, '. . . called you a cook. I'm calling you a wanker. Go fuck yourself St John.'

This was marvellous. I hadn't had so much fun since my dad's lawn mower broke down and it took two months for the spare parts to come through. The Voice and the Legs took a deep breath, smoothed her short skirt to her hips and went back into the kitchen never to return. As the swing doors swung closed behind her, Kirk apologised to the other diners for the outburst, muttering something about 'time of the month'. Without any trace of embarrassment he looked at me and bowed.

'How long have you known about us?' he asked. I felt Gina stiffen from across the table. This was something new, something that wasn't in my plan. It was a surprise that I suspected I wasn't going to like.

'Kirk,' Gina interrupted quickly, 'fancy seeing you here.' She mugged like a bad character actor in an old British B movie.

'What do you mean, "us"?' I asked.

Kirk looked at Gina, but his pride had been badly hurt and he wanted revenge at any cost.

'You got home safely from your conference, then,' he asked Gina, smirking as he said the word 'conference'.

'Gina?' I asked, helpless and desperate for someone to put me out of my misery, preferably with a twelve-bore shotgun.

'Didn't she tell you?'

'Kirk, don't, not yet, I've got to tell him about the . . .'

'Gina was with me yesterday.' He threw his final spear and it caught me in the ribs, just above the heart.

'But, but, what about Sheena Muller?' I asked, placing all my hopes in the hands of a fat cow who wouldn't be happy until I was neutered.

'I left at lunchtime, after her speech. I always leave at lunchtime.'

'We both leave at lunchtime,' Kirk said. 'Once I've sorted out the catering. That's what I do you see, I'm the caterer. I've got a company in London.' He handed me his business card, it had nice silver writing on a dark-blue background. It read 'Kitchen Sink Revolution, Plc.'

'We do all the radical conferences, hippie shit usually, loads of wheat dust and chickpeas, but it's paid for all this.' He waved a deliberately limp hand around his French provincial empire. The other diners were listening to him in rapturous silence, hanging on his every pompous word. This was what they had come for, the angry young man of the kitchen range.

'I'm . . .' I could see that in her own way Gina was struggling to say sorry. '. . . Pregnant,' she said. 'We're pregnant. Me and Kirk that is, not me and you. Obviously.' It was the word 'obviously' that stung the most.

'My side of the family have always been very fertile,' Kirk boasted to the crowded restaurant.

'I don't know what to say,' I said, not knowing what to say. Then I thought of something. 'But he's such a . . . such a . . . cowboy.'

'Don't you mean cow person?' Gina asked, even in adversity finding time to adhere strictly to her feminist creed. 'It was only meant to be casual, but it kind of developed.' She made an effort to be sensitive which, as usual, failed miserably.

'Into something more causal,' Kirk added, as sensitive as a packet of Saxa emptied on to a third-degree burn. 'Tell you what, what do you say to this one being on the house. Have what you like, I'll pick up the tab. After all, I do own the frigging place. It'll be my way of saying thanks. For Gina. And the baby.' Kirk actually believed he could buy his way out of trouble.

'Thanks,' I said, weakly. I got up and went to the Gents' toilet, grateful now that it was so handy.

There was a terrible rushing sound in my ears that was like white noise without the hum-along quality. I was hot and sweating, yet cold and shivering. I wanted to throw up. I wanted to pass out. If there had been a doctor present I would have got enough sick notes to see me through to New Year. I splashed my face with the bottle of sparkling water that Saint's provided by the Victorian basin for what reason I wasn't sure, and stared at the bloodshot mess in the mirror for what felt like two hours. They were the kind of hours you usually come across on a dismal boring Sunday afternoon. In February. When the only thing on television is horse racing. Or Crufts. Deciding my life was probably over, I went back out. We agreed to deal with the situation in a mature manner, after which they set about nibbling each other's ears and were soon oblivious to my presence, so I ordered two bottles of the most expensive champagne on the wine list, got my coat and, pausing only to phone the fire brigade and pass on an anonymous tip that there was a suspect package inside Gina's cardigan, went home alone.

Nine

It was supposed to be a lost weekend, obscured forever in the mists of excess. Unfortunately this particular weekend had the sense of direction of your average nomadic Laplander herdsman and consequently found its way back, uninvited and unwanted, into my consciousness sometime around mid-morning of Sunday 14th February, 1982. St Valentine's Day. Despite the nuclear meltdown of my hang-over the irony wasn't lost on me

It began what felt like several eons before, on Saturday 13th February, 1982. It was on the almost empty and freezing terrace of City's Cattle Shed End and Churchill and I were suffering the torture of watching a turgid 0-0 draw against a team so unfancied I hadn't heard of them before. From what Churchill was shouting I'd have guessed the club was called 'Come and have a go if you think you're hard enough you great hairy arseholes United'. At least he was enjoying himself. We'd been smoking some industrial-strength cannabis, an activity I had begun to indulge in again purely for recreational purposes, as in those bits of the day between waking up and going to sleep. This had the unfortunate side-effect of appearing to slow down the passage of time. The football match went on for a week. Every goal kick took an hour, every terrible pass forty-five minutes. It was no wonder the opposition saw every attack coming and were able to stifle it with time to spare. After a while I gave up with the game and watched the grass growing, which was marginally more exciting. When the final whistle finally blew, an action that took the referee two hours and ten minutes to complete, we left the ground and Churchill insisted on engaging in a minor scrap with half a dozen half-hearted United fans. It soon became clear that the pain of supporting terminal losers was something we shared with the opposing fans, so he made it up and we took them for a drink in the nearest pub. Churchill raised his pint of lager to mine.

'Howay the lads.'

Life without Gina was pretty much like life with Gina, due to the fact that three months after walking out she hadn't gone very far. She and Kirk had decided that it was ridiculously bourgeois to fall out over a stupid thing like adultery and that we were much too intelligent to do anything so petty. So they vowed to keep in touch, an act which, for most people, marks the last occasion when they ever meet. Kirk and Gina were not most people. At least once a week they would drop in to the flat and spend an amiable couple of hours drinking my cheap coffee and pulling their 'its poison' faces to each other, before insisting that I go to their apartment, which was actually a rather poky flat over Kirk's restaurant. Occasionally I'd give in and go and endure a three-course meal that was so pretentious it made a Duran Duran video seem modest.

On these occasions it was hard to tell who was with who. Kirk would reminisce about the good old days when he and I hung out in the band, and Gina would pat her bump and chat happily about the things she and I did together (which as far as I could remember had absolutely nothing to do with the bump). I'd smile and kid myself that I had enjoyed the time with each of them as much as they obviously had with me, although for the life of me I couldn't remember when it was

'We're friends, so it makes sense,' Kirk and Gina would insist to anyone who queried the odd relationship.

'It's fucking daft, you should beat the bastard up,' Churchill said, who spent most of his free time querying the relationship

'That's Kirk, though, that's the way he is,' I would say, apologetically.

'Who said I was talking about Kirk?'

I'd used the time since Gina had left me to reconsider my career. The first thing I noticed was that I didn't have one. I had the job at Joshua Kindside and I still enjoyed it but I was starting to want more. More money for instance. More responsibility. More time off. There was only one thing for it, I would have to seek a more senior position, one that gave me the benefits I required without also giving me too much to do. It was a simple solution that had only one flaw. I would never get a sniff of promotion while Attila the Hen was in charge because she saw me as an idle, disrespectful troublemaker. She was as mad as a hatter who has 'By Appointment to Broadmoor' on his label, but this didn't stop her from being dangerously shrewd.

So nothing much had changed in my life, except for Saturdays. On Saturdays I went to football, taking my life in my hands by going with Churchill to watch City in their annual battle to achieve mid-table ordinariness. City's football was slightly less attractive than ten-day pigs' liver on a maggot farm but it was still a wonderful feeling to stand on a cold, wet, windswept terrace and insult men who were twice my size.

'You fat tosser, you play like a fucking woman.'

'Mind your fucking language . . .' someone yelled back

from a group of supporters fifty yards away, 'my young lad's here.' It was great, I could be all the things Gina hadn't let me be for years, perfectly safe in the knowledge that I wouldn't be arrested by the gender police. Not only that but Saturday afternoon had been a Gina and Kirk time when they called round to impose on my hospitality, so I was doubly grateful to City for an excuse to be out.

Churchill and I were both on the outside of twelve pints of lager and several blue pills – which I'd thought were uppers but were actually Smarties – by the time we got to Iacono's Pizza Parlour for Linda's leaving do. Linda had been at the Joshua Kindside Geriatric Rest Home for eighteen years and she left approximately every two years. She'd resigned three times to have children, twice to get married, once through illness and three times when she'd told Attila the Hen to fuck off and die. On this particular occasion she was leaving to settle in New Zealand. She had left and then come back so many times her leaving present was a yo-yo. Yo-yo was also her nickname, not coined for the same reason but rather because of her apparent willingness to share her sexual favours with any man who had a large amount of tattoos and small amount of brain cells. It referred to the action of her knickers which allegedly went up and down, up and down.

That was the main reason why we had agreed to go. Churchill was hopeful of achieving what most Bradworth males had already achieved with Linda. I told him he was sad and pathetic while judging that between him and Ken I might pass as a decent option and get lucky.

We were the last to arrive. The group of fifteen staff had been waiting half an hour but had loyally refused to order until we came. It was a noble gesture and one which we wouldn't have reciprocated. Churchill and I both ordered pizza for six with side salad, chips, garlic bread and coleslaw. The effect of the cannabis on our stomachs ensured that Mr Iacono would be able to buy another Giorgio

Armani suit on Monday. Linda was looking particularly
fetching with short spiky hair, earrings in her eyebrows, top
lip and nose (but none in her ears), blue eye-liner and green
lipstick. She also wore a remarkably short pink ra-ra skirt
and matching leg warmers, which were always a favourite
of mine.

'He's so desperate sheepskin slippers with zips up the
front would turn him on,' Churchill said to the whole group.
Ken and Attila the Hen were both there, giving me their
own particularly sour look of welcome, the one that said 'I
thought you were dead, what a shame I was wrong.'

Linda was off her head, which Churchill took for a good
sign. He gave me the internationally recognised wink of
dirty intent. Several carafes of wine arrived in what looked
like urine sample bottles.

'Tastes like piss as well,' Churchill toasted. I grabbed a
carafe and set about drinking it quickly so as to ward off any
possibility of sobriety. To be sober in the company of Ken
and Attila, who sat either side of me like bookends from
hell, would have been too hard to bear. Surprisingly, I found
that after four glasses even piss could have a sharp raspberry finish with a luscious buttery aftertaste.

Attila the Hen, closer to me than she'd ever been, immediately made up for lost time.

'I need to review your performance. Monday morning,
nine a.m. My office. If you're not there I'll use the time to
find your replacement.'

'Cheers,' I said, toasting her, trying to make it sound like
'go fuck yourself, you sad lonely cow'. It sounded like my
bid for a senior position in the hierarchy had been put on ice,
the kind of ice that one finds in the vicinity of liquid nitro-
gen.

Ken nudged me and sneered. 'Oh, oh, sounds like someone's in trouble.'

'Bill,' Churchill bellowed across the table from where
Linda was draped over his shoulder like someone who has

made a special study of the 'Kama Sutra', 'I won't be sharing a taxi home, mate.' The lucky bastard.

'Thanks, mate,' I whispered under my breath and gloomily poured another half-pint of vino de pissoir.

I didn't remember going home. I didn't remember going to bed. What I did remember was the sex dream. It was the sex dream of a lifetime. Every taboo was explored and exploded, every fetish was enjoyed and exploited. It was long, hot, wet, sticky and immensely satisfying. I woke up still smiling at the thrill of letting go of all my inhibitions and exposing my innermost desires. I was thankful that it had only been a dream, and I was on my own. Anything that exposed the hidden self so explicitly was dangerous stuff indeed. The bedroom door opened

'There's no milk left, so I've made us some toast, lover.'

It was Attila the Hen, naked except for my ridiculously short bathrobe, which provided such inadequate cover that she was, by any reasonable criteria, still pretty naked. I'd never noticed before just how tall she was. She loomed over the bed like the Eiffel Tower, only with bigger tits.

'Move over, lover. It's breakfast in bed. And I'm not necessarily talking about the tea and toast.' She went off into a stage laugh of fruity whoops that were in danger of choking her to death. If she carried on doing it much longer I'd be in danger of choking her to death.

'Last night was . . . well how was it for you?'

'Me?' I asked, still not sure that this wasn't all a horrible mistake, as if she'd taken the wrong turn from her kitchen through a blip in the space–time continuum and ended up in my bedroom. But then the dream was replayed in glorious widescreen format before my eyes. I tried shutting them but it was still there, on the big screen, the sight of me drunkenly urging her to join me in a range of sexual gymnastics that would have won triple gold (all with personal bests) at the Pervert Olympics. Previously I'd thought she had an allergy to the penis but I now knew this was simply a lack of acquaintance. In one drunkenly debauched night she had made very good friends with mine.

'Oh God,' I said, unable to disguise the depth of my despair.

'Oh God?' she asked, seeking clarification on whether I meant it as in 'Oh God, it was brilliant' or 'Oh God, your very presence revolts me'.

'Oh God, it was brilliant.' I lied so badly I thought I'd need a hacksaw to get my nose down to a reasonable length. But I needn't have worried, Attila the Hen was almost as desperate as me when it came to seeking sexual gratification and her bullshit detector had been switched off, unplugged and stored in a backroom somewhere with an old fondue set and a Teasmade.

'Attil . . . Henrietta?'

'Yes, lover?' She looked up from pouring tea. I could see right up into the depths of her cleavage and the dark interior that lay hidden beyond the mountains.

'What should I call you?'

'I liked it when you called me "Queen Pussy" and promised to serve me.'

A picture, in slow-motion action replay, appeared in my mind. Oh no. I did too. And worse.

'I mean, normally, every day. I can't call you Miss Swallow.'

'You can when I'm doing that thing you like. You know, with your bottom just before you moan and . . .'

'Right, yes,' I interrupted, unable to bear the truth, 'but at work for instance.'

'Call me Hen. I feel comfortable with that.'

'I'm sure you do.'

We ate breakfast in silence, Hen basking in the afterglow of sexual fulfilment, me concentrating on a plan to get her out of the flat, and then out of my life, as quickly and cleanly as possible. It would mean giving up all hope of promotion, or even of ever working again, but that was a small price to pay for a night of rampant indiscretion with someone who made the criminally insane seem as reasonable as Mother Theresa. And then she spilled marmalade down the front of her robe. Butter and marmalade dripped on to her cleavage. She looked up slowly and saw me jealously watching the progress of the sweet sticky drip.

'Would you like seconds?' she asked. It was a damn shame because I had just come up with a fool-proof plan to get rid of her, but marmalade on hot, buttered breast was my all-time favourite.

We finished screwing about four-thirty in the afternoon and had finally got dressed and were about to go out in search of food (having eaten the last of the yoghurt off each other's buttocks) when Gina and Kirk arrived.

'Hi,' Gina said to Hen with so much suspicion she sounded like Columbo hot on the trail. I introduced Gina and Kirk, rather untruthfully, as friends.

'Oh, he's embarrassed,' Gina laughed, with a vicious glint in her eye. 'We're much more than friends.' She then told Hen all about me, including some of my sexual foibles, to which Hen nodded along too as if to say, 'Yes I noticed that one last night.' Kirk eyed Hen and kept looking at me as if to say 'Can't you do any better? I hope to God she's good in bed.' At least he didn't ask her if she was the mad bint from work that I was always moaning about and threatening to kill. I tried to distance myself from her. I sat next to Gina and Kirk on the sofa and we looked like an interview panel. I talked about her as a colleague rather than someone who, twenty minutes before, I'd been eating tinned pilchards off. Hen didn't seem to mind, she was just happy to be in the company of people who didn't obviously despise her, a rare event outside work.

'You must bring Hen to the restaurant, I'd love to have you,' Kirk said. I tried hard to detect anything suspicious in the phrase 'have you' which, if I hadn't known him better, I'd have believed was quite innocent. Hen was dying of happiness, she'd had sex, conversation, and an invite out, this was the high point of her social calendar. It was a calendar that probably went back to 1969.

That evening I sat in the darkness of the sitting room thinking through the previous twenty-four hours. I fast forwarded through the embarrassing bits, which reduced it to about eleven minutes. I attempted to retrieve something from the disaster my dick had led me into. Hen was company. That was about all I had come up with. Sure the sex was great, while we were doing it, but afterwards, in the cold light of day, it made even me feel a bit queasy. So, she was company, someone to be with and share with. She was also my boss so we would be together all the time, twenty-four hours a day. There was nothing else for it, I'd have to kill myself.

I went out to buy some fags while I considered the best way to do away with my miserable self. So far the only option I could think of was another night with Hen, which would hopefully shag me to death. I went to Skinner's Early 'til Late store at the end of the street. Inside a young woman was serving. She was wrapped from head to foot in a nylon overall, cap and hairnet, a sartorial nightmare that was the shop owner's obsessive response to food hygiene regulations.

'Pack of Bensons, please.' If it was to be my last ever cigarette then it may as well be a proper one. She handed them to me. Her hair was scraped back out of sight in the cap and all I could see were her eyes. They were a clear dark brown and stirred something in the depths of my soul.

'One pound twenty, please.'

I knew that voice. I looked over the counter. Below the hem of the nylon overall I could see her legs from the knee down. It was the Legs as in the Voice and the Legs. Now I knew she also had the Eyes. And the Bent White Teeth which gave me the Lopsided Smile that swept every other thought clean out of my head.

'From Saint's to Skinner's,' I said, pleased with this quick thinking.

'What?'

'You're her. From Saint's, Kirk's place.'

'Oh shit. It's you, you called Kirk a cook.'

'Yep that's me,' I agreed as if I was acknowledging I was the man who shot Liberty Valance.

'Is he some cunt or what?'

I had heard plenty of women swear before. Gina and her friends swore a lot when they were talking about men, but it was always sixth-form swearing, the sort that sounded affected, as if the swearer was slightly worried about being caught and given detention. But this woman swore like it was a natural part of the language. She wrapped her blood-red thin lips around the word and spat it out as if she didn't care what anyone thought. Which she didn't. And yet she still retained an innocence as if she didn't quite understand the full meaning of the swear words that she used freely. I hadn't heard many men swear as frequently and fluently as she did.

'I'm not sure you should use the C word; it's very demeaning to women.' If I was Sooty, then it was Gina's hand up my arse. 'But you're right, he is.'

'Complete fucking cunt to work for too.' The C word was gratuitous this time, in a 'piss off and mind your own' kind of way. I minded my own.

'Obviously. That's why you're here.'

'This is due to my uncle. He's the Skinner in "Skinner's". He gave me the job to help out.'

'So, you've gone from Saint's to Skinner's.' It was the best joke I'd made in a while and I was going to labour it.

'I'm a Girlington.' She gave the joke even less notice the second time around. 'Trish Girlington. Uncle Jack is my mum's brother. He's a bit of a wanker actually, at least Kirk gave you a decent meal at the end of your shift. It's all Scotch eggs and salmonella here, but I need the money.'

'Oh.' She was extraordinary, and that wasn't my dick talking. That was still lying dormant in its lair in my boxer shorts, exhausted from the exertions of the last few hours. No, she was extraordinary in a refreshingly honest sort of way. Her wonderful eyes, her lopsided grin, her frank speech. I instinctively knew that this was a woman I respected. I also fancied her like mad.

'Would you like to go out?' I asked, unable to believe that I was asking her to go out only seven minutes after deciding to end it all because of the poor state of my relationships with women.

'What the fuck was the deal between you and Kirk? I didn't stay around to see but I realised something was going on,' she said, seemingly oblivious to my question.

'Well . . .'

'Never mind, you can tell me about it over a gin and tonic.' She rang up the till, took out a bundle of five-pound notes, and winked at me.

'Uncle Jack daren't tell my mum that I'm a thief. He's such a clit. Come on, Skinner's is early 'til even earlier, today.'

She tossed her nylon uniform behind her, threw off her cap and let a waterfall of lovely black hair fall out all over the place, before ushering me out of the shop.

Ten

Although my lost weekend had despair at its core, despair that was only slightly offset by the hint of hope given by meeting Trish Girlington, it didn't stop me from seeking out Churchill at work first thing Monday morning and bragging about what had happened to me.

'You cheap tart,' he said, partly out of excitement and partly out of jealousy. He had walked Linda home after her leaving party only to find that her morals were about as loose as a battery hen.

'All I got was her new address in New Zealand, and the promise of a bed in the spare room if I ever go over there.'

I gave him my rarely used smug-bastard-cat-that's-inherited-not-only-the-whole-dairy-herd-but-also-the-entire-cream-factory smile.

'I'm going to need a spare bed to fit all my women in, the way I'm going,' I said, choosing to forget for a second that I didn't necessarily want all of my women. Speaking of the devil she duly appeared, and Hen entered the room in search of someone to volunteer for cleaning-up-sick duty.

'Bill, a word, please,' she summoned me over with her well-practised fascist dictator attitude. I went over, hoping the word would be goodbye As I got close she bent down and blew in my ear.

'Don't make that face,' she said, in a tone that was the dictionary definition of cheeky.

'What face?'

'That face. I know that face, I saw it the other night. Your come-and-get-me face. It isn't fair.'

'No, you're right, it isn't fair. I won't do it again.'

'Oh go on, Mr Misery, do it for me.'

I made an excuse that my skills for changing colostomy bags were required on the top floor, and once there I claimed sanctuary in a long-forgotten linen cupboard.

The evening out with Trish had been nice. We had talked. Or rather I had talked and Trish had sworn, eaten peanuts, drunk pints and sworn some more. But at least she'd paid for everything, which was something I wasn't used to. Or at least Uncle Jack had paid for everything, which was something Trish was very used to. I'd left her at the bus station and she'd promised to call round and see me sometime, which was about as definite a commitment as she was prepared to make. All the time I was with her I hadn't thought about Hen or Gina once, and even my dick never woke up to meddle. It was uncanny.

I didn't know what I was going to do about Hen, so while I waited for inspiration I avoided all possible contact. When we did meet at the end of the day I made sure I was in the middle of a large group of staff, knowing that Hen wouldn't dare drop her professional image as a murderously mad autocrat in front of the *hoi polloi*. She called out to me but I pretended to be interested in Ken Dubbin's in-depth description of Mrs Dixon's urine infection and made my escape.

'Serves you right, you slag,' Churchill said, reassuringly. Churchill calling me a tart and a slag in the same day did make me think of pots and kettles racially abusing one another.

'Yes OK, but what am I going to do?'

'Hot sex with your boss and a regular date with the angel of mercy and you want advice?'

'In case you've forgotten, our boss is Attila the Hen, the same mad cow who made you take Mrs Doughty to the shops without a wheelchair.'

'She'd only had the one leg amputated, and Mrs Doughty hops better than any eighty-year-old I know. Anyway, I could manage.'

'Don't stick up for Attila, she's a fruit cake.'

'If she's a fruit cake then I hope you made a wish when you were stirring her. Some would say you protest too much.'

That was all I needed, Churchill misquoting Shakespeare. My world had truly turned upside down.

I took the next day off sick, rather pleased with my excuse that I had a touch of phthisis, a form of pulmonary tuberculosis that meant I was progressively wasting away. I'd been steadily working my way, alphabetically, through the medical dictionary for several years, moving on to the next letter every time I needed an unplanned day off. I felt phthisis was an apt description for my current predicament. I was wasting away, emotionally if not physically.

I was sitting down to a tea of sausages (a whole packet), chips (three potatoes worth), fried eggs (half a dozen) and beans (a whole tin) when Hen walked in.

'Feeling better, lover?' she asked in a strange voice.

'Feed a fever,' I said, quickly pointing at the plate of food as if it was the last thing I wanted but which my weakened condition had forced on me.

'Cold,' she corrected

'What?' I asked, not paying much attention as I was more puzzled by her presence in my kitchen. 'How did you get in?'

'It's feed a cold, starve a fever. Has my lover got a poorly cold?' Her voice still sounded strange and then I realised what it was. She was being sympathetic and affectionate and the result sounded like a wounded animal just before it was shot by the vet.

'Saturday night,' she continued with a vampish wink.

'What?'

'How I got in. You told me you never wanted to be apart from me again. You gave me a spare door-key and then we made love on this.' She tapped the kitchen table with her forefinger and I blushed.

Appetite all but gone, I offered to share my food. She greedily helped herself to half of it, pointing out rather unnecessarily that chips were her favourite. I watched her big lips as she spooned in mouthful after mouthful. While it made me feel sick, it was also strangely sexy. It was like watching a hungry lion, you knew it was dangerous but it also looked sweet enough to stroke. I summoned up my inner strength.

'Hen, I'm not sure this is going to work.'

'I know.'

'You do?' Perhaps this was going to be easier than I anticipated. I vowed to use my inner strength more often.

'Yes. The more I think about it, the more I think you're right.'

'You do?' What did she mean, think I was right? She never thought I was right. Right about what? 'Right about what exactly?'

'Moving in with you. It's a good idea. It would solve all my poorly lover's problems.'

'Moving in?' I said weakly.

'On Saturday night, silly Billy, don't you remember anything? You said I should move in with you and never mind the gossip.'

I was starting to realise that I hadn't only spent Saturday night screwing Hen, I seemed to have spent quite a bit of time screwing up my life.

We spent the rest of the evening planning our future

together, or rather Hen planned and I listened, and then I agreed at what I judged to be the correct moment. She decided what new furniture we should buy (everything), which of my furniture we would throw out (all of it), and what the new decor in each room would be (crinoline ladies). Hen liked crinoline ladies, on wallpaper, on curtains, on printed toilet-seat covers. I knew that my mum was going to love her. Resigned to a fate worse than death, I resolved to gain something from the evening and persuaded her to join me in a re-run of the kitchen table affair, only this time I made sure I didn't do anything stupid like giving her my door-key afterwards. Unless you count asking her to marry me, that is.

I helped her move in the next day and then took her to meet my mum. As I expected, Mum did love Hen. They had so much in common. A deeply religious faith in Persil, for instance. Mum was happy that at last I'd met someone who would look after me, just like her. I knew she was right too. Even Dad agreed.

'Whhggz,' he grunted in encouragement. Hen chatted in her sing-song way throughout our visit, happily putting away several dozen tinned-salmon sandwiches and half of Mum's date and walnut cake, extended family size.

'Ooh, I do prefer you to that slut Gina,' Mum said, unbiased as ever. She smiled at me to show that I had finally brought honour to the Wrose family name. I chewed on the lumpy slice of date and walnut darkly. During the meal I said even less than Dad. Afterwards Hen confessed that they reminded her of her own parents.

That explained a lot, I thought.

Hen was working a late shift on the Thursday and I revelled in my first taste of freedom since she'd descended on my life like a cloud. What was worse, the only silver lining this cloud had was colour-coordinated crinoline ladies printed on it. There was a polite knock on the door and I put out the illicit cigarette and hid the can of Special Brew in the fridge before answering it. With Hen I knew that I couldn't be too careful. I opened the door and saw Trish, who was smiling and waiting to be welcomed in. I'd not only forgotten about her promise to call round, I'd forgotten all about her existence on the planet. Hen had that effect on me, under her spell I forgot anything even remotely pleasurable.

I smiled back at Trish and thought as quickly as three cans of Special Brew would allow. If Hen did catch us together it was possible that it might just get me out of a hole that was deeper and blacker than any current model in the latest Calcutta range. I showed Trish into the sitting room and under the pretext of opening a bottle of wine (the only alcohol Hen allowed me to drink), I untidied the flat as much as possible, partly to give the impression I was a man who lived alone but mostly to look as if I had a semblance of basic good taste. The latter was particularly difficult as, even after only four days, evidence of Hen was everywhere. There was the poster of a horse looking over a stable door which said 'Life is what you make it'. There was the copy of The Desiderata framed in a flowery picture frame, along the bottom of which was written, in Hen's manic scrawl, 'I promise to try'. There was also the table top full of anti-depressants and general happy pills that Hen took at particularly stressful times, like on days which ended in Y. After two minutes of frantic endeavour, it looked as if the flat was inhabited by a man with severe mental depression and a bad dose of terminal sentimentality.

Trish was wearing black ski pants and a white mohair coat. She looked both odd and totally wonderful. I told her so.

'Fuck off, you smooth-talking bastard,' she said, almost affectionately. I took her coat which felt very warm and offered her a glass of dry white wine.

'Got any Lambrusco?' she asked. 'Can't abide that dry

shite.' I hadn't so she put a hefty spoonful of sugar into the glass and stirred it. We sat down and I groped around inside for some residual inner strength to explain what had happened since we last met.

'What happened to your kitchen table?' she asked, pointing at the pile of broken matchwood in the corner of the sitting room.

'Woodworm,' I said from somewhere behind a mask of radioactive blushes. I heard the front door opening. It was Hen home early and I was going to die. At least if I was dead I wouldn't have the embarrassment of being exposed as a two-timing cheat in front of Trish. I prepared myself for the storm that was about to break, stupidly believing that my life was capable of following the instruction book.

'Hi,' Gina and Kirk said together, in a smug, caught-you-with-your-pants-down kind of way. Why was it that those who had a key to my flat were the very people I didn't want to have a key to my flat? More to the point, why didn't I take Gina's key away and stop them coming round? Because I was desperate to appear to be handling our break-up in a mature, I'm-glad-she-and-Kirk-are-happy-and-we-can-still-be-friends kind of way? Because I still had hopes that Gina might come back and I'd get even with Kirk? Or because I was weak and stupid? The truth was probably a combination of all of the above.

'It's you,' Gina said, as if Trish were a well-known and deadly virus. Kirk looked over Gina's shoulder and winked.

'It's you,' he said, in a completely different tone to Gina's. His was more along the lines of 'get your knickers off'.

'It's Cocksucker Kirk and his little friend va-Gina. What are they doing here?' Trish asked me. It was a good question and one that would have left me in need of a good lawyer had not Gina decided to set herself up as my advocate.

'We're his friends. We are always here. But what is she doing here?' Gina asked imperiously, pointed an accusing finger at Trish.

'Well . . .' I began, without any idea of how I was going to finish.

'How's life treating you then Tish?' Kirk asked, smoother than a baby's bottom that's just come back from a buffing at the hands of an award-winning French polisher.

'It's Trish, you fornicating bastard. I'm OK. I trust you're not.'

'Look I'm sorry but Trish and me, we've got things to discuss,' I said in an attempt to gain control of the situation.

'What's happened to Hen?' Gina asked suspiciously, as if Hen was bricked up behind a fireplace somewhere. Some hope. 'I liked her,' she said.

'She's . . . not here,' I stammered.

'She can't have gone, she only moved in on Sunday.'

'Hen? Moved in? Sunday? You bastard,' Trish summarised with the ease of a tabloid newspaper.

'Indeed, Bill. You seem to have treated this little lady rather badly,' Kirk said, implying that if Trish wanted to seek solace in someone else's arms his were open twenty-four hours a day, seven days a week, and not only that but you got saving stamps every time you used the facility.

'Anyone want to watch TV?' I asked.

Gina and Kirk, never noted for their sensitivity, had been surprisingly understanding when I asked them, as politely as you like, to fuck off so I could speak to Trish alone. I'd put on the television and immediately Kirk became the Secretary General of the United Nations and insisted on leaving us in peace to sort out our troubles.

'Come, Gina, these young people have big decisions to make. Plus I wouldn't mind catching the end of *Top of the Pops*.'

When they had gone we watched television in silence. *Top of the Pops* started and lots of groups I'd never heard of came on and mimed to their latest hit.

'So?' Trish finally asked.

'Well, there's this girl that I don't really like and who I asked to live with me but now I'm trying to get rid of and she's sort of my boss and . . .'

'Oh very nice. Am I part of the plan to get rid of her?'

'No,' I lied. 'You just happened.'

'And Sunday. You asked me out on the same day you asked her to live with you.'

'Look, she and me, it just happened.'

'Lot's of wild and wacky things just happen to you, don't they?'

'Yes,' I said, truthfully. 'I was drunk.'

'Oh, that's all right then. I thought Kirk was a cheesy prick but as overripe Gorgonzolas go, you take the biscuit.'

'Look . . .'

'No, you look . . .'

'No, I mean look.' I pointed at the television.

'What?'

'Him,' I said, still pointing at the screen. On stage in the full, grey glory of my ancient black and white set, a grown man was dressed in what looked like an old curtain. He was dancing very badly and miming with even less conviction. The song had a rueful kind of melody which sounded like it wanted to be doing something else, something that was more worthy and noble, like advertising a breakfast cereal. It gave up and died away peacefully, to be replaced by hearty applause from the two dozen or so audience who were being rudely shepherded around the studio by a ruthless floor manager. The toothy grin of the DJ came back into view, pre-pubescent girls glued either side of him to try to achieve an image of being a fun-guy around town.

'And that's "Shiver Me Timbres", a new entry for Fear Factor Five, featuring Don One, The Pirate King.'

'Its not pronounced "Timbers", its . . .' I began to correct him, before I realised there was something else, something more familiar about the title.

'And now from a pirate song to a song I rate, it's Soft Cell with . . .' The end of his weak link was drowned out by my primal laugh, which evolved into a primal scream, which developed into a primal kick through the TV screen. This was rapidly followed by sparks, smoke and severe burns on my leg, followed even quicker by primal screams of a more painful nature and a lot of hopping.

The nurse drew back the curtain and showed Trish in.

'The doctor just needs to take a look and then you can take your husband home.'

'This dozy shag isn't my husband. He's some twat who claims to have written "Say Hello, Wave Goodbye".'

'Well, as long as he doesn't stay here annoying us you can do what you like with him, love.'

The nurse went off in search of other wounds to scrub a little too firmly and dress a little too tightly. I wondered if she was a distant relation of Hen's.

'Well?' Trish asked, interrupting my reverie.

'It was Chopper. Don One was, I mean. The Pirate King. It was Chopper. He used to be in my band, and that sounded a lot like one of my songs, only much more wanky.'

'I quite liked it. Very New Romantic. But then I like Diana Ross, and that doesn't answer my question which was "Well?" As in "Well, what the fuck are you playing at?"'

I knew I should be taking her anger seriously, I knew she had every right to be upset, and I also knew she was some-one that I didn't want to hurt, but unfortunately I had a bad leg, a broken telly and a private life that made the average can of worms look simple and uncomplicated.

'It's not my fault.'

'Seems like it never is. You're as bad as Kirk.'

'That's not fair. He's always fucking up my life, too. He'd have you if he got the chance.'

'He fucking wouldn't.'

'Honestly?'

'Honestly. I wouldn't go with him again.' The word

'again' hung around like a love bite after an unfaithful liaison. Use any toothpaste you like, put up your collar, wear an embarrassing cravat, you couldn't hide it, disguise it or remove it.

'Again?'

'Yes. Didn't he tell you? He usually liked to brag about his conquests. Every waitress went with him. It was practically part of the job description. Not a particularly big part from what I remember. He chooses the waitresses on whether he fancies them or not. As he fancies anything in a black skirt it probably doesn't unfairly discriminate against anyone. Very equal opportunities.'

'How could you?'

Well, I didn't know that was how he operated. He can be very charming, you know.'

'Believe me, I know. How many times did you go with him?'

'God only the once; what is this?'

'It's him, the bastard. I'm sorry.'

'So am I. It was only the once, thank God, which as far as I'm concerned is only one time away from none at all, so it's practically never.'

'I suppose so. Was he any good? And if he was I don't mind if you lie.'

'He was all right. I mean he started crap but he got better. By the thirteenth time he was OK.' She was never less than painfully honest.

'Thirteenth time? You said you only did it once.'

'We did. We did it thirteen times on the one night we spent together.'

I tried to explain that, to me, once meant one time and thirteen meant thirteen times but she disagreed, arguing that any amount that happened within the confines of one night counted only once. We argued like a couple of schoolchildren until the doctor came and threatened to call hospital security and have me expelled from the casualty unit. Out in the car park we carried on arguing to the point where we walked away from one another both saying it was over. Unfortunately the hospital was on the wrong side of town and we had to wait at the same bus stop to catch the same bus back into Bradworth. There was no one else on board, but common decency forced us to sit next to each other. Trish got off first.

'I'll see you around,' I shouted through the narrow window that only opened a couple of inches so as to avoid draughts.

'Not if I see you first, bollock face,' she said, smiling ever so slightly.

The next morning I went to the local record store and asked for the latest single by Don One (The Pirate King), and the young assistant gave me a glance that said 'wow you're cooler than you look – but not much'. The record came in a cover which pictured an embarrassed-looking Chopper waving a cutlass and wearing an eye patch.

'Not so much a New Romantic, more a bleeding old pillock,' I said to the man looking at a Kate Bush album and fiddling in his trouser pocket. I took the single out of its cover. I could hardly bear to look but I knew I had to.

'Shiver Me Timbres' claimed to be written by someone called E. David. But I knew it was my song and some bastard had stolen it. I also knew that bastard was called E. David but I had no idea who that bastard E. David was. Life wasn't so much unfair, as totally bastard corrupt.

'Yes,' Kirk screamed from the other end of the phone line.

'Were you busy?' I asked, pleased to have pissed him off.

'I'm in the middle of filleting fresh dace for tonight's special.'

'Dicing with dace, eh?' I joked. To have Kirk angry and at my mercy was a pleasure rarer than a friendly letter from the bank manager.

'Get on with it or fuck off. By the way, who is this?'

'It's Bill,' I said, realising too late I'd fallen for his feigned ignorance. Angry, I demanded to know what he knew about Chopper and his new career.

'Nothing, mate.' He was calling me mate, which confirmed for me that he must have a guilty secret. 'I'd heard he was doing well, the old bastard. Who'd have thought it?'

'Quite. Carving out a successful career would have been the last thing I'd have thought him capable of,' I said, pointedly.

'And you say it sounds a bit like one of our songs?'

'No, one of *my* songs. And it doesn't sound a bit like it, it sounds exactly like it. Word for word. Who the fuck is E. David?'

'Don't ask me. I've no idea. It's probably one of Chopper's many aliases.'

'Like Don One. Funny how he chose that name. It used to be your stage name, didn't it?'

'Did it? I don't remember. What a low life, he'd nick anything. Anyway, can't hang about, must dace.' He arrogantly threw the fish joke back at me and hung up.

'I gave the record to Hen when I arrived at work.

'A little present to show what I think of you,' I said. We were alone in her office.

'I'd have preferred "Daddy's Home", but this is very nice. I've also got a surprise for you. We had a little appointment last Monday, but you were too ill to keep it, remember? So I've rescheduled it for after lunch today, in my office please.'

I could feel panic rising and filling the space where my backbone used to be. Hen had made several suggestions during the height of passion about how much fun it would be to have sex in her office. The anglepoise lamp on the desk looked like it had some nasty sharp edges and I hoped to God she wasn't about to turn these fantasies into reality. I needn't have worried. Hen was an insecure and sometimes insane person but, at work at least she was the same old obsessionally hierarchical bastard. The nearest she got to a good time in her office was the sensation she got when cutting the staff overtime.

I ate lunch feeling like a condemned man, only with slightly less chance of a reprieve. Aggie and Alf sat with me and wished me well.

'Give her one for me,' said Alf, again showing an astute awareness that constantly surprised me. I knocked on the oak office door as quietly as I could, hoping she wouldn't hear.

'Come,' she yelled in her best I'm-in-charge voice.

I came, in the non-biblical sense. Hen wasn't alone. There was a man in a very smart suit and tie with her and I tried to remember if she had mentioned troilism as one of her fantasies. She'd said something about a Welsh rugby team but this man was thin and weedy and would have been unsafe in a summer breeze.

'Wrose. This is Mr Airdrie.' He smiled a smile so thin I wouldn't have got a cigarette paper between his lips. He had an angular chiselled face which was crowned with a mass of black hair that was either dyed or a wig, I couldn't tell which. It was so black and such an odd style it couldn't have been natural. It looked as if an unkindness of ravens had enacted a Jim Jones-style mass-suicide pact on top of his head. His empty colourless eyes showed a complete lack of interest in me, making me think he was typical senior management, people who never wasted time talking to underlings if they could possibly help it.

'Mr Airdrie is the Assistant Director of Geriatric Services.' Hen licked her lips as she said 'services', and a wicked sparkle shone in her eyes. I felt a compulsory throb in my groin, which quickly collapsed, fed up with making the effort.

'Mr Wrose.' He licked his lips in the fashion of the average anal retentive. 'I understand from Miss Swallow here that you are skilled in the technique of memory relocation?'

'I am?'

'Yes, you are,' Hen said firmly, 'you regularly lead the old folks through their memory sequence, helping them recover lost information and thus aid their space-time re-orientation.' She'd been reading text books again which was always a bad sign.

'Well, I talk about the war and stuff with them.'

'Quite so. Excellent technique,' said Mr Airdrie, nodding at Hen so hard I thought his stupid head might fall off.

'Good, good,' Hen agreed. I looked from one to the other and tried to work out which was the most ridiculous. I concluded it was probably me for going along with this charade.

'Congratulations, Mr Wrose. You've passed.'

'Passed what?' A loose stool, a kidney stone, the last hope in hell?

'Passed your interview. He's just the man for this team, eh, Miss Swallow?' Mr Airdrie gave her a dangerous wink, that, if I hadn't wanted her dead, would have made me exceptionally jealous.

'You're the new Deputy Officer In Charge. I'm already looking forward to our first supervision.' She gripped my hand like a boa constrictor and I remembered why I was frightened of upsetting her. Mr Airdrie also shook my hand, his grip as limp as eight-day-old lettuce.

'Deputy? You jammy twat,' Churchill congratulated me. 'Hey, that means you're in charge of the duty rota. Can I have Tuesday off? And Wednesday? And next Saturday? Say yes and I won't tell anyone about you and Attila.'

'Too late, some bastard has put it in this month's house magazine.' The latest copy of *Old Times* had a less than cryptic piece under the heading 'Love Amongst the Bedpans'.

'Sack the editor, I say,' Churchill said.

'You're the editor,' I pointed out.

*

'Deputy?' I asked Hen after work. We had no television to occupy us, thanks to Don One, so we were indulging in conversation, and I could see that we were going to get on about as well as a seagull in an oil-slick. As we chatted Hen bathed my leg wound in a salt-water solution that was slightly stronger than sulphuric acid.

'Yes. Good news, isn't it? More responsibility, more freedom, more money. And of course we can spend more time together.'

'Great news. Great. The three things I always wanted.'

The next week we went to Saint's for a meal. This was at Hen's insistence, which was similar to having a bayonet held at your shoulder blades. She also insisted that Kirk and Gina join us, feeling that they were the kind of people we should be cultivating for our social circle, reinforcing our new-found status. Kirk said it was on him. On him in the sense that he cleared the table at short notice; the rest, such as paying the bill (including an extra charge for clearing a table at short notice), was my responsibility. I thought, and secretly hoped, that Gina and Kirk would mention Trish, but I was disappointed. When Hen made one of several visits to the toilet, a condition brought on by her latest course of tranquillisers, Gina said that she wasn't going to say anything because she thought Hen was good for me and she didn't want to do anything to hurt her. I thanked her for being so considerate. The supercilious cow. Later, when Hen and Gina had both gone to the toilet, presumably to laugh about something they had in common (like knowing about the unusual bend in my penis), Kirk asked me for Trish's whereabouts.

'I've tried her old address but she's moved, the little honey. She had such pert little breasts, like poached eggs. I wouldn't mind making her acquaintance again, as you've kicked her into touch.' He poked his tongue out and waggled it up and down.

'I don't know how women can resist you.' It was only then that it had dawned on me that I was kicking Trish into touch. I felt more like kicking myself.

The main course arrived. It was *chou rouge landais*, which roughly translated as fancy frankfurters in a sauce that was so rich a Labour Government would have put it straight into the super-tax bracket.

'Kirk loves to emulate Elizabeth David, don't you, darling,' Gina boasted on her beau's behalf.

'Well, why not. If you want to be the best, then you only keep the best company,' he boasted back, ten fold.

'Who?'

'God, Bill,' Gina mocked with the strutting arrogance of one who knew about these things. 'Don't you know anything? Elizabeth David, the greatest of all English cookery writers.'

'She was the person responsible for saving this country from the tyranny of artless food,' Kirk said, and completed all the necessary biographical details for me.

'I didn't know that,' I admitted as shamelessly as one who didn't give a monkey's about the tyranny of artless food, 'but I do know that E. David is the person who claims to have written Chopper's latest hit.' I gave Kirk a look that was meant to search his conscience like a flashlight and expose even the smallest shadow of guilt. He gave a disarming smile which side-stepped the full destructive force of my stare.

'What a coincidence,' he said in a lazy voice and then shouted at the waitress to get another bottle of Merlot. As she scurried off, the front door burst open and several men dressed like a rack from Laura Ashley's January sale roared into the room, laughing and singing. The loudest of the group, who was in a long, flowing gown of green velvet with daisy-patterned shawl wrapped around his head, searched the room with his one good eye (the other was covered by a tartan eye patch) until he saw our table.

'Har, har, me hearties,' he chuckled like a character from a bad provincial pantomime, throwing the shawl back to reveal bleached-blond dread locks.

'My man Kirk. We did it. You did it. We're number fucking one. In fact we're number fucking Don One.' From inside his velvet cloak Chopper – a.k.a. Blackburn Woodcock a.k.a. Don One The Pirate King – pulled a bottle of champagne, which he duly opened and sprayed over the diners.

Kirk looked at me without the slightest trace of guilt or embarrassment. 'It was going to be a surprise,' he said.

'Don't apologise,' I said with a calmness that surprised even me, 'it still is a surprise. You cheating –'

'I like your shawl,' Hen said, interrupting me. 'That pattern would go lovely in our bathroom, wouldn't it, Billy?' I couldn't give her an opinion on this as, due to the usual 'musical differences', I was too busy throwing a table at my former musical colleagues, followed by a selection of sharp cutlery, before ripping off Chopper's eye patch which, for some reason that made perfect sense at the time but not afterwards, I then ate. Having had everything in my life ripped off by this pair of thieving pirates, it was the first time I'd been able to rip something off them, and even though it wasn't exactly big or important, it still tasted good.

Eleven

> I don't want you to think I'm taking the piss
> but when it comes to being happy
> who is . . .?

Don One sang on 'Positively the Last Song I'll Ever Write About Pizza'. It was ironic that it wasn't even the first song he'd written about pizza, or about anything else for that matter, as it had been written by me. It was from his Greatest Hits album, 'The World Owes Me a Living', released after he had split from the rest of Fear Factor Five. He'd had two minor top forty successes since leaving the band and not a lot else, so the greatest hits formula had all the hallmarks of a career in decline. At least that's what I hoped.

I sang along with lyrics that were still being attributed to E. David (but which I knew had been pirated from me) while I shaved in the bath. I also knew E. David was Kirk St John, but several singles as well as years had passed and I had yet to receive any share of the royalties. That was unless you counted one free meal at Saint's that Kirk claimed was more than adequate compensation for what he saw as the very small part I played in helping him write the original song. My assertion that the small part I played included writing both the music and lyrics caused him to laugh, slap me on the back and say that I always did have a good sense of humour. At least he still had the scar on his forehead caused by a flying table as it reached the peak of its parabolic curve.

Outside in the sitting room I could hear Hen getting ready for work. It sounded like a particularly disturbed psychopath attacking a conference hall full of Freudians with a chainsaw. I turned up the radio and mimicked Chopper's nasal whine. Hen and I still lived in the same flat that I'd shared with Gina but it now had a new range of furnishings that marked the battle lines of our relationship. Black leather armchair versus broad flower-print sofa, top-of-the-range TV versus china-doll-in-national-costume collection. Framed football programmes versus sketches of pink ballerinas, crying. It was the Cold War of interior decor. Living and working with Hen caused all sorts of problems, not least the black despair of sharing every hour of my life with someone I wouldn't usually share a continent with. To say we argued would be like accusing a Caribbean hurricane of being a bit draughty. Our relationship was the verbal equivalent of the Trojan Wars, only with a touch more gratuitous bloodshed. We went to work separately and, where possible, worked separate shifts. The only real area of contact we had was sleeping with each other.

Hen and I had been brought together by that most powerful of emotions – sexual attraction. The one thing we had in common was that we both had a previous sexual history that would barely fill one side of a postcard. A postcard that already had Wish You Were Here and a big postmark obscuring the rest of the available space.

'Fill your boots, mate,' Churchill said, describing sex that was for the sake of sexual gratification alone and didn't have anything stupid, like love, to obscure its purpose. So we'd filled our boots. But our boots had long ago overflowed and now our turn ups were damp, soggy and cold. Sex, especially the sex we had, needed something to set it in relief, such as mutual respect. That was where the trouble started. Hen's chief desire was to have a career. She believed a relationship was something she had to have as a prerequisite for success. It was as essential for defining status as having a good job, getting qualifications, or owning a toasted-sandwich maker. My role was to serve as a tick in the box marked 'boyfriend'. In time it was obvious to both of us that I'd become an annoying little tick. Love and affection never did figure greatly in our relationship, and nor did happiness.

'Are we happy, darling?' she asked me as I dried off and dressed for work. It was a question she asked me at least once a week so I'd had plenty of practice in making my lies sound convincing.

'When it comes to being happy, who is?' I quoted Chopper and Co., plagiarising me.

'Pardon?'

'Of course we are,' I said quickly, spotting a violent argument on the horizon unless I took immediate evasive action.

'How happy?' she asked. I hated this question. I always underestimated the amount she required me to define. If I said 'this much' and held my hands apart like a weekend fisherman, she would sulk like a teenager because it wasn't enough. In order to properly satisfy her expectations I'd need to hold my hands so far apart it would permanently dislocate both shoulder blades.

'Very.' I was quite pleased with the answer; it said a lot without ever coming close to a definition.

'How much is that?' she asked, pedantic to the end.

'A lot. Bags full. Infinity. I couldn't be happier if I was a cowboy and you were Laramie.'

She screamed like a bloodcurdling cacodemon and ran at me. I instinctively threw my hands in front of my face for protection but she brushed them aside as if they were wisps of straw. I waited for the blow that would probably break my neck. Instead she planted a big wet kiss on my lips, nose and cheeks. It was like walking into a room of very friendly red setters. Then she pulled away and gave me her serious look. It was one that she didn't get to practise much, which was why it always made her look like she was under the influence of white spirits.

'Are you being serious?' she asked. I thought about what I'd just said. I had to admit her reaction was more than I'd expected but I couldn't see any reason why I should change my point of view. She blew me a kiss which was almost as wet as the previous one. It sprayed across my face and made me close my eyes. Meanwhile she ran off into the other room to phone her mother. I finished dressing and listened in to her conversation.

'He just came out with it, Mum. I couldn't be happier unless you were to marry me. That's what he said. Yes, Mum, he is being serious, he just told me.' She squealed again and I thought I heard a similar squeal echo from the other end of the line.

Without thinking, I put on two shirts, probably in case I shivered when the executioner raised the axe above my neck. A couple more squeals later the phone was crashed on to its stand and she came rushing back to me.

'This is amazing,' she said.

'Isn't it just?' I agreed.

'Why now?'

'I don't know,' I said honestly, 'of course I don't expect you to say yes.'

'Yes.'

'Well, not immediately anyway.' I was now grasping at straws.

'Yes. Yes. Yesyesyesyes.'

'If you wanted more time . . .'

I'd asked her to marry me many times before, but only on the point of sexual release and shortly before the cold reality of our relationship reminded me how this was the very last thing on earth that I actually wanted to do. I'd never expected her to take me seriously. The fact that she had accepted was probably because it came at a time when there was nowhere else for our empty relationship to go.

As Hen had needed to have a 'boyfriend' so I had to have a 'girlfriend', but there the similarity ended. My ideas for a fulfilled life were more abstract, and included things like getting drunk, having a good time, and waking up where I fell. Soon after we got together I'd realised the futility of sharing my life with Hen and had even gone in search of Trish, but Skinner's Early 'til Late had become Munir's We Never Close and the trail went cold. Meanwhile Hen and I continued to have great sex, nasty, brutish and short sex, increasingly more occasional sex, but great sex nonetheless. Yet it was amazing how the one thing I had sought for so long gradually became the one thing I wanted to avoid.

These days we ate our food off dinner plates, rather than parts of one another's anatomy. Only the night before we'd had sex for the first time in many months. Hen didn't know we had, but we had. She'd thought I was asleep and had masturbated in bed next to me. The sensation of someone indulging in secretive sexual fulfilment just inches away had made me realise how much I'd missed the physical side of our relationship. In other words it turned me on like crazy. So much so I joined in. When she reached orgasm she wrenched the quilt over her side of the bed. I came with her as the cold air hit my body. I bit the pillow to contain my giggles as I'd realised that this was probably the first time ever we'd come together, not counting the occasions she had pretended to come at the same time as me, or indeed, the occasions I'd pretended to come at the same time as her.

I drove into work with Chopper's greatest hits tape playing but all I could hear were church bells. The fruits of success that my promotion had brought (and bought) were all around. The car, second-hand but in reasonable condition, despite all my efforts, the smart woollen suit, that my mum loved because it made me look like a newsreader, the briefcase made out of fine calf leather, in which I put urgent paperwork to take home where it stayed unread until I took it back to work again. Personal, emotional and sexual relationships aside, things were going pretty well, considering.

As her boyfriend, Hen liked to control my every movement, but as her deputy she had given me a completely free reign. She was so busy trying to be the consummate senior manager that she didn't have time to do any real work, so she left it to me. Given the opportunity to be creative and change things, I set to with a vengeance. I introduced the 'personal plan', where every resident had one member of staff to give them special help, such as with shopping, personal care, or telling their money-grabbing relatives to fuck off and leave their savings alone. The idea was simple. I'd based it on my experience of spending years hiding in cupboards. You simply gave the staff something to do, something that you could check on later to see whether they'd done it, and this reduced their opportunities to skive by a minimum of seventy-five per cent. The scheme had become a major talking point around Bradworth Corporation and had received fair praise from the people at the top. I had been a bit pissed off that Hen's name had appeared to be rather too closely associated with the idea, as in 'Henrietta Swallow's Personal Plan Scheme gains merit award at national level'. But I figured that if it was good for the old people it was immaterial who got the credit. At least, that's what I said in public. In private I'd cleaned the toilet seat with her toothbrush and then enjoyed a cold dish of revenge every morning as she cleaned her teeth.

Churchill was waiting for me when I arrived at the Rest Home. His arms were folded across his chest in the aggressive fashion he now adopted with me. This was a bad sign.

'I want to discuss these rumours with you now.'

'What rumours?' It was the nature of my job as Deputy Officer in Charge that I was always the last to know anything. My job was great, some responsibility, but not much, some contact with the residents, but not much, better pay than most of the staff, but not much. I was given license to keep my head down and tell others what to do and I excelled at it. So much so that I had very little idea what actually went on in the place. Rumours had a tendency to be hard fact enshrined in legislation by the time I got to hear about them.

'Janice knows someone at the town hall who knows someone in the Labour group who reckons privatisation is on the way. Is it true?'

Churchill and I had grown apart since I'd been with Hen. He didn't feel comfortable hanging out with the Deputy Officer, particularly when the Deputy lived with the mad bitch Officer in Charge. Instead he'd thrown himself into the role of Union Steward, which meant that he could give us both a bloody hard time from a safe distance.

The week he had been installed as Shop Steward he had taken up the cause of Noreen, the domestic. Noreen spent most of her shifts safely ensconced in the domestic store cupboard, where she sold a wide range of produce from free-range eggs to large cartons of bleach and mop heads. She earned three times what she was paid for cleaning floors and many of the staff did their weekly shops in her cupboard. Hen had finally grasped the nettle and suspended her, not for gross misconduct so much as for overcharging for the cans (catering size) of beans that she regularly bought off her. The terrible deed then done Hen handed responsibility for the problem over to me to deal with. Churchill had put on his Union Steward badge, licked his lips and set about terrorising me. After several months of battling, Noreen had agreed to resign as long as she was offered the franchise for the small tea bar which operated in the

entrance hall of the Rest Home. Bruised and battered by the
fight, I'd agreed immediately. It cheered me up no end to
think how the news that Hen and I were to be married
would piss him off.

'Come on, Churchill, does privatisation sound likely?
Who'd want to buy this dump?'

'Since the Tories got control of the council anything's possible. They sold off The Magnolias last year.'

Once upon a time hearing Churchill talking politics would
have been about as likely as a Winter Olympics at Ayers Rock.
But now he was the Che Guevara of the incontinent classes. A
blue enamel badge with 'Union Steward – Here To Help You'
written across it in gold letters was, as always, worn proudly
on his chest. I thought it made him look a pillock but I didn't
dare share this opinion. To have done so would have resulted
in facing a mass picket of angry domestics all waving bottles
of bleach in my face every time I went into work. As Union
Steward the domestics were Churchill's Praetorian Guard.

'The Magnolias situation was different, the Corporation
explained that.'

'Sorry, I was forgetting, you are the Corporation now,
aren't you,' he sneered and walked away.

'That badge makes you look a right pillock,' I shouted at
his retreating figure. I knew he was right to worry. I was also
concerned about what the future might bring, but I wasn't
going to let the irritating little git know that.

Aggie was alone in the television room. I stopped for a
chat in an attempt to prove to myself, and anyone who
might be watching, that I was still down-to-earth and
approachable.

'And how are you, Aggie?' I asked, patronising bastard
control knob turned on to maximum.

'Who are you?' she asked suspiciously. She was hardly
on planet Earth these days but I had a sneaking suspicion
she was taking the piss out of my efforts to be a man of the
people.

'Has that nephew of yours been in lately?' I asked, knowing it would get her going. She hadn't got a nephew.

'Only Prevent comes to see me.' Prevent was what she called Ken Dubbin. No one knew why but we presumed it was some fuddled term of endearment from her past. Either that or the fact that Ken's personality was the thing that would prevent anyone from ever finding him the slightest bit interesting. Ken was one of those care workers who claimed their reason for being in the job was that they loved old people. I didn't love old people. I didn't even claim to like them very much. As far as I was concerned they were just like other people, only older. They could be nasty, deceitful, vicious, they could make me laugh, they could annoy me, the only difference between them and younger people was their expectations They never expected much beyond their next meal. Life for them was just like life on Death Row only with less basket-ball practice.

'Well go and see Noreen for a cup of tea and slice of cake. That'll cheer you up until Ken gets here,' I said. Ken spent a lot of time cheering Aggie up. That was what he claimed he was doing anyway. Ten minutes with Ken wouldn't have cheered me up, it would have driven me to suicide. But then I wasn't a batty old woman with no friends and no caring relatives. Well, I wasn't a batty old woman anyway.

'Can't afford it, got no money,' she said, before holding up the television remote control and turning up the volume so loud that the glass in the windows began to rattle ominously.

I spent the day ordering incontinence pads, completing the financial records, working on the holiday rota and sending off the monthly mortality returns. According to the text books it took special interpersonal skills to be able to care for those less fortunate than oneself, but I'd have settled for a degree in accountancy. A satisfying day of skiing down a mountain of paper over, I dragged myself home with a sense of terrible foreboding. Not only was I engaged, but I was going out to celebrate this horrible state of affairs at Saint's, with Kirk and Gina.

Unfortunately contact with Kirk had continued despite our violent disagreement over royalties and I had little choice but to endure it. If I was honest I suppose I was also secretly hoping for an opportunity to exact some terrible, complete and final revenge on Kirk. Until then I grinned, bore it, got pissed and ate the best food in the North of England. It wasn't a difficult compromise. Hen had begun an almost obsessive friendship with Gina and had insisted on regular contact as a 'foursome'. As with all of Hen's obsessions I didn't dare disrupt it. Becoming bosom buddies, they found they had so much more in common besides making my life a misery, although that was a good start. It didn't take Einstein to work out why they got on so well, they were the same person – opinionated, bossy and selfish. And that was just their good points.

'Try this,' Gina said over dinner that evening, spooning a mouthful of spinach with ginger and red-currant sauce towards Hen, which I managed to intercept.

'Lovely,' I said, trying to make it sound like I was lying even though it was, in fact, surprisingly lovely.

'I'll just do the rounds,' said Kirk. He got up and went around the tables in Saint's, like a shepherd tending his flock, a flock that was about to be put on the lorry and taken to the abattoir. He asked everyone if their meals were all right, never expecting anyone to say no. No one said no, instead they fawned over Kirk who was now something of a local celebrity. He was the reason why people came to Saint's. They came to see him in action, taste his extravagant creations and, if they were really lucky, see one of his famous tantrums where he picked on some unsuspecting youth trainee in the kitchen, and beat seven shades of shit out of him. The male diners liked to show off to their female company that they were regulars and could afford the ridiculous prices. The women came to swoon over Kirk and, occasionally, write their phone numbers on napkins and press them into his hands. Kirk let it be known via a range of elaborate winks that he would follow some of them up. It was easy to tell that things were going well for Kirk, his meals were getting smaller while his prices were getting higher.

He and Gina now had a daughter who they'd called Escoffier. A name which I thought was grounds for the child to be taken into care. I mentioned this to Hen and she picked a fight with me, declaring to the whole restaurant that I was an arrogant, obnoxious pig with poor sexual technique. She then refused to speak to me for ten days. I hoped Kirk and Gina would have lots of children and call them all stupid names so that this glorious state could be repeated. Fatherhood didn't change Kirk but motherhood did affect Gina. Since the birth of Escoffier, Gina had acquired a permanent worried look and had become more dependent on Kirk. She still read *Spare Rib*, but whereas it had once been her bible, now she joined in with the mocking laughter of the whole restaurant when Kirk opened it out, turned it sideways and pulled a leering face as if viewing a centrefold.

Two years after Fear was born – the nickname Escoffier had to suffer because her infant demands had put the fear of God up her emotionally ill-equipped parents – all my wishes were granted when Kirk and Gina had a son, Roux. Gina had thrown herself into full-time motherhood, while Kirk threw himself into establishing his reputation as a restaurateur, which seemed to require him throwing himself into as many women's beds as he could.

My meals at Saint's were horrendous affairs, mitigated only by the fabulous food, which, I continually reminded myself, I was supposed to hate. Gina and I would talk about babies, Hen and Kirk would talk about work, and Hen and Gina would talk in hushed tones about I knew not what. Kirk would occasionally whisper to me about the women he was 'seeing to'. Out of academic interest I asked him whether he was going to tell Gina about these affairs.

'Why? That would only give them a level of importance that they don't merit And anyway, Gina's got too much on her plate at the moment, what with the cholic.' He was as charming as herpes, but that didn't stop women from throwing themselves at him.

'If you're so worried about what Gina would think, you could always try to get her back,' he added with the arrogance of someone who had it all, and if there was anything he didn't have he knew he could get it.

'Are you being serious?'

'I'm deadly serious, it's you that's the joke.' He gave me a steady stare before diving off to refresh the salt cellar of a young blonde girl in the corner who was smiling invitingly in his direction.

'Fatherhood . . .' he said over his shoulder as he left me. '. . . turns you into a fanny magnet. You should try it.'

Half an hour of adulterous flirting later, Kirk returned with a man in tow. He was expensively dressed, in an old-fashioned sort of way, aged around fifty-five and, judging by the gold rings that were extensively wrapped around his podgy fingers, possessed the one thing that Kirk found more attractive than a young woman with hinged legs. He had an obscene amount of money.

'This is Ralph Crowe. I said he should meet you, Hen, he's big in the care of the elderly. He owns Swansong.'

'Is that right?' Hen was using her 'please patronise me I'm just a silly little girl' voice, the one she wrongly assumed made people like her.

'Hen, is that short for Henrietta? That is absolutely my favourite name,' Ralph Crowe smarmed. He liked her. She giggled, it was a sound that made me grind my teeth.

'Well, my dear Henrietta, I do have one or two investments in the old folks business.'

'Don't be misled by his modesty . . .' Kirk said.

'I'm not,' I said, and a gust of air brushed my legs as Hen's sharp heels swept by in search of a victim.

'. . . Swansong's number one in this region,' Kirk droned on like a dull promotional campaign.

'And several other regions,' Ralph interrupted, modesty forgotten by his pompous need to correct the inaccuracy in Kirk's biography.

He sat down and chatted with Hen for the rest of the evening. I was ignored to the point where I began to think I was invisible. I put this state of affairs right by drinking so much of the wine that Ralph Crowe insisted on paying for, that I threw up over the linen tablecloth.

Arriving at work on Monday morning I was still smarting from a two-day-old hangover, the shame of putting several dozen diners off their lime sorbets, and a return to the old hostilities with Hen as she sought violent retribution for embarrassing her in front of Crowe. I'd just managed to score a five-quid deal of Andrew's Liver Salts from the drug cabinet in the office when Mr Airdrie arrived. He closed the door behind him and opened his briefcase as if it contained instruments of torture.

'Glad you're here, I wanted a word.'

How about dickhead, I thought.

'I'm concerned about what's going on here.'

'What is going on here?' I asked as nonchalantly as I could, fearing he might discover the awful truth that I was actually the last person to know what was going on here.

'How can I put it, there's . . . um . . . discrepancies.'

'Um . . . discrepancies? You mean someone's been nicking the paper clips again?' I joked, guiltily remembering the three dozen Biros and several notebooks in my drawer at home.

'It's more systematic than that.'

In Mr Airdrie's world the more impenetrable the vocabulary the bigger the problem. This was obviously pretty serious.

'Money is disappearing from accounts.'

'Shit,' I said, horrified that there was actually a problem and it wasn't just Mr Airdrie making his usual complaint that the toilet paper in the staff rest-room was being used.

'Quite. But at least it's only the residents' accounts and not the main budget.'

'What?' I was even more horrified. Apparently someone had been siphoning off the old people's savings, taking just a little here and there so that it was hardly noticeable. Despite Mr Airdrie's lack of outrage at the theft of the old people's money, I vowed swift and terrible retribution.

'I'll phone the police.' I reached for the phone.

'Now don't be too hasty, Mr Wrose. We don't want to raise concerns, or awareness. Not at this stage.'

'What do you mean?'

'I think we can deal with this by taking a closer look at procedures and . . . um . . . access.'

'Um . . . access?'

'Yes. Who has access to the accounts, for example?'

'Well, I do for one.'

'Quite.' So that was it. He thought it was me. I was shocked at his lack of confidence in me but I wasn't particularly worried. I knew my fiancée would support me through thick and thin.

'I don't think it's wise for us to carry on with our wedding plans given the circumstances,' Hen said, after Mr Airdrie had left to pursue his investigations with the enthusiasm of a ferret faced with a trouser leg. In this case, the woollen trouser leg of my suit.

'Given what circumstances?' I shouted.

'Mr Airdrie thinks –'

'What the fuck has our marriage got to do with that intellectual pygmy?'

'Now, don't get angry with Mr Airdrie, it was his suggestion in the first place that it may help my career if I were to be married. It may even help yours too,' she said, as if that were about as likely as Lazarus getting a refund from the Co-op funeral parlour.

'What?' I couldn't believe any of this was happening.

'And similarly if there's a problem with honesty then marriage to you may damage my career.'

'What about me – I might go to prison?' I asked, anger rising in my voice.

'Listen, pudding, it makes sense to postpone until you're in the clear.'

I don't know why I was annoyed. I'd been racking my brains to find a way of avoiding marrying Hen.

That afternoon Janice called me into the television room. Aggie was still there. She was wrapped up in sheets and blankets and surrounded by her suitcases.

'This is where I live now,' she insisted when we tried to remove her cases. Nothing we did could convince her.

'I'll get Prevent to come and see you when he gets here.'

'I don't want him all over me again.'

There was something about what she was saying that caused me a minuscule amount of unease. Nothing significant, but enough to want to know a bit more.

'All over you?'

'With his blooming tongue and his thing. You know, his thing. I don't want that near me again. I had enough of that nonsense with my Harry. Except that my Harry never made me pay for it. I'll stay here from now on thank you very much.'

Mr Airdrie kept looking at the file like it was an exciting novel even though it contained only one sheet of paper and on that were two meagre paragraphs – the bare bones of my conversation with Aggie. Aggie could remember the war, when houses cost two hundred quid, and when the height of luxury was an outside privy with a lock on the door.

Unfortunately, she couldn't remember what someone who molested people was called. She knew it had a P, an E, an R and a V in it, but she was buggered if she could remember the order. So she called him Prevent. Not only because that's what she wanted to do, to prevent him coming near her, but also because that's what he was, Ken the Pervert. Not just that, he took money from her bank account to pay for services rendered. He'd been doing it to all his special residents.

'It's not as if it's an official complaint,' Mr Airdrie finally said, his impossibly black hair hanging in mid-air like a Babylonian allotment.

'Official complaint?' I shouted as reasonably as I could. 'He's been shagging the residents. And when he's finished shagging them, he's nicked their money.'

'Bill, let's be calm about this,' Hen interrupted smoothly, a mark of someone who got ninety-five per cent in the 'Managing Conflict' module of her MBA. 'You've not actually got any proof.'

'Don't you mean "we"? This is not about me, it's about us, what we do. Aggie said he's been going to see her in the night. She described what he did. And he's always taking her out. Out to the shops, out to the park, and especially out to the bank.'

'He certainly takes the "Personal Plan" approach seriously,' Mr Airdrie said. While he nodded emphatically, his hair stayed put.

'If it hadn't been for the "Personal Plan" approach, Ken wouldn't have had so many opportunities for doing whatever he may or may not have done. And we . . . you mustn't lose sight of the fact that it was you, Bill, who designed and implemented that very scheme,' Hen said, deciding that now was the time to give credit where it was due and clearly write my name in the box marked 'Person Responsible For This Mess'.

'So you're saying this is my fault?'

'No . . .' said Mr Airdrie, interrupted as one who was about to say but with a capital B.

'– But, well, this is bad timing.'

'Bad timing? Should we ask Ken to shag the old folks at a more convenient time? Is it simpler to blame me for stealing the money than the person who's actually been doing it?'

'Bill. Sarcasm doesn't help,' said Hen quoting from 'Module Seven, Lesson Six, Assertion without Aggression'. But she was wrong because it helped me. I was surprised that she wasn't supporting me, which was pretty stupid because I should have known that Hen supporting me in anything was about as likely as a vulture insisting on a decent burial for a dead wildebeest.

Mr Airdrie listened to my statement while closing the file, and then he opened it again, as if something new had caught his eye at the last second, something that would show that this was all a silly misunderstanding that could be amicably dealt with over a nice cup of tea. Unable to find such evidence he closed it again.

'You've done well Mr Wrose. This will be followed up at the highest level and the matter will be treated very seriously. I would like to thank you on behalf of elderly people everywhere for your efforts. This will not be forgotten.'

It felt like I was being metaphorically thrown out of the office. And then I was actually thrown out of the office, politely but firmly, as Hen and Airdrie 'had things to discuss'. She refused to talk to me about it afterwards, saying it was all now subjudice.

'Can you say if the wedding is back on, or is that also subjudice?' I asked, not really wanting to hear her answer.

'This has been a good learning experience for both of us. I think we'll be stronger as a result,' she said.

'Is that yes or no?'

'I think I've made my position very clear. I have nothing but the strongest of feelings for you.'

'So it's yes?'

'We need to take a close look at the reasons why we want to get married, just to reassure ourselves they remain valid.'

'So it's no?'
'Maybe.'

Two days later I was called into the office again. Mr Airdrie was still there, in the same suit and smiling the same bland smile. I wondered if he'd been home in the meantime.

'In recognition of your vigilance and diligence, Wrose, the Corporation wishes to reward you. It's my proud duty to inform you that your name has been successfully put forward for the "Middle Management Course, level one" in Hull. A four-week residential course of intensive study in the theory of management.' He made it sound like a punishment.

'Thanks,' I said.

'On behalf of the Corporation, I thank you. I'm sure it will revolutionise the way you think. I envy you, I really do.'

Hen had sex with me that night. I think it was to stop me asking any more questions about Ken. Afterwards as she snored gently I lay awake thinking about the dull stodgy stew that my life had become and realised that I had completely forgotten to ask her for an apology for ever doubting me.

The following Sunday, I drove the seventy miles to Hull completely unprepared for the revolution in my thinking that was waiting for me there.

Twelve

The group was watching a video in the darkened training room of the hotel's conference suite. It was an introduction to Management Studies and several people were already asleep. Their gentle snores reverberated around the group of strangers who had yet to break the ice of the first Monday morning and speak to each other. Having overslept I crept in late and took a seat at the back. The video waffled on about how easy it was to deal with conflict and was clearly made by people who had never actually had to deal with conflict. The film ended and Kevin leaped up to try and switch off the video. Kevin Fry was the senior trainer in charge of the group, he was earnest, eager and had a hair cut that could have been sued for plagiarism by any self-respecting haystack. The video speeded up and then went into reverse. Several of the men in the group couldn't resist cheering and applauding this incompetence. The video finally stopped and breakfast television news came on, very loudly.

'It's the fucking red button on the fucking right,' said a laconic voice from the middle of the room. There was no doubt, even in the dark. Especially in the dark. It was Trish Girlington.

It took me until mid-morning break to get near enough to speak to her.

'Remember me?' I asked hopefully.

'Sure, I saw you in the corner at breakfast. You came in late and knocked the orange juice over.'

'I didn't think any one had noticed that.'

'It was hard to miss the torrent of liquid pouring off the table. I thought you'd pissed yourself.'

'You still swear a lot, don't you?'

'Do you still two-time your girlfriends?'

I hoped I was about to find out.

'So you do remember me,' I said, neatly side-stepping her question.

'He said, neatly side-stepping my question.'

Before we could say any more, Kevin called us back in for the role play. Trish was to be a dissatisfied customer, so I immediately volunteered to be the manager dealing with her complaint.

'This is fucking useless,' she said, holding out a metal tea tray to improvise the damaged goods in question. 'What's more, it's broken.'

'I beg to differ, madam, it's not broken . . .' I said, pleased with my well-honed oil-on-troubled-waters technique. She hit me hard over the head with the tray.

'It is now.'

'OK, OK, people, let's debrief,' Kevin squawked anxiously.

The rest of group cheered at the suggestion of debriefing. The sound of dirty laughter merged with the ringing in my ears.

I joined Trish, who was sitting alone when I arrived at the hotel dining room – probably because the rest of the group were afraid of her – for the evening meal.

'She's a lesbian,' Steve Bright, a junior manager from

British Home Stores had said, with the air of someone who knew.

'How do you know?' I asked.

'My wife went off with one.'

Intrigued though I was by this explanation, I was inextricably drawn towards Trish's table. She smiled and welcomed me, almost as if she was happy to see me.

'Of course you can join me. Sit your fat arse down.'

She was now managing her Uncle Jack's new chain of mini grocery stores that were sprinkled across Greater Grimsby.

'Greater Grimsby? Isn't that a contradiction in terms?' I asked, two glasses of wine making me believe I was Oscar Wilde. Trish carried on as if I hadn't spoken.

'I'm in charge of six shops, which is great.'

'It must be a real challenge running six businesses.'

'It gives me six chances to borrow from the till.' She winked and I wasn't sure if she was joking or not.

Three bottles of red later I was outside her hotel room desperately trying to get an invite in.

'Can I stay to breakfast?' I asked as innocently as I could, but coming across like Casanova in a convent.

She opened her door and ushered me in, saying:

'You can stay if I can phone your home and tell who ever answers what you're doing.'

'You're too smart for your own good,' I said and laughed. She flicked her dark hair out of her dark eyes.

'Ah, the truth at last, there is someone waiting for you?'

'Yes, 'fraid so.'

'Is it still what'shername? Hen?'

'Yes, 'fraid so.'

'At least your level of honesty has improved.' She paused. 'Would you like continental or full English?' She got up, put off the light and went into the bathroom. Without a second thought, I drunkenly scrambled out of my clothes. My boxer shorts got stuck on my shoes and in trying to free them I fell down the far side of the bed. She stuck her head round the bathroom door.

'I hope you're not getting undressed in there. Just because you're staying the night doesn't mean we're having sex.'

Of course it doesn't, I thought.

She wore a T-shirt and knickers, which embarrassed me in my naked erectness. As we kissed a 24-volt kiss I ran my hands down to her knickers. She pulled my hands back to the safer territory of her breasts. That was my tenth and final attempt. I admitted defeat.

'I had to try.'

'Try?'

'To get into your knickers. It's in the "Guy's Code". If I didn't try I'd be letting guys all over the world down.'

'And if you hadn't have tried, I'd have thought there was something up with you. Now shut up and snog me, clit face.'

I rang Hen and told her the course was so invigorating that I wanted to stay on over the weekend and add a few extra tools to my manager's tool kit. Hen didn't seem bothered. She said there were a few things happening at work that needed her attention and that I wasn't to worry. Unworried in my deceit, I bought a bottle of sweet fizzy wine from the hotel bar and went back to bed with Trish for the best sex of my life. I used every technique I'd learned and developed, with other women and on my own, over the years. It was going pretty well and we were almost at the ten-minute mark (including foreplay of course) when Trish opened her eyes.

'How long does this go on for?'

'Sorry?'

'Well I don't want to crush your feelings but it's all a bit . . . mechanical isn't it?'

We stopped and drank a little more wine and talked about sex. She talked about Kirk and one or two others, and I talked about Gina and Hen.

'You see, that's it. I don't want to be made love to. I want to be involved.'

'OK, I'll give it a go,' I said.

That was when I had the best sex of my life.

'That was the best sex of my life,' Trish said. 'Mind you most of the sex I've had has been crap so that's not saying much.'

'Do you fancy another go, just to make sure?'

'I'd rather have a bag of chips.'

'Actually, so would I,' I said, laughing.

Later we tossed the empty chip papers to the bottom of the bed and did it once more, just to make sure. There had been no mistake, it was the best sex of my life, again.

Kevin was using his considerable expertise in a variety of management techniques.

'You see, Bill, Trish, it's not me.'

'It's not?' asked Trish.

'No, oh no. You must believe that. It's the rest of the group.'

'First rule of management, blame the others,' I said and Trish nodded in agreement.

'No I'm not. But the others, they see you two together, never attending anything, and it gives them ideas.'

'But surely that's good,' I enthused.

'Yes, they were a lot of fucking morons before, and now they're having ideas. You've done your job well, Mr Fry,' Trish said.

'Ah, yes, well, but you see, it's bad for morale. There's the issue of secondment you see. Your employers are paying for this. They expect value for money.'

'Take it from me,' Trish said, looking at my groin and licking her lips, 'they're getting it.'

'Hah, hum . . . right.' Kevin pretended to get the joke. 'Well, I felt it was important to share these feelings with you. Perhaps we can address the issue of morale building in your personal-action plans,' he added, a flush of excitement dappling his cheeks at the thought.

'Right,' I said.

'Right,' Trish said. But we had both already forgotten he was there.

The final session of the course was 'Good News, Bad News Feedback', as Kevin insisted on calling it.

'If you are to achieve the goal of every manager,' he whispered, breathless with excitement at the thought of achieving every manager's goal, 'then honest and open feedback is essential. So, one more time, what is the goal of every manager?'

'Not to get caught?' Trish offered from the back row, where she was unashamedly reading a gory crime thriller with a blood-splattered cover. Kevin swung his lifeless fringe out of his eyes and tried to ignore her.

Steve Bright put up his hand.

'Transparency, Mr Fry.'

'Exactly so.' Kevin applauded his model pupil. Trish mimed putting her fingers down her throat.

'In that case, Steve, you must be the perfect manager, because I can see right through you,' I shouted.

'Transparency.' Kevin raised his voice from weak and ineffectual to timid and ineffectual. 'In short, a healthy organisation is one that gladly welcomes progress and change, reducing the barriers and boundaries between its constituent parts, making them transparent. Thus ensuring that the strategic aim of each individual mirrors the strategic aim of the organisation.'

'That's in short?' I asked. Like the thoroughly professional management trainer that he was, Kevin completely ignored me.

'But in order to achieve this ultimate goal . . .' He held out his hands, palms up, in a welcoming manner.

'. . . We must first hear what people are saying. So I want

you all to think of one piece of good news and one piece of bad news about your experiences on this course and then share it with everyone.' He swallowed hard as if he was about to do something dangerously foolish. 'And I'd like to start with Trish.'

Trish unhurriedly finished the page in her book and then put it down thoughtfully. As she did so she looked around at everyone in the room in turn. Most people shuffled uncomfortably under her inspecting gaze.

'You, Kevin, apart from talking utter shite most of the time, have got unquestionably the worst hair cut it has ever been my misfortune to witness. Four weeks in close proximity to those dull, lank locks may have done me who knows what deep psychological damage. But it's not just me, everyone here calls you "quim wig" behind your back.' Trish neglected to add that it was she who had dreamed up the unflattering, yet uncannily accurate, nickname.

'Criticism should never be personal, Trish, I would have thought our session on "Coping Strategies in a Changing Market" would have taught you that, but if that's the worst thing you can say about the course then so be it. Now what's the good news?'

'That was the good news, dick breath.'

When it came to my turn, Kevin was a broken and defeated man but he was still pretending he was in control.

'Bill, what have you learned?' he asked, almost sounding as if he really wanted to know, which of course he didn't.

'I've learned that no matter how bad things get, it's always possible to find something that can relieve the complete, unmitigated gloom.' I looked at Trish, who did her fingers-down-the-throat mime again, before blowing me a kiss.

After the course finished, Trish and I stayed on until the Sunday. We left then only because someone else was booked into our rooms. We kissed in the car park for about an hour and then went back into the hotel and found a deserted seminar room for a final quick shag. Temporarily satisfied, we parted and made our separate ways home. As I drove along the deserted M62 from Hull (the longest cul-de-sac in the world, as Trish called it), I wondered how I was going to break the news, which would also break Hen's heart.

The flat was empty when I got back. Empty as in no furniture whatsoever, apart from an old smelly mattress, some worn carpets and a cardboard box full of my clothes. A short note was propped up on the tea chest that now served as a kitchen table.

> Sorry to spring this on you but I've had a great job offer and I'm not here because I've taken it. Guess what! I'm now Area Manager for Swansong, Southern Region. Ralph Crowe offered it to me. We've spent a lot of time together recently. I know you'll understand. All the extra time you've spent on your course will have taught you that you must seize every opportunity. Well this is mine and I'm taking it.
> Best wishes,
> Hen.
> p.s. I tried ringing you at the hotel but you were never in your room.

I should have felt elated, but oddly enough I felt the opposite. It was like life had spat in my face, stuck its finger in my eye and then, as a final insult, stuck its tongue out at me. I went to work at the Rest Home the next day. In my briefcase, next to the potted-meat sandwiches, was a framed certificate which announced that I was a graduate of the Middle Management Course, level one. To confirm this, Kevin had scribbled his signature in the corner under the ridiculously pretentious seal of the 'Western European Management Skills Development Programme'. The sight of it didn't make my heart well up with pride, but the clash of fluorescent blue and orange, which the certificate was printed in, did make my head ache.

The sign outside work also gave me a head ache. It told me that it wasn't just in my private life that things were changing. It read:

Crowe House, part of Swansong Plc.
Where all your troubles are old ones

A dark cloud was swirling in and fogging up my mind.

'What the fuck is going on here?' I asked, walking into the office. The row of mops and buckets stood embarrassed and unwilling to answer. 'My office, it's a broom cupboard.'

'The office has been moved.' It was Alf. Thank God something was the same. I looked closer. Alf wasn't the same.

'Alf?' I asked. He was wearing an orange and maroon boiler suit with a 'Swansong' badge on the breast pocket. Under it was a label that announced 'A Meacher, Janitorial Issues'.

'What . . . are . . . you?'

'New job, mate. I'm in charge of the cleaning supplies. Mr Airdrie says it offsets the cost of my care package.'

Mr Airdrie. I should have guessed. He was waiting for me in a new, plush, grey and pink office on the first floor. It used to be the upper sitting room but he'd cleared out the miserable old sods who sat in there day after day watching *Blockbusters* and made it his own. He was looking out the window at the breathtaking view of the moors as I went in. Before I could speak, he held up a finger and pointed at the empty chair to indicate that I should sit down and shut up. In that order.

'William. This is not what you think. You think you've been usurped, that things have been done in your absence. But you are wrong.'

I wanted to point out the incontrovertible evidence to the

contrary, but his finger held me spellbound and silent; it was like a cane in the hand of a mentally unstable teacher.

'You are wrong, I promise you.'

Under the circumstances Mr Airdrie's promise seemed about as reliable as an ocean-going colander. I decided it was time to make my stand.

'What is happening here is immoral, it goes against everything I care for and believe in . . .'

'It's the future.'

'It's not my future. I'd rather die than accept this.'

He smiled a thin maggoty smile from under the dark shadow of his hair, got up from the chair, which sprang into a rest position without making a sound, and walked to the door that I had just come through and slammed shut in my fit of pique. He gently opened the door to a point where I could see the other side. There was a plastic sign; of the slide-in sort that could be easily replaced, that I hadn't noticed on my way in. In big black letters it said:

WILLIAM WROSE – OFFICER IN CHARGE

Mr Airdrie came up behind me.

'Should I ring the undertakers?' He smiled. 'Believe me, William, someone up there likes you.'

'You mean God?' I asked, barely able to believe that he of all people was going to go religious on me.

'No, I mean the higher echelons of Swansong.' He pointed to the desk. 'I think you should read that sheet of paper. It's your new contract. And those noughts on the end are your new salary.'

I looked at the figure in front of all the noughts. Maybe the future wouldn't be so bad, I thought, not with the right man in charge, and maybe I was that right man. It might just work. I took out my Middle Management Course, level one certificate and hung it on the wall behind my desk.

*

Churchill was angrily scraping up burned fat from the hot plate when I found him.

'No truth in the rumours about privatisation, eh?' he mocked.

'I had no idea.'

'Oh yeah, like Attila didn't mention the new regime, or your promotion while you were shagging her brains out. I'm assuming the dopey cow actually has brains.' He hadn't talked about Hen like that for years. At least not to my face. Not that I minded.

'No she didn't. Nor the fact that she was going off to Reading and taking most of my furniture with her.'

That shut him up. I told him about Hen, elaborating the story to gain maximum sympathy, which wasn't a lot where Churchill was concerned, and then mentioned Trish, only briefly, so as not to destroy my image as a man wronged.

'Do you want to come to the football?' Churchill asked, unexpectedly .

'Football?' I asked, as if the concept was a new one on me.

'Me and you. I wouldn't ask if there was any danger of you bringing Attila, or worse, Kirk and his old tart, but as that isn't going to happen, I can.'

'Thanks. Yes, all right.'

'Hey, did you hear what happened with Ken?'

'I'd forgotten Ken,' I said, trying hard not to give too much away, as I assumed it was still subjudice, 'what happened?'

'He's disappeared. One day he was here, next he'd gone. No one knows where.' He looked at me very carefully . 'Or why.'

'Good riddance,' I said, without too much emotion.

'Funnily enough, that's what Aggie said.'

When I got back to the flat there were signs of life that threw me into a panic. Lights were on and bags were strewn throughout the hall. Somewhere from the far end of the flat I could hear the sound of at least two children having atomic-strength tantrums. At least it couldn't be Hen, I consoled myself.

'Hi there.' It was Gina. 'Surprise!' I opened my mouth but, not having prepared any statements for such an eventuality, I closed it again.

'I rang Hen in the week, she told me about you two. I'm sorry. However . . .' she said, using the word 'however' as if it was a link to some bright new future, one which could, if I played my cards right, include her and the screaming brats, 'I've decided to leave Kirk. He's a no-good bastard. You were right. He screws anything that moves and quite a few things that don't. I can't stand it any more and I knew you had a spare room and you never did take your key back, so I didn't think you'd object . . .' She was looking at me the way a butcher's dog looks at a tray of sausages.

At that moment, Fear hit Roux over the head with my sole remaining china ornament and it shattered into a thousand worthless fragments. Then the phone rang.

'What the hell's going on in the background, is that Hen screaming? Did you tell her?'

'Trish.' Perfect timing as usual. 'No, I haven't told Hen, didn't need to as she'd already gone.' I lowered my voice. Gina was giving me her well-practised suspicious stare, the one that made me want to confess to every wrong deed in the history of mankind, including a plea bargain on the original sin. 'But there've been other developments.'

The front door was now being pounded by what sounded like the SAS on a routine visit to the Iranian Embassy. I covered the phone.

'Get that, Gina.'

'Gina? Don't tell me that tight-arsed turkey neck is the other developments?'

'OK, I won't tell you. Look this isn't my fault. My life is so complicated and none of it is my fault.'

'It never is, is it? Listen, you know my number, sort out what you want and if that includes me, give me a call. But if not, then bye bye.' The phone went dead.

'Trish?' I said to the disconnected tone, even though I knew it was pointless.

'Bill. It's Kirk.' Gina led him into the sitting room. Fear and Roux stopped fighting and looked at the new arrival. This should be interesting, they thought.

'Gina you've got to come back. I'm sorry, I really am. But it's really important you come back.'

'It's not just what I think now.' She gave me a look that hinted now was the time to speak up and claim her. I tried to look like I couldn't wait to see the back of her and her dreadful children, which didn't take a lot of effort.

'Bill. I know she's important to you but you don't know what's going on here,' Kirk said, before turning back to Gina. For a moment I thought he was going to go down on one knee. 'Hob Knob rang earlier. They're a TV production company,' he said for my benefit. 'They were confirming that I've got the morning-show cooking slot. This is the big one. There's even a sniff of a solo series, prime time. I want you there to share it, Gina.' He turned back to me and gave me a slow wink of victory .

'Sorry, Bill, mate.'

'Yes, I'm sorry, Bill,' Gina agreed, slipping her arm around Kirk's waist. I wondered who these people were who thought they were so important in my life, and whether the time would ever come when I could honestly say they weren't?

'My name is William,' I said with some pride. 'William. It says so on my office door, so it must be true. And I think you two deserve each other. Oh, and, Gina, can I have my front door-key back before you go.'

'Cheers, mate.' Kirk came over and shook my hand. 'Look, would you have the kids for tonight, I think Gina and me need some space. Good man.'

And with that they were gone. I looked at the two deserted children standing among the shards of my broken belongings and felt almost sorry for them.

'My mum calls you the "Doggy Man". Why?' the older one asked in a tone that reminded me of her dad.

Thirteen

Giving me the job of Officer in Charge was a bit like giving a catwalk model the keys to the diet-pill cupboard, only slightly more foolhardy. For the first time in my life I was in control. I made the decisions that mattered, such as how late I would get in to work, how early I would leave and how long I would take for lunch. I didn't so much abuse my position as slowly murder it.

'Your hands are so soft you'd get a blister from wanking,' Churchill alleged, in an off-duty moment, when we were watching City go down four-nil at home to a bunch of part-time plasterers from the dark depths of non-league football. But it didn't matter as the less I did the less Mr Airdrie bothered me. Mr Airdrie (I couldn't find out his first name and he made sure he didn't tell me) had been given the post as Area Manager with Swansong, in recognition of all his help in the transfer negotiations.

'A bribe,' as Churchill put it, just after the fourth goal had gone in.

Mr Airdrie was not a cheerful man but he was a moderately happy one, so long as my behaviour didn't kill anyone,

and the beds were full. In fact, as long as the beds were full
I don't think he was too bothered about me killing people.
Crowe House had a more relaxed feel to it since Hen had
gone, and this made it popular with relatives already awash
with guilt at putting their dribbling, incontinent and sometimes intensely irritating elderly relatives away into a home.
I was making a name for myself at Crowe House, and for
once it was a good name. I had pioneered a daring new
management technique that I called 'Radical Positive Non-
Intervention', which required me doing fuck all about a
problem until it went away. It was amazing how many problems did go away when you ignored them for long enough.
This was particularly true in the case of care for the elderly
because time was the thing they had the least supply of. For
them everything went away sooner or later, and usually
sooner. 'The Swansong Procedure Guide for Senior
Managers' stated in its introduction that if business was
busy, then business was good. I wasn't quite sure how I was
doing it but at Crowe House business was very good indeed.

I bought a selection of cheap suits with index-linked waist
sizes, a better car and a new bed. I sat back to enjoy the
fruits of my success. But success or no success, Trish still
refused to move in with me .

'I'm not living anywhere where that pair of pissy pussies
lived,' she declared, meaning Gina and Hen.

So I also bought a house. It was a large Victorian villa, five
bedrooms and a big garden. It had potential, as the estate
agent, who was a man of vision but not the 20-20 variety,
described it. It also had a mortgage that would have caused
the smaller Third World nations to hesitate.

'Can I afford it, honestly?' I asked.

'Do you ever want to sleep with me again?' was Trish's
reply. The deal was done.

Number 5 Halcyon Row was in the select area of Bronte
Bridge. Select as in the place where people lived who were
on their way up to somewhere better, or on their way down

to somewhere worse. I wasn't sure which we were. It was also the small town where Kirk had his restaurant, something that put me off at first, but I was convinced it was going to be all right when Trish gave me her list of conditions for agreeing to move in.

'You let me share the mortgage and other costs, you get rid of all those bloody awful records that give me a headache, you don't suck your stomach in when teenage girls walk past, and we stop pretending we're best of friends with your witchy old girlfriends and that anus mouth Kirk.' How could I refuse? We moved in and forgot all about Kirk and Gina.

This wasn't hard as Kirk, Gina and the kids (now with a Michelin and an Egon added to the number) divided most of their time between their flat in London and their retreat in Umbria and only came up to the restaurant occasionally. These occasions usually caused a stir in the local newspaper, the *Bronte Bridge New Dawn*, which was otherwise starved of celebrities. So we were warned in advance to avoid Saint's and its surrounding area, when the evil brood were likely to be in residence. Kirk had become an established presenter on *Morning Glory*, a weak excuse for entertainment provided by day-time television, where he cooked up exotic dishes from ingredients that most viewers wouldn't ever be able to spell, let alone afford. The programme was shot in a converted ice factory somewhere near Billingsgate Market. As this seemed a safe enough distance away, I would watch him, if I was late in to work, or home extremely early, and I'd grate my teeth as he ranted and raved while physically assaulting the latest trend in raw Japanese fish, or South American monkey poo. He was the 'Punk Chef', and had adopted a ridiculous spiky hair-style to set the image off. The very sight of him made me spit and I had to calm myself down by saying over and over that he was, after all, just a fucking cook.

*

With both of us working full time, Trish and I were in great danger of becoming middle class very quickly. Trish's unabashed love of salacious language showed no signs of receding with age so I didn't think the middle classes would be very happy with our impending arrival. I needn't have worried. After about four years together, Trish came home one Friday with a bunch of flowers, a card and a large gift-wrapped package.

'What's that?'

'My leaving present.'

'Leaving present? What have you left?' If I was in the dark then Trish was about to put on the light in her own unique way.

'My job. Well, work in general actually.'

'I . . . I don't get it?'

She gave me the package. I unwrapped it carefully. Life with my father had taught me to be meticulous about saving gift paper for future use.

'Nappies? Why would they buy you nappies? You're not pregnant.'

'Not exactly.'

'Either you are or you aren't, and you aren't because you're on the pill.'

'I'm not on the pill. I stopped taking it three months ago. I was going to tell you but I didn't know how you felt about the idea.'

'Are you kidding? No, you're not, are you? I think I'd like to have children with you. I mean . . . this is so sudden I don't know what to think. When's it due?'

'Well, it's not . . . that's what I meant by "not exactly". Nothing's happened yet.'

'Why didn't you tell me about this?'

'You know me, I don't believe in all that talking about feelings shit. Shut up and put up, that's me.'

'So what will you do?' I asked.

'I want to concentrate on . . . well, becoming a mum.

That's why I've given up my job, that and the fact that Uncle Jack was becoming a bit of a bore about me keeping proper audited accounts. I'll have time to run the monthly Traidcraft event in the village hall. Those do-gooders have their noses so high in the air they'll never notice my fingers dipping into the profits.' As usual, I couldn't tell if she was joking so I kissed her anyway. She kissed me back. When we finally pulled away from each other she was crying.

'Bastard hayfever,' she said, wiping her eyes.

'It's October,' I said, a little too pedantically.

'Shut the fuck up and get my tea. I'm a woman of leisure now.'

For the rest of the weekend I thought about the idea. Me, a dad? It was scary. I didn't exactly have a good role-model to follow and I didn't want to be the kind of father to my child that my father was to me. I looked at the evidence. Four years in our house at Halcyon Row, and I was already spending an inordinate amount of time out in the garden with the strimmer. I'd even caught myself measuring the grass length with a ruler but I'd put that down to heatstroke caused by the recent long hot summer. Maybe I was destined to repeat history. You can't hide from heredity.

By Monday morning, I had distilled all my doubts into one issue. Trish came down to breakfast, late as usual.

'Trish. Do you think you'll ever leave me?'

'I will if you insist on frigging talking over breakfast.'

'No, but really? Every woman I've ever been with has left me. Apart from my mother and she's the one that I wish would go. There's only you who's stayed and we've never really formalised our relationship have we?'

'Formalised our relationship? You sound like that pillock of a boss of yours. Pour me a cup of tea, pronto. What is it? Do you want to get married or something?'

'Married? Shit I don't know. Do I?' Marriage. It started

with her sinking into his arms and ended with her arms in
the sink. Marriage is an institution, and who wants to live in
an institution? Marriage is for life, you get less for murder.
The clichés echoed around in my mind like a late-night fart
in someone else's toilet.

'Yes, I think I do,' I replied.

'OK. Is that ginger marmalade? Pass the twatting stuff
here then.'

And so we got married. Churchill, now married to Janice
and restored to rank of best friend because Trish found his
earthy coarseness very like her own, was my best man.
We walked out of the Bradworth Register Office under an
arch of bedpans presented by Crowe House care staff.
Trish had insisted that only close friends and relatives
were there, to keep the numbers to below thirty.
Unfortunately the criteria wasn't strict enough to exclude
my mum and dad.

'You'll know for next time,' Trish joked. At least I think
she was joking. Mum did the catering. She did enough food
for five hundred just in case. Just in case of what I wasn't
sure. Just in case they were all greedy bastards with bad
doses of worms maybe. Dad insisted on taking the official
photographs, which meant that every shot took half an hour
to compose.

'Smile,' he said, without engaging in any eye contact with
me or the other guests.

'Why the fuck should I?' Trish snapped back. 'I've just
promised to forsake all others.'

Trish insisted on making a speech after the meal.

'Right you hairy-arsed bunch of fucking scroungers, I
want to propose a toast,' she began, causing one elderly aunt
to have a near fatal attack of the vapours.

'Today, not tomorrow,' she said, and drank a big gulp of
wine and then threw the glass behind her where it smashed
on the pile of presents.

Back at the hotel, I finished off the job of getting pissed on champagne.

'Do you think we'll be together for ever?' I asked.

'I fucking hope not,' Trish replied from somewhere under the duvet.

'Me too,' I laughed. When it came to consummating the marriage I was so pissed I couldn't get it up but Trish didn't notice because she'd already passed out. The next morning, picking over a fried breakfast that taunted my stomach like a school bully, I reviewed the situation.

'I've got the set.'

'Put it on the thank-you list then,' Trish said, desperately trying to keep down a mouthful of toast.

'No not that sort of set. A life set. I've got a career, God knows how but I have. I've got a house which costs the national debt to maintain to the standard of the average derelict slum. I'm thirty-one years old and I've just got married. It's official. I'm in the early stages of being middle aged.'

'Is that bad?' she asked. I thought about it.

'No, it's not bad. It's all right. Yes, it's all right.'

'And you haven't got the set.'

'No?'

'No. You haven't got a family. That's what you need for a full set.'

'Finish your toast then, we'd best get upstairs and get cracking.'

We kept on cracking for the next three years. Eventually we began to realise that crack as we might, nothing was going to happen. Before, birth control had never been something Trish took very seriously at the best of times, and at the end of each month her packet of pills usually had had five or six left over.

'Do you think I could get a refund?' she joked. But even with an approach to contraception that made Sellafield look leakproof we never realised there may be a problem. Eventually we went to see our GP who told us to relax, not to worry and to try to enjoy it. We tried that for a while and it didn't work, so we went to see a specialist who took our obscenely large cheque and then told us we really ought to stop worrying and relax.

'Thanks for your help,' I said, implying heavily that if I came across him when I was driving late at night, he'd better get the other side of a car-proof protective barrier.

'You over-priced vaginal rash . . .' Trish began to say, before I put my arm lovingly across her mouth and dragged her out of his office, backwards.

We went to a fertility clinic where we handed over a cheque for an amount so obscene it made the previous one look more like the brassière section from a home mail-order catalogue.

'I suppose everyone's told you to relax?' the doctor asked. He was about fifteen and seemed terribly keen. I nudged Trish to stop her from going into her 'listen, fuck face, have you any idea what it's like to be a woman' routine.

'Stupid, isn't it? How can you relax when all you can think about is making a baby.'

I nodded in agreement. Sex had become something we had to do at a certain time in a certain way. It was like being a connoisseur of fine wines washed up on a desert island with only a container full of vintage reserve to drink. We still appreciated the contents, but continually pulling out the cork seemed a real chore.

'Have you any other pressures, such as work?' the teenage doctor asked.

'Well, work is, you know, work,' I said. He looked a bit blank.

'The doctor won't understand what you mean, dear, he's only just out of short trousers and he spends every day with one hand up women's fannies,' Trish said, as sweetly as possible. The doctor, despite spending every day with one hand up women's fannies, went red. Trish could make Caligula blush and say 'Aw stop it.'

But work was work. Things had been good in the 80s, money had poured into Crowe House and I had been the toast of Swansong, Bradworth Region, or I would have been if Mr Airdrie hadn't stolen all the glory. But now the cold wind of change was blowing a gale down the draughty corridors. Money was no longer available to pay for expensive beds and income had fallen like a television from a pretentious rock star's hotel window. Mr Airdrie was now taking a much closer interest in my level of performance. The staff nicknamed him Polly, because he could usually be found on my shoulder. Even Alf had given up and died before the going got too tough. The death certificate showed that he was a hundred and nine.

'Damn. We missed a major publicity opportunity there.' Mr Airdrie shook his head in disbelief at my ineptitude. I pointed out that making an old man aged one hundred and nine work for his supper by handing out caustic cleaning supplies would have been a publicity opportunity of epic proportions. Mr Airdrie gave me his cool look, the one games' teachers adopted as standard when sending the asthmatics on a ten-mile run, and then ordered me to fill the bed by the weekend at the latest.

So I was under pressure at work, but wasn't everyone? What difference would that make?

'Research shows that the sperm count can be seriously reduced by stress, and motility can also be affected,' the doctor said, glancing worriedly at his watch. *Blue Peter* was due to start in ten minutes.

'Hang on, hang on. Are you saying this is my fault?' I bristled.

'Please, Mr Wrose, Mrs Wrose . . .'

'Ms Girlington,' Trish corrected. Ever the thoroughly modern Ms, she'd refused my surname because, when combined with her first name, it made her sound like a sneezing fit. 'And don't try blaming me either.'

'This isn't about fault. You mustn't think like that. If you do then you are merely adding to the pressure on the both of you.'

'Right,' I said.

'OK,' Trish said.

'So who's fault is it?' we both asked together.

It was mine. I had a good sperm count, sixty-three million of the little buggers, and as the doctor pointed out, it only took one to do the deed. Unfortunately the little buggers all had the motility of a brick. A brick that was in serious need of swimming lessons. They were willing enough, they just didn't have the legs, or the flippers, to complete the task. There was no doubt about it, I needed some help. The fertility clinic were keen to help provided I handed over another cheque with more 0s in it than the chorus of a Supremes' song. I took the receipt, intending to give it a cursory glance, but something about it made me read the small print.

'The Pregnant Pause Fertility Clinic, a sub-division of Swansong Plc.'

I made a mental note to get my money back by stealing the equivalent amount in cleaning materials and paper clips from Crowe House.

My first appointment was at seven-thirty in the morning. The nurse on duty was far too pretty to be in charge of the wank session. Or maybe she was the perfect choice. I wondered how many fantasies she had fuelled as she handed out the black plastic bin liner with a small jar and a pack of tissues in it. She was the Helen of Troy of fertility clinics, she was the face that launched a thousand hand jobs.

'Please write your name on the outside of the jar,' she said.

'I certainly won't be writing it on the inside,' I joked, feebly. She gave me a warm smile that she'd been able to practise during years of hearing feeble jokes from panic-stricken men.

'It's the room at the end. The door locks on the inside. When you've finished, seal the jar and leave it in the blue box outside pathology. You can take as long as you like; do you have to get off in a hurry?' Her poor choice of words hung in the air like a swear word in a Sunday sermon and both of us blushed redder than a lorry load of beetroot.

'I mean if you need a hand . . . I think I'll shut up.'

'If you would,' I said gratefully.

The room was a cell with a chair, a sink and a bed. The window looked out on to a small courtyard where a couple of men were noisily repainting the fence. It reminded me of a cheap American motel. On the bed was a pile of magazines. My mistresses for the occasion. The magazines had clearly been chosen by a woman who had a stereotypical view of what men liked. None of the women had a chest size less than the water displacement ratio of the average oil tanker, and all of them seemed to think that wearing cheap nylons and sticking their tongues out represented the height of eroticism. Even the copy of *Teenage Temptress* was a special edition focusing on a group of women who had been teenage temptresses, once, sometime in the early 1950s. All of them had 38 DD chests, were dressed up in standard cheap nylons and pulled the same silly faces. I tried and failed to get aroused by them. Outside the painters were laughing over a dirty joke and I could hear every chortle as if they were in the room with me. So I thought about the pretty nurse and very soon afterwards sixty-three million freshly released sperm were happily exploring their new environment in the jar. Next to the blue box outside pathology sat a man who was trying to read a newspaper. He caught my eye as I added my jar to the other seven or eight that lay there.

'Pervert,' his eyes said.

'Get fucked,' my mouth said.

In the plush waiting room I worked through the pile of magazines, reading about lifestyle and home interiors, which was far more enjoyable than looking at bad photos of fat old women with big tits. Trish was somewhere in the hidden wards having several battery eggs removed from her Fallopian tubes. They'd been chemically encouraged by sniffing drugs for four weeks, injecting drugs for two weeks and taking drugs through vaginal pessaries for one week. All this intrusion in her female cycles had enabled Trish to develop a whole new range of swear words that she could have easily sold to a regiment of troopers. While she was undergoing further humiliation at the hands of the medics, I was reading about the best ways to get the most from your dado rail. I flicked over the page and was confronted by Kirk and Gina and the rest of the St John progeny smiling back at me.

'Kirk and Gina with their family on honeymoon in the Napa Valley, a *Hello!* magazine exclusive,' it said. Gina had given birth to child number five (they'd run out of names connected with high cuisine and instead had plumped for the rather more desperate name of Spatula). They had decided to celebrate and take the lot to California, and then get married. Gina looked old and harassed. Like all the rich people who appeared in these magazines she hadn't realised that expensive make-up and designer clothes couldn't hide the tell-tale signs of life. Kirk had a three-hundred-dollar hair-style chosen to try and make him look young and energetic. It bloody did too, the bastard. 'Kirk is excited about his new television series which represents a major departure for him,' the bland copy waffled on. 'Recovering alcoholic Kirk sipped his glass of still lime and told *Hello!*, 'I can't say too much, but it expands the cooking format to new heights.'

'New lows more like,' I said out loud.

'Pardon?' said the pretty nurse from the desk. I couldn't meet her eye as I was still embarrassed by the sordid sexual acts which I'd had her perform in order to help me reach a climax. 'I've never done this for any other man, but there's something really special about you,' she'd said as she unbuttoned her crisp white uniform. From the corner of my eye I saw her smile. It was the self-satisfied smile that said, 'By the look on his face I've just starred in another fantasy.'

The photos showed the family proudly exhibiting Escoffier's first tattoo, which was a chef's hat with the words 'Born To Cook' underneath it. Kirk and Gina said that all the children would have tattoos just as soon as they were old enough.

Kirk had turned up more often than Toulouse Lautrec's trousers. Even today he was there. The day I was to father my first child, with a little help from a Petri dish and a few million pounds' worth of hospital equipment. He could always be relied on to stick his big fat face where it wasn't wanted. The magazine gave me just what I needed least, which was a reminder of what a clever, successful, fertile bastard he was. I stuck my tongue out at the picture of Kirk and Gina and threw the magazine into the bin. When it came to dealing with difficult situations I could be as mature as the next three-year-old.

Fourteen

The phone call from Kirk, when it came, caught me off guard. It had been several years since I'd had any sort of contact with him and I had hoped it would be several decades more before I did again. Trish was eight months' pregnant and every time my office phone rang I automatically struggled into my coat in order to make a quick getaway to the maternity unit.

'Bill?' It had to be someone I hadn't seen for years as no one called me that any more. Even Churchill had given it up in favour of an extremely sarcastic rendition of 'Boss'.

'Kirk?'

'Hi. I didn't know if you'd still be in that dead-end job,' he joked, a little too early on in the conversation for my liking.

'We can't all live fabulous superstar lives,' I said, making it clear that I didn't mean him.

'It's not as great as it looks. I have pressures.' Yeah, like which part of Italy to buy next. 'Anyway I'm sorry to ring you at work, but I need to ask you something.'

I should have hung up. Every bone in my body told me I should, my waters begged me to and my sense of smell said only one word, which was 'rat', but I was intrigued. Kirk wanted something from me and that put me in a position of power for the first time ever in our relationship. That feeling alone was enough to blind me.

'I'm doing this new cooking series for TV, it's going to blow the fucking lid off the genre . . .'

'It's expanding the format to new heights?'

'Yes, quite so.' He sounded impressed at my knowledge of the mystical inner workings of television.

'It's called *Kirk St John's Hot Kitchen* . . .'

'Anyone in it I know?' I said, wasting valuable sarcasm as he ignored the interruption.

'It's basically a filmed dinner party. The first part is me preparing the food, the second part is the conversation with the guests as they eat my food. Like a kind of chat show.'

'Only with more crudités.'

'Absolutely, yes. And it's going to blow the fucking lid off chat shows. That's why I want you for the first show, you'd be perfect.'

'Me? Why me? No one knows me.'

'No, but everyone knows me,' he said, clearly unfamiliar with the concept of modesty. 'You see, as it's the first one, we thought we'd do a kind of sentimental journey about me and my life. There's plenty of people who want to know about that sort of stuff. You and me go back a long way. Ten years or so.'

'Sixteen.'

'Is it that long?' he asked disbelievingly. I remembered the *Hello!* article in which he had claimed he was only thirty-two. Lying bastard.

'Whatever. People would be interested in finding out about my past from the perspective of someone who was there. What do you say?'

'Are you sure?' I asked, already an idea forming that here was my chance. Sure it would mean letting Kirk back into my life, but that would be a small sacrifice if I was able to publicly expose the man who had made his living out of stealing mine.

'Sure I'm sure. And it would be a good way to revisit our past, patch up our differences, that kind of stuff. We've got so much in common and yet we've drifted too far apart over the last few years, mate.' Not far enough, mate. I thought.

'I'd need to think about it, and talk to Trish of course.'

'Trish. You don't mean Tish, do you, that bimbo waitress?' Kirk asked, as always with the sensitivity of a Sherman tank.

'No. Another one,' I said, not able to be bothered with blowing the fucking lid off the Trish/Tish issue.

'Good. Gina would be really pissed off if she thought that tart was on the scene again. She's a bit sniffy about the old extra maritals these days.'

'Really? I wonder why?' I said. Like a hardened artery acting on the blood supply the furred British Telecom line sieved out all traces of irony from my tone.

'So you'll think about it?' he insisted. I agreed to think about it knowing that he'd interpret it as a definite 'Yes I'll do it'. But I'd already decided that I would do it. I'd do it and blow the fucking lid off sham TV chefs.

Having left it there, I then got on with being a panic-stricken father to be. So busy was I sleeping in my clothes in case Trish went into labour suddenly, or making up endless supplies of cheese sandwiches in case I wouldn't get the opportunity to eat for twenty-four hours, or constantly checking the oil, tyres and battery on the car, just in case, that I completely forgot about Kirk's request. When Trish did go into labour, I went into such a spiral of panic that, at that moment, ground-breaking TV series were at the bottom of my list of priorities, just below renewing my subscription to Reader's Digest.

I was at work, settling in two new residents to the home. Dolly Watkins and Maurice Marlowe had never met before but they had one thing in common. They had both lost their grip on reality. Dolly was in her nineties and hadn't seen her teeth since the birth of the Welfare State. She had a limited amount of fine white hair that was thinly spread over her freckled head. She was underfed and frail and carried a handbag that weighed several hundredweight, thanks to the eighty-seven pounds in ten-pence pieces that it contained. Maurice Marlowe was a large, flamboyant man in his seventies who smoked endlessly, sometimes three at a time. He had yellow fingers, burn holes in his cardigan and smelled strongly of smoke. He had more symbols to link him with cigarettes than a Formula One racing car. Apart from smoking he loved to tell tall-tales of his past. He divided everyone that he had ever met into either heartless bastards or lovely, lovely human beings. He was more theatrical than an actor at an awards ceremony. He was old, incontinent, and had less marbles than the school weakling after morning playtime.

I was trying to explain to a bemused Maurice how to use a toilet when Mr Airdrie stuck his head round the door. He was leaning at such an angle I felt sure his daft hair would slip right off.

'Hospital rang, your wife's in labour.'

I dropped Maurice's ancient cardboard suitcase and sprinted past Mr Airdrie, pausing only to pick up my Tupperware box of cheese sandwiches.

'What about the rest of your shift?' Mr Airdrie called after me, in a tone that suggested he'd already accepted that he would have to shove his shift up his arse.

I hadn't been looking forward to the birth. This was because I wasn't sure about my ability to withstand the sight of someone else's blood. Also I thought Trish's vocabulary at the primal effect of childbirth would get us both ejected from the hospital grounds. I needn't have worried. When things were at their most tense and Trish was in maximum pain, she dug her nails deep into the soft fleshy parts of my hand and shouted at the assembled midwives and doctors.

'Flipping heck, this blooming hurts.' It was unusual to say the least. It was as if the antiseptic atmosphere of the childbirth suite had washed her mouth out with soap.

'Crikey, doctor that nipped.'

The labour went on and on like a Conservative government. Except that, unlike a Conservative government, I loved all the blood, the pain, the terror. I decided that childbirth was definitely invented for men. It was like an extremely realistic horror movie, only with better effects. Then, suddenly and with little ceremony, a baby appeared and was presented to me. I held the bloody mess in my arms, kissed it and cried.

'Bloody hayfever,' I said.

'It's been a fucking warm September,' Trish said from deep in an exhausted coma, quickly recovering her usual powers of speech.

We called him Charlie, after the scent Trish had been given for her sixteenth birthday. I didn't know why that was so significant and I didn't dare argue. She had too many hormones, both natural and artificial, rushing around in her body, as well as free access to sharp surgical implements. I ate all her toast and drank her tea and then, shortly after she had told me to fuck off, I left the hospital. I was still in a daze brought on by the combination of becoming a father and not having had any sleep for thirty-six hours. I drove home and automatically picked up the ringing phone.

'Yo, Billy! it's Kirk. Where the hell have you been? I've been ringing for two days.'

'Hospital.'

'Hope you're feeling better,' he said, with as much concern for my welfare as a wooden club shows when hovering over a baby seal.

'Listen, it's today. I'll send a car round to collect you at four.'

'Today? Collect? Four?'

'See you later.' Click. The phone went dead and I followed its example shortly afterwards.

At four, the car arrived and a smarmy young man with several hundred poorly disguised spots on his face knocked arrogantly on my door. I was awake but not alive.

'Yes?'

'Hi, I'm Simon and I'm your travel aide today. We need to leave by four-ten latest, there's a terrible snarl-up on the M62.'

'Who the fuck are you?'

'Hi. I'm Simon . . .'

By four-thirty I had almost finished dressing, washing and shaving. Simon was on his mobile phone and pacing around in my sitting room. Occasionally he would pick up an ornament and give it a look of disgust. He never stopped talking.

'Yeah, sure, I know. I do, Mandy, but you tell Mr St John that this guy's being very obstructive. Says he doesn't know anything about the bleeping show. Between me and you, I think he's got some sort of problem you know, the chemical sort. It's a real bleeping drag. I'm supposed to be going raving with Marcus this evening . . .'

My squeaky leather shoes, reserved for job interviews and funerals, grassed up the fact that I was just outside the room.

'Hi there, feeling refreshed?'

'Simon, my bleeping travel aide, switch that bleeping thing off because I feel like giving someone a bleeping hard time, and if you say one more word it will be bleeping you.'

As I got into the back of the black Ford, Simon sat in the front, sniffed and dabbed his eyes with a monogrammed hanky.

We got to the studio in Manchester by seven and I was told to go straight to the green room and make myself known to Kirk's personal assistant. I staggered off and met a young girl in a short black skirt in the corridor. She was sex on legs. I nodded to myself that she had all the required talents to be Kirk's personal assistant.

'Hello, I'm Amanda, I'm Mr St John's PA. You're late.'

She'd obviously learned her manners from Kirk.

'I had a baby this morning. You're lucky I'm here.'

'What are you, some kind of doctor?' she said, with the kind of disgust that was usually saved for paedophiles or necrophiliacs, or people who weren't in TV. I followed her into the green room.

The green room was actually decorated in blue candy-stripes which, to my tired eyes, merged together in a moving pattern that was like something from Bridget Riley's worst nightmare. The room was very dark on account of there being no windows, and as it was situated in a basement deep under the studios, it had all the atmosphere of a coal mine that had been closed by the Tories for ten years. I instinctively looked around for something alcoholic to numb the pain of sleep deprivation.

'No alcohol. Mr St John's orders. Since he bravely came out and declared his alcoholism, he's very insistent that none of his guests is allowed to self-abuse. He doesn't want to be responsible for causing them any harm.' I resisted the obvious joke about it being a bit late for that. She reminded me of Gina. Kirk deserved her.

'So Kirk's a piss head. I guess he needed something to work on day-time television.'

Amanda gave me a look which could have been used in circumcision ceremonies the world over, took out a mobile phone that wasn't ringing and answered it.

'Hiya, Katie. Tell me it's on.' She looked at me, noticing my puzzled expression. It was hard to believe she had a sixth sense when I hadn't thought her capable of having the previous five. She covered the phone with her hand.

'It vibrates. Doesn't disturb the guys in the studio.'

I wanted to say something so obscene it even made me blush, but some thread of decency helped sew my gob shut.

While Amanda chatted on the phone to Katie, I sat slumped in the corner nursing a sparkling apple juice that tasted like the horrible boiled sweets my dad ate all the time. It made me feel sick. A familiar figure entered the room; the subtle lighting meant I couldn't quite make out who it was until he was right in front of me.

'Chopper.' I was awake now. At least I thought I was.

'No, I'm Blackburn. How's it going, man? Do I know you?'

'William Wrose. Billy.'

'Didn't we meet in the ambient tent at Glastonbury this year?'

'No. But I feel as if I've written the sound track for your career.'

'Groovy.'

'I'm William, you know, Billy Petrol from I saw Warsaw.' It felt strange saying those names again, I hadn't said them for about sixteen years, like I had a mental block about that whole period in my life.

'Oh yes. Right man. I remember. Were you the drummer?'

Chopper was so far out of it it would have taken a long-haul flight to get him back to somewhere near reality. I was surprised how absent-minded he was; I figured it was probably the years of habitual drug abuse and living the rock-star life. Or possibly it was living with the constant pressure of being a total arsehole who had as much talent and original-ity as a common yellow duster.

'Are you on tonight,' I asked.

'Sure, man. You?'

'Yes. It's like a reunion, isn't it?'

'Reunion of what, man?' he asked, while searching in his breast pocket for a pinch of cocaine. He found some and offered it to me.

'No. Thanks all the same.' I was more used to scoring deals at Oddbins these days, where the drugs on sale had buttery flavours with a blackcurrant and pineapple aftertaste. I wanted to ask him what had happened to my royalties but they had probably got right up his nose. I decided to bide my time and ask him in front of the millions of misguided fools who would be watching the show.

I'd just dropped off to sleep again when I heard Amanda yelp from the other side of the room.

'Tonya, great, hi.' She was crawling in an animated fashion to a tall, elegant, young woman in a short black taffeta dress which had WESTWOOD embroidered on the lapels. The elegant young woman was ignoring her with the ease that comes naturally to the upper classes.

'No booze?'

'Ah no, sorry. But I could send out for some,' Amanda offered. I was surprised she couldn't hear my teeth grinding from the other side of the room.

'Shag,' she said. I knew how she felt. She stood around for a couple of minutes giving me a look that said 'What's the matter, don't you recognise me?' and I returned it with my best 'No, who the fuck are you?' Then she was called through. I asked Amanda who the fuck she was. Amanda was horrified at my ignorance.

'That was Lady Tonya. She's the daughter of Lord Barkingside.'

'Oh,' I said, none the wiser.

She lowered her voice as if describing a particularly disgusting episode of human history. 'The tabloids call her the "Punk Princess", she's engaged to Prince Ijaz. You know, the Sheikh of Q'wmcuat.'

Now I remembered. She was an outrageous debutante who wore expensive Punk jewellery, outrageous haute couture dresses and swore at public events in order to guarantee regular column inches in the popular press. She had also surprised everyone by recently getting engaged to Prince Ijaz who belonged to the ruling family of one of the smaller, least stable Middle Eastern states. The press suggested the engagement might have more to do with him being the thirty-fifth richest man in the world or maybe because he owned a world-wide chain of trendy night-spots called 'Dogruffs', where those famous for being famous, such as Tonya, hung out and teased the paparazzi. These suggestions, as well as the leaking of Tonya's comment, spoken off the record, that she would convert to Islam just as soon as she could give up the fizzy stuff, had resulted in the arrest and subsequent deportation from Q'wmcuat of several journalists. I was so excited at meeting her in the flesh I fell asleep almost immediately.

When I awoke, Amanda was climaxing into the phone. I assumed the vibrator must be full on.

'Ohh, Yes!' she said, nodding excitedly into the black plastic handset. 'Okay, Katie, excellent.' She switched it off and came over.

'Sorry, Mr Writhe, there may be a hitch,' she said solemnly.

'Oh yes?'

'Well, the thing is, your slot may have to be reduced.'

'Reduced slot?' I asked, managing to stop myself from making an 'Oo-er matron' kind of wise crack.

'That was Katie, Nigella's PA. She's got her to do it.'

'Mandy, one thing I need to ask.' I could feel waves of sleep rushing in to drown me. I didn't have long left before high tide.

'Sure thing.'

'Can you please speak English?'

There was a long pause while Amanda wondered whether Kirk would sack her if she killed me then and there in cold blood. Probably not, but she didn't, instead choosing to spare me for some future horrible humiliation.

'There's been a change of plan because we've managed to get Nigella Marten to be a special guest on tonight's show. She's been upstairs recording a show of carols for Christmas. She's a big fan of Kirk's.'

'Nigella Marten?' I asked. I had once been aware of the

name, a long time ago in the days when I used to get eight
hours sleep a night.

'You know, the singer, she won a Tony last year for the
musical "The Bell Jar". Her Sylvia Plath was awesome,
apparently.'

Something akin to an uneasy feeling was whispering
insinuations into my ear. 'When you say reduced my slot,
what exactly do you mean?'

Amanda brightened up considerably; my horrible humiliation time was here already. 'Well, Nigella Marten doesn't
condescend to sing on TV too often. This is a big honour.'

'I'm not going on, am I?'

'I'm sure we'll get you on, for a moment or two. Maybe at
the end.'

'Fancy, I've been stood down for a Tony-winning singer,
my mother will be so proud.' She would too.

I watched the programme begin from the comfort of the
green room on the big TV provided. A lively audience was
applauding because a cardboard sign was telling them to.
The main sound stage of the recording studio was decorated to look like a French country kitchen. In the middle of
the set Kirk sat around a fake rustic table. I was pleased to
notice he was at least a stone heavier than the last time I'd
seen him. This pleasure was slightly tempered by the fact
that I was two stone heavier. The audience fell expectantly
quiet.

'Welcome to my kitchen. And it's going to be hot tonight.'
This made them noisy again, as if he'd announced world
peace.

'Now I'm known to all you millions as the "Punk Chef",
and I was once a top punk singer. From this experience I
have learned that fame may come from arrogance, but great-
ness comes from being humble. Which brings me to my first
guest, a fellow member of my band and one-time pop
singer, Don One.' The words 'one time' were like a derisive

nudge in the ribs, as if to indicate that it was a time in pre-history when dinosaurs still walked the earth.

The audience were ordered to applaud and they obeyed.

Blackburn staggered the three yards or so to the kitchen table and sat down heavily. Kirk shook his hand as if it was the shitty end of a stick.

'Yo, Blackburn.'

'Hi, Kirk man.'

Kirk winked at the camera whose red light winked back.

'I was going to chat first and then eat, but from the looks of you, if we don't eat now we might not get another chance . . . so *skate au poivre* in a prune sauce.' The audience clapped madly, as a lackey, another pretty girl in a short black skirt, brought on a tray of food. Kirk served it with a flourish that was well rehearsed and the audience made 'yum yum' sounds as they watched. It looked cold and stodgy, as if it had been prepared several hours earlier.

'How is it?' Kirk asked.

'Tastes like shit, man,' Blackburn said automatically. The audience gasped, a few even booed. The floor manager waved his arms and pulled his finger across his throat. Kirk took the skate off Blackburn's plate.

'Come on, Blackburn. Get a fucking grip. We'll do that again.'

So they did, the food was brought on again and the audience clapped even louder just to show they didn't blame Kirk. The skate looked even colder and tougher than before.

'Tastes fine,' Blackburn said when asked a second time, his blocked brain sensing the possibility of a lynch mob being formed by the audience if he didn't behave.

A group of men and women from another studio had joined me in the green room.

'I took my time-sheet to Harry and do you know what he said?' the small woman with mousy hair asked the other two. 'He said I was to get it countersigned by Rick.'

'Harry bloody Hitler,' said the man, who had no hair but

lost any sympathy this may have engendered by sporting an enormous overgrown hedgerow of a beard.

'Quite. It wasn't like this on *The Classic Serial*,' the other woman said, in between pushing her long blonde hair up and checking the impact in the reflection on the glass door.

'That was a real team. Oh look,' she said pointing at the screen, 'fish cakes with a mango salsa. He's a real original, isn't he?'

I watched the monitor in stunned silence as Nigella Marten came on and she and Blackburn sang a duet of 'Not Waving, But Drowning' from her Tony-winning show. A man I didn't recognise came over and stood next to me.

'She's marvellous, isn't she?' he asked. It didn't sound like he was talking to anyone in particular so I ignored him.

'Great range.'

'I wish she was home on it,' I quipped.

'I happen to be her musical arranger, if you don't mind.'

'I don't. Rather you than me, mate.'

'And you are?' he asked, as if he was about to beat the shit out of me. I realised it was time for conciliation.

'William.'

'I'm Dennis.' He held out a hand for me to shake and it seemed mean to refuse.

'Not your cup of tea?' he asked in a more convivial tone now we were acquainted.

'I prefer something a bit more . . .' I left him to guess what I preferred a bit more of, a bit more silence in Nigella's case.

'A bit more . . .?' he insisted.

'Rocky, Punky, Funky. That kind of stuff. Stuff that ends in Y.'

'Noisy ends in Y.'

'So does lousy,' I said, looking towards the screen. 'Now that would be a challenge. I bet even you couldn't arrange a Punk song into this middle-of-the-road shit. Which, by the way is where it belongs, in the middle of the road. Imagine it, Punk for the Radio Two generation. Or what about classical? Get an orchestra to play Punk hits. It could be a whole new market.' I started giggling insanely. He gave me a strange look that was halfway between contempt and admiration.

'You're one in a million,' he said, obviously wishing I was even rarer. He began making notes in a little red book like a vindictive traffic warden, as I fell into a sleep that was so deep most hospital consultants would have diagnosed it as a coma.

The sound of enthusiastic applause roused me and Amanda stood over me beckoning with a crooked finger. As if sleepwalking I followed her out of the green room and into the studio. As I walked on to the set Kirk welcomed me with a handshake and Blackburn saluted me without any trace of recognition.

'Hiya, Billy. Glad you could make it.' Kirk greeted me cheerfully enough

'Thanks I . . .'

'Right. Now I've got a surprise for you, Billy. Watch this.' Kirk clicked his fingers and all over the studio the monitors showed my face filmed secretly minutes earlier in the Green Room, fast asleep, mouth open and head thrown back. The audience went crazy and Kirk had to hold his finger to his lips to try and restore order.

'This is Billy. He was in our band and I've waited ten years to get even with him. He thinks he came here to be a special guest at our little feast, but what he didn't know was, he is the feast. Watch this.'

The picture of me was instantly reduced to a corner of the screen while a short film ran to which Kirk provided the voice-over.

'Billy Petrol was the guitarist in I saw Warsaw and was probably the main reason they never found the success they deserved.' An old photo of me in very tight trousers grabbing my groin in mock rock-star pose appeared in full view. The audience began to giggle.

'But Billy wasn't satisfied with being a mediocre guitarist, he had set his sights much higher. He decided to steal our songs.'

Blackburn, who was trying hard to follow the story, suddenly caught up. 'Hey, I remember that bit. You were the drummer, weren't you? Kirk wrote the songs. Is that right Kirk?'

Kirk gave him a cool look.

'I certainly did write them.' A picture came on the screen of a gold disc for Don One's Greatest Hits with the name E. David in big letters on the label.

'Not only that, but he stole all the earnings from our tour which he had the nerve to take away in my van.' The audience were caught not knowing whether to laugh or cry; they looked around helplessly for a sign to tell them what to do.

Kirk continued. 'It took a few years to find success but we did find it eventually. Didn't we, Blackburn? And what's more, we deserved it.' The audience cheered. 'And that's no thanks to Mr Petrol, who having failed to steal my songs, set about trying to steal my girlfriend. Once more he failed but that didn't stop him trying again when she was my wife.' As one the audience drew a shocked breath. 'As well as the mother of my children.' A few boos went around the room.

'Your van?' Blackburn asked, merely seeking clarification for his muddled mind rather than insinuating any wrongdoing.

'Yes, my van.'

'I thought it was the drummer's van. The real drummer's van, I mean.' He shut up as Kirk gave him a look sharper than a Stanley knife.

'All in all he's been a nasty blight on my life and that's why I've decided to get even. Do you think I was right to get even?' He appealed to the audience who were already looking around for the nearest lamppost to hang me from.

'*YEEESS!*' they screamed.

'Sorry, Billy, looks like you're outvoted. Say goodnight to our dish of the day.'

Kirk stood up, gave a signal and quickly moved away as the audience reached under their chairs and pulled out a wide range of food left over from the television studio canteen. They then began throwing it at me. Most of it hit Blackburn who was too doped up to even think about moving. Tired as I was, I managed to duck and dive and only received superficial damage from a three-day-old baked potato and a cup full of beans.

'He was a crap drummer too,' I heard Blackburn say as I staggered out of the firing line.

The audience burst into spontaneous applause, spontaneous in the sense that a pretty woman in a short skirt was walking round with a sign that had 'clap now' on it. I was led away by Amanda who was armed with a towel. In the background Nigella went back on and sang 'I'll be your Velvet Girl if you'll be my Iron Man', another of the dreadful songs that had somehow won her awards around the world. My alleged misdemeanours forgotten, the audience were now waddling down to the front of the stage to taste bits of very cold leftovers. This was the studio-audience equivalent of receiving a papal blessing.

Once in the corridor Amanda turned to me.

'Stay on to the post-show party. There's always lots of leftovers.'

But I politely declined and I had gone long before Kirk finished soaking up the appreciative plaudits from his admirers. I asked Simon to drive me straight to the hospital so that I could see Trish and Charlie before either went to sleep for the night. As we approached Bradworth city centre I told him to slow down. I wound down the window and leaned out.

'I fucking hate you, Kirk St John. You are a pretentious, conniving, thieving, lying bastard, and I'll get you one day,' I promised the empty city streets.

'Good, Delia Smith is much easier to follow,' an unseen figure echoed back – from where I couldn't say.

'Where the fuck have you been, arse face?' Trish shouted, almost her old self

I tried to explain.

'You've been making a television programme?'

I had to admit it sounded pretty stupid, now I was fully awake. 'Not exactly making it, more suffering it.'

'When's it on?' she asked, betraying a hint of interest.

'Not straight away, tonight was just the recording.'

'I'm going to tell everyone about this so they can all see what a stupid, selfish, pig-headed bastard husband I've got. I'm even going to break the habit of a lifetime and talk to your mother so she'll know about it.' Her hormones were out in force, like a mob of drunken squaddies on a Saturday night in Aldershot.

'Darling . . .' I began.

'Don't bother, I can see the skidmarks on your tongue from here.'

Inside his plastic fish tank, Charlie began midnight scream practice.

'Your son's crying. I'm off to sleep now. Night, night.'

Fifteen

When the episode of *Kirk St John's Hot Kitchen*, on which I was humiliated, was finally shown some months later, I didn't watch it. This wasn't out of pique or embarrassment, it was because I had yet to achieve a sleep pattern that allowed for more than four hours a night. It was true that I was pretty piqued off and embarrassed to buggery, but thanks to Charlie and his amazing lungs, which promised him a wonderful career as a pearl fisherman, Trish and I were in bed by eight p.m. every night. The programme went out at nine-thirty p.m., which to us was a time of night experienced by only the most decadent of dirty stop-outs.

Churchill watched it, of course, and the next day at work he was full of it.

'You were wonderful, darling. Your perfectly measured lack of credibility was so . . . telling. Very Pinter.'

'It's Pinter as in winter, not as in pint,' I said, correcting his pronunciation more to divert the conversation away from my own stupidity, rather than out of any genuine interest in the use of English.

Mr Airdrie was more supportive but not much. 'Such a shame you didn't stay for the after-show party, it would

have been marvellous to have met Nigella Marten. I have
several of her records, you know,' he said, smoothing down
the wilder waves of his jet-black hair with such vigour that
I thought I saw the whole edifice move from side to side on
his head.

'No, I didn't know, but somehow I'm not surprised.'

Mr Airdrie had moved in to share my office as a temporary measure to save costs while we rode the financial storm
that raged around us. A year later he was still there, the
financial storm was now a nuclear winter and he claimed he
had to keep a closer watch over strategic affairs. In other
words he had nothing to do and was so scared that people
higher up the Swansong foodchain would find this out, he
kept busy by inventing jobs, like spying on me. He'd always
been a bit of a bore, in the way a sheep is a bit stupid, and
he'd been too long a Bradworth Corporation man to ever
aspire to anything more dynamic, but his attempts to look
active merely highlighted the fact that he did absolutely fuck
all. For years he'd relied on me to do everything for him,
contenting himself with making occasional lazy statements
about 'commitment to quality' and the need for 'investment
in human resources', things which sounded dynamic but
were emptier than a promise made by a politician in a room-
ful of babies. When the rumours started to creep out that
Crowe House wasn't achieving its outcomes, whatever that
meant, Mr Airdrie's statements took on a different tone, one
of barely contained panic.

'We've got to run harder just to stand still,' he told me as
I worked late to try to correct his childish errors in the petty-
cash book. Life in Crowe House had prepared me for things
falling out of old people's bottoms, usually straight on to my
shoes, but now the bottom was falling out of the old people.
Everyone over seventy was staying at home and being cared
for by home-helps or relatives with 'sole beneficiary' written
in their eyes, rather than rotting away in places like Crowe
House

'We have to be creative, efficient and effective in our efforts,' Mr Airdrie waffled on. The first two pretty much ruled him out, and if you included the third one, then he was in real trouble.

'Mr Airdrie . . .'

'Please, call me Forfar,' he said.

'Why?' I asked, wondering if this was some bizarre Celtic fantasy that he wanted me to engage in with him. Then it dawned on me that Forfar was his first name. I realised things must be serious if he was going to go all informal on me. He was trying to make me like him which meant that he was probably going to need all the friends he could get. If I'd dared ask he'd probably have let me in on the secret I had always wanted in on. His ridiculous hair, was it wig or bottle?

'Forfar. How bad are things? I mean with Swansong.' I made the distinction just in case his new-found openness strayed into revealing the nasty, sticky, personal problems that I'd always suspected he'd harboured.

'Well, if we can improve efficiency and effectiveness . . .' His repetition of the same old platitudes was an attempt to convince himself that there might be a grain of truth in them. 'Then we have nothing to fear. Indeed one day all this could be yours.' He waved at his desk, the centrepiece of which was a miniature dry-stone wall he had made out of rolled Blu-tack during a slack month or seventeen.

He was right too. The very next day Swansong announced its 'Forward Into The Future' strategy, which was a radical realignment designed to shape the organisa-tion for the next millennium. This meant cutting half of the management structure and making the half that remained work twice as hard for the same money. So the next day Mr Airdrie was radically realigned and I was given all his duties. He put on a brave face, the one which shouted surrender from every pore and waved a white flag in his eyes.

'Bloody glad to be going, if the truth be known. This is just the kind of opportunity I've been hoping for.' Which broadly translated as 'This is the end of my pathetic empty little world and all I've got is the minuscule lump-sum the bastards have promised.'

Worse was to come. Frank Lardis was to come. Frank Lardis was nicknamed 'Lard Arse' by Churchill in a moment of rare incisive irony. Frank Lardis, who loved marathon running, healthy food and a fast-paced lifestyle, was sent by head office to sort things out. He wasn't so much a new broom as a butcher's knife. To call him a bastard would have invited a wave of writs from bastards everywhere claiming defamation of character. He was a horrible loathsome man, made even more unbearable by one thing.

'You hate him because he's only twenty-eight,' Churchill mocked, hitting nails on the head like a time-served joiner. I tried to deny it but he knew me too well.

'The writing's on the wall, just as you've made it to the top of the greasy pole up pops Lard Arse to knock you down again.' He laughed as only one who was free of ambition could laugh. If he carried on like that for much longer he'd be free of teeth, too.

On his first day Frank Lardis toured the building oozing oily charm in front of the residents, while consulting a financial ledger to see how much they paid for the privilege of being exploited in our care. If he was happy with their financial circumstances he put a little blue tick next to the name, if unhappy he put a red cross. As he did this I studied him. There was no denying it, he was eleven years younger than me and, despite his prematurely greying hair and lined face, he looked eleven years younger than me. He was fit and muscular, and had a healthy glow that took me several pints to achieve. To make matters worse, he treated me as if I was eleven years younger than him, calling me 'son' or 'laddie'. How I wished a psychotic old gimmer would lunge at him with their plastic medication spoon and lacerate his silk chess-board-effect tie.

At the end of the tour he looked up from the books and pointed the red pen at me. I felt a chill shoot down my spine.

'A thought, Willy, my son. Think throughput. Your problem here is throughput.'

'My problem?' I asked. This didn't sound a very promising start. Mr Airdrie was an annoying tit but at least he was a slow-thinking annoying tit. This guy was different, he had smart-arse whizz-kid woven into the very fabric of his soul, and whatever problems he uncovered it was already clear that none of them was going to be his.

'Too many beds are filled by the kind of people who are too expensive to look after.'

'You mean, old people?' I asked innocently.

'Think incontinence. Look at Watkins.' I'd rather not, I thought. Dolly Watkins, everyone's favourite toothless ninety-six-year-old, who wore not only her heart but also her bodily fluids on her sleeve. She was the sort of resident who tested the capabilities of the laundry service to breaking point. Nice woman. Smelly, but still very nice.

'They're all nice people, despite their . . . impairments,' I said, brightly.

'Willy lad. Incontinence is an expense we must do without,' Lardis explained with a cold logic that made me think of martial music and trains running on time.

'Extra staff, cleaning materials, laundry, it all adds to the cost of caring.'

'And that's bad, is it?' I asked.

He gave me a withering look that toxicologists with a ten-year government grant would have been hard-pressed to analyse completely. I didn't know what he wanted me to do but it was clear that whatever it was I should be doing it.

'What exactly do you want me to do about it?'

'That's entirely your decision and I don't want to interfere. You won't find Frank Lardis stepping on toes,' he said,

obviously about to jump on mine, 'but one thought springs
to mind. Heat.'

'Heat?'

'It's hot in here. Too hot. That means big heating bills. You
could start by knocking the heating down by a notch or
two.'

'But then the more frail residents may catch cold. That
could be fatal to some people.'

He gave me a knowing wink. 'Two birds, one stone' it
read. 'Well, of course we wouldn't want that to happen,
would we?' he said and smiled.

'I could leave the bedroom windows open at night if that
would help,' I said, intending to be sarcastic.

'I think you and I will work well together,' he said and
patted me on the shoulder.

He went back to studying the books in more detail than
Mr Airdrie had ever done before.

After an hour of silence he leaned back in the chair and
threw his pen on the desk. 'A dark thought, Willy, my boy –
this place is depressing. I look around and all I see is old
people.'

'How perceptive of you.'

'Take my word for it, old people, if they are not properly
packaged, are depressing. What this place needs is an image
that's more hopeful, more positive. I want you to see to it.'
With that command, he ushered me out of his office putting
a Do Not Disturb sign on the door handle as he closed it
behind me.

I thought about the problem of throughput. I then thought
about the old and infirm who lived at Crowe House, like
Dolly Watkins and Maurice Marlowe. In Frank's new order
people like Maurice and Dolly were an expensive luxury
and it was now my job to get rid of them. If I didn't have the
stomach for that the alternative was to try to give them an
upbeat, upmarket image. It wasn't much of a choice.

*

While the world was trying to make up its mind what to do about Bosnia, before giving up and concentrating instead on the more important question of Blur or Oasis, which was best?, Chopper, who'd always had a great sense of timing, chose that moment to die.

It was a small headline buried in the middle of the newspaper but it still shouted at me louder than the *'Eastenders'* Love Rat Confession' on the opposite page. 'Pop star dies,' it said simply. And he had. 'Pop star, Don One, who had many hits in the '80s [well, three anyway], died yesterday in a drug-related incident. Real name Blackburn Woodcock, he formed the infamous I Saw the Sea Shore punk band before finding his solo success.'

Over the next few days, more details of Chopper's life and death emerged. He had been dependent on drugs for years, apparently even when I'd known him, and he'd spent all of his money-making deals to fuel his habit. All the newspapers agreed that he was a weak pathetic excuse for a man.

'So tell me something I didn't know,' I said to Churchill, with as much sympathy as the early bird has for the worm's next of kin.

His death had been an ironic tragedy. Early in the morning, while on the way to his usual drug dealer in Brixton, he'd stepped out in front of a milk-float. Bang (or perhaps that should be Clink) and that was it. Very Pinta-esque.

'You won't be going to his funeral then?' Churchill asked. I thought about it. They'd all be there, Kirk, Gina, all of them. Yet more wounds to be opened up in the full gaze of the press and public. It wasn't exactly tempting, but how could I refuse? I might just be able to save some of the face I'd lost on Kirk's show, even though to merely break even I'd need to save more faces than could be found on the Eiger, but I had to try.

'Yes, I guess I'll be going.'

'Good. That means I don't have to.'

After my experience on the *Hot Kitchen* show, Kirk was the

last person I wanted to meet. His career was going from strength to strength and the show was now into its third series, as he achieved a God-like status for the 90s' gourmand generation. Even the incident with the granny had helped raise his stock with the viewers. It happened when he'd brought on an elderly woman who was celebrating her eightieth birthday and her granddaughter had taken her to the show as a treat. Kirk asked her to prepare a hollandaise sauce while he got on with the game chips and baked red mullet. Already famed for his tantrums in the kitchen, he turned on the elderly woman when she tried to boil the sauce. He didn't exactly strangle her, not hard anyway, but she and her granddaughter still made an official complaint. No action was taken because of the support from food fanatics everywhere, as well as a campaign in the tabloid press to whom the 'Punk Chef' was a regular contributor and valuable provider of column inches. The television company realised that, to the public who watched Kirk's show, attacking an old woman for stupidly trying to heat hollandaise sauce was a punishment that aptly fitted the crime. So, as my career arrived in the doldrums with lowered sails and no spare oars, Kirk's had caught the perfect wave and was now confidently hanging ten.

I took the day of Chopper's funeral as compassionate leave, much to Frank Lardis's disapproval.

'Death is a fact of life, Willy lad, like redundancy,' he said.

Kirk and Gina looked satisfyingly miserable as we stood in the church listening to the vicar drone on endlessly about someone he'd never actually met (on account of Chopper never having set foot inside a church). We sat out of view at the back. Trish nudged me.

'Have a go at this.'

It was a bottle of Jim Beam that she'd secreted away in her giant handbag.

'Good for shock,' she insisted

I took it off her and went outside for a quiet drink to

remember the good times with Chopper. This didn't take long but I still felt a sense of regret at his passing. I drank some more and reflected on the frailty of life. This sent me into a bit of a panic so I finished off the whisky.

The rest of the mourners came out and we filed our way reverently to the graveside. As we stood around watching the coffin being lowered into the grave, Kirk and Gina looked even more miserable and I was gratified to think that this might be more than just sadness at Chopper's death. It might be because they were unhappy with one another and their lives together. That possibility cheered me up no end.

'And now a tribute to a very talented man.' The vicar pressed the Start switch on a large ghetto blaster. Chopper's whiney tones came warbling out as he sang 'Shiver Me Timbres', his biggest hit. I'd never liked his version much but I couldn't help humming along to it, and then joining in with the chorus

> Fell out of my life but you fell on your feet
> Love got lost when you got cheap.

I suppose I got carried away but it was my song and suddenly I was enjoying myself.

'God, you're disgusting,' Gina said, and Kirk gave me a look of disapproval that he usually reserved for his most junior of assistants, just before he hit them with a metal spoon. I tried to work out what was so disgusting about singing and then I realised that I wasn't just singing, I was dancing. Worse, I was dancing on Chopper's grave, or at least by it. The vicar switched off the tape and the mourners looked at me in hostile silence.

'It was a tribute. My way of saying goodbye. He made good dance records,' I said, trying to justify my behaviour. I could see Trish giggling at me from the other side of the grave.

The vicar continued and started throwing soil around and

wittering on about ashes and dust. My attention began to wander and that was when I noticed the wreath. It was from the dairy whose milk-float had run Chopper down and killed him. They had sent a wreath of white flowers shaped like the tags you put around milk-bottle necks when ordering an extra pint. On it was a simple message. It read: Praying for Your Safe Delivery to Heaven. I began to laugh. It was gentle, controlled laughter at first but then, thanks to the bottle of Jim Beam inside me, it became more uncontrollable and irrational. The vicar had to shout the closing passages of the service over my braying cackle. As he finished I lost complete control of both my laugh and my balance and I slowly slid down the freshly dug soil until I stood on the polished oak lid of Chopper's coffin.

Trish's face appeared above me.

'You got yourself into this hole, you can get yourself out. And can you hurry up because I don't want to miss the ham tea.'

Over the funeral tea Kirk spoke loudly to anyone who would listen, which was everyone present, about the evils of alcohol and his brave struggle to kick the habit. I chewed guiltily on the stale ham sandwich while Trish made one last public attempt to defend me.

'William doesn't have a problem with drink, actually. It's being pissed he can't cope with.'

'Thanks for your support, Trish,' I said in the car on the way home. 'You were a big help.'

Chopper's death didn't really hit me until a few weeks later. I was desperately trying to make the yawning deficits of the Crowe House budget look like a fit and healthy profit when it came up behind me and went bang! It being the realisation that Chopper was the same age as me. What was worse, he was now guaranteed to remain this age in perpetuity, while I, on the other hand, was going to get older. At least that's what I thought.

I began to spend more time than was healthy with the likes of Maurice Marlowe, trying to think of ways that I might be able to improve his downbeat image and failing miserably. While doing so I suffered many long, boring stories about the places he had visited, all of the heartless bastards who had done him down and the lovely, lovely people he had met on his travels. One day, after having endured three hours of the 'best bed and breakfasts in Poole' and 'where to avoid the heartless bastards in Burnley', we were interrupted by Frank Lardis's monotone voice over the public address system. He'd had it installed soon after arriving at Crowe House, using the residents' entertainment budget so that he could purchase it from 'Executive Relief', a catalogue he subscribed to that contained the latest Japanese business toys. The slim black box with built-in microphone sat on his desk and allowed him to broadcast to every area of the building, which he claimed helped to improve efficiency. When he went home at five, as he did religiously every night, Churchill and I switched it on and stood the radio by it so that the residents were treated to the soothing tones of Radio Two in every corner of Crowe House.

'Staff information announcement, code blue. Mr Wrose to the main office, please,' Frank said with the warmth of a four-minute warning. 'Code blue' meant that whatever message followed was to be obeyed instantly. All staff had a photocopied sheet of what each colour code meant. No one bothered reading it but everyone had a copy. I duly went straight to Frank's office, pausing only to nip in to 'Café Come Home', Noreen's new coffee shop franchise in the foyer, buy a paper and espresso, read the former, drink the latter and then spend twenty minutes arguing with Churchill over who was the greatest footballer of all time. I knew Frank had bad news for me when I entered the office. He sat at his new mahogany desk looking like someone who had just decided that something horrible needed to be done, something so vile that the only option he had was to give it to someone else to do.

'Willy, young feller, I've been doing some further income analysis and it has forced me to revisit the whole throughput issue again.'

'Is that bad?'

'I'm thinking margins here. Our margins are narrower than originally predicted.'

'But surely our quality of care is still good?'

'Quality of care . . .' he said, as if the concept was new to him and it clashed with his double-breasted pin-stripe suit, 'doesn't pay your wages.'

Frank Lardis had a face for every occasion and for certain occasions, such as this one, he used both of them.

'One thought, young 'un, it would be good for margins if you were to process the termination of service provision to the likes of Marlowe and Watkins asap.'

'You want me to throw them out?'

'That sort are too expensive to care for. Sad but true. Let's look at it as a learning experience for all of us.'

'But where will they go?'

'That's your problem. I don't want to interfere in something which is clearly your decision.'

It was good to know who was in control.

That evening I thought about Frank Lardis and what he wanted me to do. The more I thought about it the more my chest started to hurt, until by eight-thirty it had become a burning pain of such intensity that I began to complain, mildly.

'Hell hath no fury like a man with a fucking illness,' Trish said.

'Fecking ellniss,' Charlie mimicked. He had learned to swear long before he had learned to talk, thanks to his mother's positive role model. Trish was hard but she wasn't entirely heartless and she called the doctor, not so much out of concern for me, but because she wanted to disturb his evening.

The GP was harassed, a state that hadn't been helped by the interruption, which meant he was missing *Top Gear*. I told him about my symptoms, and while Trish was out in the kitchen making a cup of tea to try to ease his temper, I told him all about work and, for some reason, Kirk.

'Hmmn I don't like that.'

'What? My heart?'

'No, cooking. Can't stand programmes about cooking, bloody tedious. I much prefer car programmes,' he said in a tone that was darker than a Belgian chocolate. 'No it's not your heart. All you need to do is reduce your stress levels. Relax, stop worrying and enjoy life.'

'You said that when we couldn't have a baby,' I said accusingly.

'I say it about everything. I reckon if I say it often enough I might even believe it myself one day.' With that, he clicked his Gladstone bag shut and let himself out.

'Has he gone?' Trish asked as she came into the room carrying three mugs of tea.

'Yes.'

'Shame, I've spat in his tea. The pompous twat.'

Frank Lardis was in a good mood when he called me in to see him.

'I've been thinking about things, Willy, me laddio, and the thought that struck me [and this is the most significant thought in my head at the moment] is Profile. I want to talk to you about profile.'

'Profile?' I asked suspiciously.

'We need to put this place on the map. We need an event that puts us in the public consciousness. Upbeat and upmarket, Willy, my kid. I want your input.'

I had a hundred questions to ask, starting with, 'What the

fuck are you on about, you moronic snotty-nosed little bastard?' But I wasn't to be given the opportunity.

'Something that puts me . . . us . . . Swansong on everyone's lips. Go away and work up four or five ideas by Monday. Go, go.' He waved me away as if obesity was contagious and he might put on a pound or two if he didn't clear my stomach from the area instantly. Outside, Churchill was looking for me.

'Phone call,' he said, his mime looking more like a medieval fertility rite, 'your mum. She said it was quite urgent. Apparently your dad's dying again. She'll ring back.' On cue the phone rang out around the echoing corridors. I ran into the broom cupboard that served as my office and picked up the receiver.

'Mr Wrose?' It was a voice I didn't recognise, a man's. In my head I immediately pictured a hospital consultant in a brilliant white coat ringing with bad news.

'I'm ringing with some good news, Mr Wrose.' He sounded almost cheerful and my hopes were raised as I reminded myself that they could do amazing things with medicine these days.

'Is he going to be all right?' I asked.

The voice on the other end sounded less cheerful and more confused. 'Who?'

'My dad. Who is this?'

There was a pause and then the voice said that he was Dennis the Menace and he wanted to talk about royalty. At least that was what it sounded like.

'What the fuck do you want?' My already thin supply of patience had been quickly used up.

'I'm the director of the Northern Symphonic Orchestra.' What the fuck did the director of the Northern Symphonic Orchestra want with me?

'What the fuck do you want with me?' I asked.

'Now's obviously a bad time, should I call back?'

He was trying to be friendly so I softened my hard

approach from granite to something more like sandstone. 'Go on, go on.'

'You don't remember, do you? We met a couple of years ago, back stage at Kirk St John's *Hot Kitchen* show. You suggested I do an album of classic Punk-rock songs. Well, I'm now the director of the Northern Symphonic and I'm producing an album of Punk tunes played by my orchestra. It was your idea really. There'll be a TV advertising tie-in and so on. I want permission to use a track from the "That Was Zen But This Is Nous" album. There'll be royalties, of course. You were Billy Petrol in I saw Warsaw, I believe.'

'Yes. Which track?' I asked, knowing instinctively what was coming.

'"Probably The Last Song I'll Ever . . ."'

'You need to speak to Kirk St John, or E. David as he likes to be known. He's the one credited with writing that track.'

'I know, I wondered if you could have a word with him for me . . .'

The phone made a satisfying crunch as I bashed it down and cut him off. Considering the amount of wires that spilled out like overcooked spaghetti, it was surprising that it could still ring, but it could and it did, immediately.

'Bugger off and do your own dirty work,' I spat.

'Billy, come home,' Mum wailed like a lonesome hyena.

My dad had a lovely death-bed scene, which my mum had carefully crafted by the time I arrived. The room was darkened as the curtains were closed and Dad lay there in immaculate clean pyjamas surrounded by the best flowers out of his garden. His moustache had never looked more symmetrical. Mum sat at his side, shorter and fatter than ever, leaning forward slightly as if straining to catch his last wishes. She wore a vast, pink, silk blouse and matching dress and a wide-brimmed straw hat. She looked like a bottle of Mateus Rose that had been turned into a table-lamp. My entrance was like a central scene in a play. The rest of the room dimmed and a sharp spotlight seemed to pick me out as I went over to him. He motioned me to come closer. I could see he wanted to make his peace and apologise for thirty years of ignoring my existence. I bent over him and could feel his breath on my ear. I was polite enough to disguise my overwhelming feeling of victory.

'Hnnng,' he said. I took this as his way of saying 'Sorry for all the silence', but it may have been 'Where are my grapes then?'

He died a little while later, around the same time that I was at the garden centre with Trish and Charlie. Ironically we had gone there to buy a new lawn mower.

'Fucking spooky,' Trish said.

'We should have waited, he might have left me his in the will.'

I went to Dad's funeral only to find that it was actually Mum's funeral. Every detail, no matter how small, had been carefully choreographed by her. From the choice of flowers at the crematorium, to the freshly laundered union jack that was draped over the coffin. She had also ordered the cars and was horrified when they arrived.

'They're Mercedes.'

'So?' I asked.

'That's a German car, isn't it? Your father hated the Germans, so do I for that matter. He spent five years fighting the Nazis.'

'And the next fifty years married to one,' I whispered to Trish.

'Bugger off and send me a Bentley,' she shouted at the funeral director. He looked at her and realised he was up against the forces of darkness. A Bentley was on our doorstep within ten minutes. That was when I got my second surprise. Mum had me next to her as a chief mourner.

'But . . . I hardly knew the bloke,' I wanted to shout. But I

kept quiet and took the starched, crisply folded lace hand-
kerchief from Mum, who had bought a dozen just in case,
and made a pretty good job of seeming upset while actually
admiring the young women from Dad's work who looked
great in black. Afterwards we went back for a ham tea at
Mum's and I wisely refused Trish's offer of a bottle of Jack
Daniel's. Mum gave me a bag full of Dad's clothes, which
she had already washed and ironed. I looked at them and
was horrified to see things that, while dated, were not dra-
matically different from the clothes that hung proudly in
my own wardrobe.

'He's a chip off the old block,' I overheard Mum saying to
an old aunt, gesturing towards me.

'Fuck no, anything but that,' I whispered to Trish and
dragged her and Charlie to the car to get away as quickly as
possible. I cheered myself up with the knowledge that Dad's
Chaplinesque moustache would be continuing to grow,
beyond the grave, unruly and unconstrained, and somewhere on another astral plane he was probably pissing off an
unsuspecting angel (or devil) by continually begging for a
pair of hairdressing scissors.

'Chopper, and now your dad. They say these things go in
threes. Who d'you think will be the next stiff?' Trish asked
with relish. I shrugged, blissfully unaware that the stress
and strain of my demoralised life was about to make me
evens favourite in the 'Next Stiff Handicap'.

Sixteen

Over the next few days I didn't have too much time to dwell on death and dying because I was too busy going stark-raving mad. Grief and stress piled up on me like junk mail in a holidaymaker's letterbox and I was already several stops past sanity on the mad bus to La La Land. I had no idea what my reaction to Dad's death would be, and when it came it wasn't what I expected. It wasn't guilt, or pain or even sadness, it was more a feeling of being cheated.

'You feel cheated because now you'll never get your revenge. It's a classic symptom,' Churchill said.

'Revenge?'

'Yep. You wanted to teach the old bastard a lesson.'

'I think you may be right.'

'Well that's a first. You must be ill.'

He was right. It was about revenge. I wanted it badly and the trouble was I was fast running out of people to take it out on. Frank Lardis was the only obvious available target, particularly as he was increasingly making more extreme demands on my frazzled mind. I went into work the week after Dad's funeral and he took the opportunity to give me advice drawn from the depths of his maladjusted experience.

'Seems like everyone you know is dying, Willy son. You must be hanging out with the wrong kind of people,' he snorted derisively. In his world death was a sign of weakness – only losers died.

'You could take advantage of the Swansong Staff Counselling Scheme if you wanted to,' he suggested, making it clear that taking this course of action would be seen as proof that I was actually a big girl's blouse trapped in a man's body. I refused the offer with a butch 'I'm OK, it's only my dad who's died, I'll soon get another one' shake of the head.

'Good man,' he said, slapping me hard on the back to show manly approval in an overtly non-sexual kind of way.

'How are your ideas for profile raising getting on?' he asked, neatly changing the subject and indicating that I was never to discuss death or any other personal details with him again.

'Great. Good. OK,' I lied badly.

'I've had a thought I'd like to send on open-top motorcade past your book depository and see if it draws any pot shots from the grassy knoll,' he said. I tried to look vaguely interested, which was hard.

'In short, an open day. But no ordinary open day, this will be a VIP charity gala open day.' He described it as if he expected the idea to provoke me into both incontinence and premature ejaculation. It had quite the opposite effect, but I feigned interest as my only idea for profile raising involved a strategically placed explosive device in the building. I nodded in an 'I'm impressed' sort of way.

'We get big star names to attract the media.' He expanded on the idea, as if reminding himself out loud what a clever boy he was. I saw him start rubbing his hands in the way sad bastards do when they can't openly fiddle with their privates.

'Someone like . . .?' I asked. He was unable to contain himself.

'Someone like . . . royalty.' It was obvious that his thought processes had reached the outer limits of their range.

'Royalty?' I queried in a 'what royalty would come to this pissing dump?' voice. 'What royalty would . . . you have in mind?' I asked.

'Well . . . I haven't thought that through yet. Give me your input,' he asked in the shameless way men in power do when they hope you may be able to do some of the hard work for them. I recognised this approach because I'd used the technique hundreds of times. I paused, pretending to give the question serious thought and then, from the murky recesses of my insanity, an idea was born. It was only the merest outline of a sketchy plan but it was the beginnings of a seed of an idea for revenge. I struck.

'How about Princess Tonya?' I suggested nonchalantly.

'The Punk Princess of Q'wmcuat?' he said, giving away the fact that he never read the *Daily Telegraph* he brought in to work every day, but instead borrowed the residents' more salacious newspapers, the ones which happened to feature photos of young girls who habitually wore their swimsuits back to front. 'It might work,' he mused.

'You want a more positive, less elderly image for this place? There's your theme.'

'What theme?'

'Punk. What's more associated with youth than punk?'

'Punk?' The fact that Frank had switched on his echo chamber was proof he was now putty in my increasingly expert fingers.

'It's simple. The sons and daughters who are putting their relatives into homes like Crowe House were punks in the '70s. The theme would appeal to them. Princess Tonya, the Punk Princess, and . . .' I paused to make sure I had him well and truly hooked, 'we could have Kirk St John, the Punk Chef. I think I can get him,' I bragged.

'I know I can,' Frank bragged back, with several container loads more braggadocio than me.

'You can?' I was surprised by his confidence. Frank was no longer putty in my hands but quick-drying cement that was gluing my fingers together.

'Yes, Kirk is a close friend. He's also a major shareholder in Swansong. I'll put the word out. I'm sure he'll be more than happy to promote a Swansong product. Thanks for your input.'

So now I knew that Kirk owned part of Swansong. Just as I was putting together a plan for revenge, what should happen but dear old Kirk comes along and offers himself as a clear target for my mad scheme. There were many questions that I needed the answers to. How long had he been involved in Swansong? Had he been pulling the strings behind the scenes all this time? I had to know more and the VIP Charity Gala Open Day was the perfect opportunity to find out.

Frank Lardis was so happy with my plan for a punk theme to the open day that he now renamed it his plan. He put me on to operational duties (i.e. doing his job) while he set about organising the event (i.e. phoning round a few caterers and inviting all his friends from the squash club). I was now doing my job, Mr Airdrie's job and Frank Lardis's job. But I didn't mind because while he was out grabbing the glory I would use the opportunity to develop my plan for revenge. How I was going to subvert things I wasn't sure, but I was confident that some brilliant idea would emerge from the dark, dangerous swamp of my psyche.

Princess Tonya was happy to be guest of honour at the luncheon for which Kirk had already agreed to prepare the food. If he had any concerns about my involvement in the event, he didn't express them, partly because he needed to bathe regularly in the full glare of the media that would almost certainly follow two such notable guests, and partly because he had long since given up worrying about what I might think, say or do. Likewise corporate sponsors didn't worry about me, and they were also aware of the publicity opportunities such an event provided, and queued up to be wildly overcharged for the honour of being invited.

'What about the residents?' I asked Frank as the VIP Charity Gala Open Day began to take shape.

'What about who?' he asked, looking up from personally signing a pile of gold leafed invitations.

'The people who live here. Do they have a role in the open day?'

'Of course they do, Willy, old son. I was only thinking about this knotty little problem last night. How can we encourage a culture in which involvement flourishes? [Without wishing to unleash the forces of anarchy, of course.] The residents must play an integral part in the day, except for those who, shall we say, have delicate stomachs and who may produce potentially embarrassing bodily reactions to the excellent cuisine. They must be shipped out to the Magnolias for the duration. Those with high standards of personal hygiene can help out, taking coats, serving drinks, showing people to their seats, that kind of thing. It will prove our belief in people never outliving their usefulness. Unless they dribble, of course. It'll be good for our caring image. I'll leave those details to you. Make it so.'

Left alone with this task I took up residence in Frank's office (which used to be my office) and set about trying to gain access to his private filing cabinet, the one he'd moved in on his first day and which had remained locked shut ever since. I spent several days with a bent paper clip trying to pick the lock but to no avail. It was as if it contained my personal holy grail and was destined to remain impenetrable. In the fortnight leading up to the Open Day I was kept pretty busy with the task of transferring the residents to the Magnolias. Most of them were so confused they believed it was due to the danger of V2s falling on the area, and that the evacuation would be over as soon as Hitler was defeated. They found the whole exercise quite exciting so I didn't disappoint them by telling them the truth.

'There's nothing more upsetting to the aristocracy than ugly old people,' Churchill said with his usual Greek chorus accuracy. I couldn't be bothered to try to defend something that was so obviously indefensible. Instead I transferred him with them to provide additional support and so get him out of the way. I didn't need his pricks to my conscience complicating the matter of exacting bloody revenge on my sworn enemies.

'A thought for you, Churchill, old mucker,' I said in my best Frank Lardis impersonation, which would probably have fooled his mother if he hadn't already sold her, 'continuity. The residents need continuity. So fuck off out of my way and give it to them.'

The day of the Open Day was clear and bright. Winter was clocking off and spring was smoking a last fag at the gates before coming in to work. The front of Crowe House had been transformed from a grey ex-municipal old people's home into a fairy-tale castle. Unfortunately it was a fairy-tale castle that had taken as its inspiration a grey ex-municipal old people's home. A canvas portico had been erected over the entrance hall to give it a glamorous Hollywood-premiere feel, but to my untutored eye it looked like something borrowed from a scout camp, the latrine tent maybe. There was a roll of red carpet unfurled down the disabled access ramp to welcome our esteemed guests, and several barrels of lavender-scented essential oil had been poured down the corridors to try to hide the smell of piss. It now smelled like the toilet facilities of the annual convention of 'Lavender Drinkers Anonymous'. Lurking in the hall was Frank Lardis. It was difficult to tell the difference between him and the usual mad geriatrics who lurked there in order to pester visitors. He was wearing an expensive dinner suit and bow tie.

He looked like a penguin. Both the Antarctic sea bird and the chocolate biscuit.

I was wearing one of my dad's old suits which made me look faintly embarrassing. This was the whole idea, and even Charlie had pointed at me and called me a twat. I had to agree. I looked like someone who had been living in the care of the community for far too long. I wandered around trying not to recognise anyone, and failed miserably. Every minor celebrity who had appeared on a day-time chat show at some time in the last two hundred years was there, parading in front of the media circus like greedy seals after a herring. It was a charity event but most of the people were there for reasons that were far from charitable. They were there to network and show the TV people that they weren't dead but merely languishing in provincial theatre or doing voiceovers for adverts. The concept of charity was a new one on most of them and one they felt as comfortable with as a grass snake feels with a mongoose. What was the point of helping people who were worse off than themselves? If they weren't getting paid for it then they were going to make sure they got something useful out of the dreadful experience. Consequently, they spent every moment seeking out cameras and giving them their well-practised professional poses. Every flashgun was a potential career opportunity. I decided to abandon my own charitable thoughts and embark on a single-handed campaign to drink all the oak-aged Chardonnay specially imported for the occasion from South Eastern Australia.

Kirk was already in the kitchen area surrounded by the paraphernalia of television as he and several dozen underlings prepared dinner for two hundred. The usual dining-room tables had been removed and long teak tables with matching chairs had replaced them. White linen cloths covered the dining tables, and silver cutlery and cut-glass had been carefully laid on them. Candles burned everywhere and were complemented by the banks of television lights. It was a beautiful sight. The kitchen staff, from Saint's, all wore base-ball caps and yellow sweatshirts with green trousers which even next to my seriously outdated suit looked totally ridiculous. In the centre of the kitchen was an enormous cake. It was iced in the green and yellow of Swansong colours and had plastic models of two people on the top. One was using a walking frame, the other was in a wheelchair.

'Great innit? Keep your eye on that cake, it's going to be bloody brilliant,' Kirk said as he saw me staring open-mouthed at the transformation. Without waiting for an answer, he moved away to grasp the hand of the local MP. I went off in search of something to do, like causing serious damage to Kirk's car, but unfortunately found Frank Lardis, who was looking to give me something to do.

'Willy, young man. I hope you are being vigilant. Keep an eye on things, particularly old things, know what I mean? I don't want any embarrassing mishaps with the geriatrics. There's a lot riding on this.' Such as your job, he implied.

Maurice Marlowe was holding a tray of medium-sweet sherry into which he was gently dribbling. He hadn't managed to interest anyone in a glass yet and seemed to have forgotten that he was even holding a tray. I took three glasses off him and knocked them back.

'Don't I know you?' he asked blankly.

Ralph Crowe had flown in specially from his home in Jersey and he had a woman companion with him but it wasn't Hen. Except that it was. I could barely recognise her. Gone was the bowed head which belied a deep sense of insecurity, the brittle laughter designed to please, the aggressive anxiety of someone who needed to control everything around them. Even her dried-out hair, once dyed and home permed to almost complete destruction, had been replaced by a full head of chestnut brown, which glistened with a very expensive and professionally applied sheen. She had become an assured, confident-looking woman, conversing easily and meeting everyone's gaze equally. Everyone's except mine. Mine she swept past without so much as a moment's pause. I was past tense, history, I didn't exist, at least not while Ralph was around. Ralph took her arm and led her off on a tour of inspection of the nice bits of the building. It would be a short tour.

'I did used to work here, you know,' she told him, without any attempt to hide her irritation at being dragged away.

I went back to the office and had another surreptitious go at the lock of Frank's filing cabinet. That was when the blend of Chardonnay and sherry hit me and I took a metal bar from a dismantled walking frame in the corner and levered the draws open. As the lock broke, it made an accusing clank. I shrugged my 'it was an accident' shrug which wouldn't have convinced a fellow mason with a gullible streak and began to look through Frank's private files.

There seemed little to learn. There was a file containing minutes of the Swansong board meetings, which were clearly the combined work of the three wise monkeys. Kirk's name was mentioned occasionally, but it was hard to make out whether he had any direct influence on day-to-day business or not. The only thing I noticed was that Noel Davis, a senior director with an obscenely young and dangerously pretty wife, had walked out of the company three months after Kirk first arrived. Reading between the lines it appeared that Kirk had suffered a recurrence of his old amnesiac condition, the one where he kept leaving his dick in other people's wives.

There was an empty file dedicated to 'Strategic Planning' which showed the nearest Swansong came to strategic planning was to say that if it makes money we'll do it. Kirk was a director of Swansong but I couldn't work out from the scant information available whether he was active on the board or not. He certainly took his duties as a sleeping director seriously. Mrs Davis was proof of that. But the worst I could accuse him of was self-interest, which wouldn't come as much of a surprise to anyone who'd seen his show.

I reached D and found a thick file marked Doncaster across which Frank had hand-written 'Extremely Private and Very Confidential'. In it were receipts from a coach company, correspondence from half-a-dozen estate agents and several building societies, all dating from around the time when Hen had left and I had got the job as Officer in Charge.

From what I could work out it fitted together like this. In the mid 1980s, the planned electrification of the main railway line to Doncaster opened up the possibility (stupid though that reality would be) of commuting daily to London. It was boom-time down in the capital and house prices were at a premium. Confidence was high despite the fact that Wham! were saying goodbye to the world. In Doncaster, house prices were about the same as a bag of sugar until a group of men so shady they could have backed Cliff Richard bought up three hundred or so houses through several different estate agents for next to nothing on mortgages almost as cheap. They then ferried dozens of people in coaches from London to Doncaster every weekend for a month or so. These people may have been friends, acquaintances or total strangers dragged off the street and given a tenner for a day out up north. The one thing they had in common was their Londonness. Word of mouth soon spread and suddenly everyone was shouting, Londoners are coming! What was more, the Londoners were apparently buying up every house in town and paying ridiculous prices for them. Everyone started buying houses in order to make a killing when the cockneys came knocking. The shadowy group of men waited for the market to rise, and rise and rise and then, when it seemed to have reached an Everest-like peak, they sold. Profits were three, maybe four hundred per cent. Soon after they had sold up all their properties, the market realised that even yuppies weren't stupid enough to sit on a train for four hours a day and promptly did the decent thing and collapsed.

It was thin, and Kirk wasn't heavily implicated, so I didn't stop at Doncaster. I went on a further half an inch to where the next file lay. This one was named Dubbin and had 'Top Secret' written on it in Frank's self-important handwriting. It revealed that Ken Dubbin hadn't secretly left after being unmasked as a thief and sexual pervert as I had assumed at the time. He'd been bought off. There in the file was proof, a copy of a letter setting out the details of the agreement to pay him and the conditions to ensure his silence. The letter was on 'Kitchen Sink Revolution Plc' headed notepaper, Directors K. St John and R. Crowe, Company Secretary F. Lardis. Ken had been given ten thousand pounds to disappear; they'd even given him a new identity and supplied glowing references to help him get established. The new identity was William P. Wrose. The room wobbled around me like a bad special effect in a low-budget movie. I left the office and went downstairs in search of more alcohol.

Two more bottles of Chardonnay safely in my possession I went upstairs again where I found Maurice Marlowe. He'd been released from his dribbling duties by a horrified Frank Lardis and was now asleep in front of the lunchtime edition of *Home and Away*. I explained what I wanted him to do.

'But I'm an embarrassment. That's what Lard Arse said. Not allowed downstairs today because I'm a disgusting old man. The heartless bastard.'

I reassured him that disgusting and embarrassing was just what I wanted, and led him out into the corridor. It was quiet apart from the occasional cough and somewhere a confused resident shouting something about the war. I pushed Maurice towards the lift. As we entered it, he looked at me.

'Take it up as far as it'll go, I want to see if there is an afterlife,' he said. I could see that in the Marlowe head it was a Bank Holiday Monday and his senses had gone to the seaside for the day.

Downstairs we bumped into Hen, who seemed to be look-ing for someone. She gave me a smile that was surprisingly friendly. Ralph Crowe was nowhere to be seen.

'How are you?' she asked.

'Don't ask.'

'Oh dear. Tell me, do you see anything of Gina these days?'

'No.' I restrained myself from adding 'Thank God.'

'She's not here with Kirk, but that's no surprise,' she said bitterly. 'I must look her up while I'm in the area.' She looked over to where Ralph had just appeared and was bossily beckoning her with a long insistent forefinger. She sighed. 'Gotta go. Nice talking to you.' I couldn't detect any obvious hint of sarcasm in her voice. She went over to where Ralph was waiting for her to join him at the hip. Although I was pissed and starting to see double, I still noticed that even though they got very close Hen made sure she didn't actually touch him.

Princess Tonya arrived with Prince Ijaz. She was wearing another short skirt. This one was brown and orange tartan and had a large padded bustle. It had a matching jacket; underneath this she wore a netting top which was daringly see-through.

'It's a Westwood,' exclaimed a breathless press woman who royal-watched for a living. Lady Tonya's underwear wasn't Westwood, because she wasn't wearing any. She had commissioned her favourite designers to come up with cre-ations that covered everything for when she visited Q'wmcuat. Some compromise had been made in deference to her recent and very public conversion to Islam, but it was of the finest lace and was as see-through as her blouse. She waved to the crowds of onlookers who had been drawn to the spot by the heady combination of minor celebrities and television cameras.

Frank Lardis welcomed her and quickly handed her over into the care of Ralph Crowe. The success of his career depended on not hogging any more of the limelight than was actually necessary. His primary role that day was to make sure the honoured guests didn't see anything that might offend them, such as an old person.

'Hiya,' Tonya said, in a tone that was the only bright thing about her. 'Smells funny in here, dunnit?' She slipped into her fake Essex accent that had made her the darling of the under-privileged classes.

Maurice and I elbowed our way through a sea of minor celebrities who were all talking about themselves, unaware or unconcerned that no one was actually listening to them. After hearing about two dozen of their potted autobiographies, Maurice and I reached the kitchen where an impromptu press conference was being set up. The press were gathered around Kirk, who had been joined by Princess Tonya. He was stirring empty pans solely for the benefit of the cameras and she pretended to taste the non-existent results. I stood at the back of the crowd and waited for my moment.

'Why were you so keen to come here?' a journalist asked without looking up from her notebook. 'Isn't it true that since your marriage to Prince Ijaz you've been resting from public engagements?'

'Nah. Kirky is the reason. He's such a blast. I really admire his art.' She paused, searching for the bite-sized quote that might get her into tomorrow's dailies. 'I think he's stonking marvellous and I love him to bits.' The crowd of corporate ticket holders who stood behind the press pack gave her a spontaneous burst of supportive applause.

'What about you, Kirk?' a fawning scribe asked.

'This is about morphic resonance, you know. All these caring people is like a force field of communal energy. It's psychic.' Kirk's well-rehearsed gobbledegook was part of a deliberate strategy to expand into the New Age markets. 'I love these people.' He waved at the minor celebrities who were too busy loving themselves to notice. 'They call me the

"Punk Chef" and this is to show I'm a punk who still has
some spunk.' The crowd seemed to part to make way for the
look he shot at me. As I met his eye, he winked a wink
which made a sound like a rusty trap-door shutting. That
wink showed me that I knew that he knew everything about
me and my life. What was more he knew that I knew that he
knew.

I shoved Maurice.

'Now, Maurice.'

'What, old boy?' He was still on an away-day with the
fairies.

'Ask them about Dubbin, Maurice. Like we rehearsed.'

'Dubbin?' Maurice Marlowe asked, looking at his scuffed
boots. 'I prefer dark tan.' This was hopeless. I tried another
tack.

'Ask them about Doncaster then.' The mention of an
English town brought some semblance of recognition into
Maurice's eyes.

'What about Doncaster, you heartless bastard?' he
shouted at Kirk in his best stage voice.

The crowd turned slowly towards him.

'What *about* Doncaster?' one of the nearest journalists
asked.

Maurice raised himself to his full height and commanded
the room. 'Bloody awful place. The Mayor wrote to the
German High Command and asked them to bomb it . . . I
stayed in digs there once, '57 it would have been, no '58, I
remember because . . .' The rest of this soliloquy, which
would undoubtedly have ended with a reference to some
long-dead heartless bastard who had done him down, was
drowned out by the sigh of fifty journalists all thinking 'Oh
no, it's one of the old nutters, who let him in?' Kirk looked
vaguely perturbed but then the same newswoman who had
identified Princess Tonya's dress stood up.

'Tonya. Is there any truth in the rumours of a rift between
you and your hairdresser?' At this Ralph Crowe appeared

from nowhere and took charge. He put his arm around Princess Tonya in a friendly, but not too friendly way, and guided her into the dining room. Meanwhile Maurice was now in the kind of form that had put Music Hall out of its misery.

'And now a farmyard impression. Get off that fucking tractor. I thank yooouu!'

At that moment a wobbly fanfare began to play over Frank Lardis's personal address system and everyone settled down to see what would happen next. Attention focused on the green and yellow cake. There was the sound of a struggle, followed by panting and then, finally a woman in a tight-fitting swimsuit with a sash across her chest burst out of the top. The crowd went 'Aarrh'. The sash read: Swansong – Caring for a Generation. The woman, now desperately out of breath, was Dolly Watkins, eighty-seven years old and a resident of Crowe House for the last six. She smiled at the camera and then rubbed her back.

'About time. I've been in here two effing hours. My back is buggered,' she said. Behind me Frank Lardis appeared.

'It went off all right then?'

'Dolly Watkins? How could you?'

'She wanted to do it, she practically begged me. It's perfect publicity, think about it, Swansong makes you feel so young. Anyway don't thank me, thank the man who had the thought and made it real.' He nodded towards Kirk who was at that moment approaching us on a collision course. He walked between Frank, Maurice and me and managed to shove all three of us roughly aside at the same time.

'I've got two hundred chocolate batter puddings to prepare,' he said, like a bomb disposal expert who'd just had an urgent call to an enemy minefield. 'And I could do without selfish spoilers like you getting in my way.'

'How could you do that?' I asked, pointing to where Dolly had her Lycra costume pulled to one side and was asking a horrified breakfast TV weather girl to rub embrocation on her thigh.

'I can do that because people do what I tell them,' Kirk said matter-of-factly.

I felt terrible. My face was hot, I couldn't get my breath and my chest ached. Kirk seemed to lurk in every corner of my life, like a poisonous cobweb, waiting to catch me and wrap me up for dinner. Then dinner started. A man in a red jacket called everyone through to the dining room, and shortly afterwards the queue for the Ladies' toilets built up as young women took their turn to regurgitate the high calorific content of their stomachs, which had been lovingly prepared by Kirk and his staff. I didn't feel hungry and instead went and hid in my favourite surrogate womb, the upstairs laundry cupboard, to try to find some sanity. It didn't do much good, although the bottle of sherry I took with me helped. Feeling more pissed than pissed off, I was snuggling up to a pile of incontinence pads when I heard a ghostly echo in my head. It was Kirk's voice.

'Come here and give it to me,' he ordered. I stood up and shook my head to make sure I was awake. I was so drunk it made me feel sick, which I took as a sure sign of consciousness.

'Sort me out. I know it's what you want and you know it's what I need,' he said, taunting me. The words were inside yet also outside my head. They were all around me. I risked a more gentle head-shake and then took another swig of sherry. Fortified I went in search of Kirk. If he wanted a final showdown then I would give him one.

I couldn't find him anywhere in the milling crowds downstairs and, assuming he'd left after the meal, I went back to Frank's office. If nothing else, I would at least write out my resignation and shove it up Frank's arse. As I closed the door behind me I realised I was not the only one present in the dimly lit office. Kirk was sitting behind the desk, the desk that was now Frank's and had once been mine.

Except that I knew it was really Kirk's because he owned it all.

'What do you want?' he asked, looking part guilty and part dreamy.

'Who do you think you are?'

'What?' He closed his eyes and I thought he'd gone to sleep.

'Tell me,' I shouted. He opened his eyes lazily.

'I'm someone who can make or break people like you, Billy. Want an example? I got you this job. How's that?'

It was my turn to say what.

'What?'

'When we took this place over, I made you Officer in Charge so that no awkward questions would be asked about Dubbin. Oh Christ. Want another example? I told Hen to marry you, and she would have done if she hadn't got a better offer from Ralph. Shame really, she'd have been better for you than that stupid tart you ended up with. I mean, she was all right for a quick one but I wouldn't have wanted her to meet my friends. Oh Yes. What's the matter, Billy mate, surprised? Surely you didn't think an idiot like you would make it on your own merit.'

'I don't believe you,' I said, but I did. For the first time ever I knew he was telling me the truth.

'Get real, get sorted and get on with your work.' He closed his eyes again and smiled.

I wanted to tell him that he was a dishonest, nasty, crooked, cheating little shit. I wanted to spit in his face and devastate him with my brutal wit. I wanted to knock his fucking head off with a wicked right hook, after first having slashed his conceit with a perfectly honed blade of verbal criticism. But instead I settled for a goldfish impression. It was a good one mind, one of my best. I would have won countless holiday-camp competitions with it. My mouth opened and closed and in between it made nice round O shapes. But nothing came out, not a single insult or witty barb. Not even a grunt with a faintly sarcastic edge. The moment of truth had come and instead of rising to the occasion I had crumpled. I had become my dad, worse, compared to my dad I had become a tongue-tied mute with the vocabulary of an ant. Mum had been right when she'd said at Dad's funeral that I was a chip off the old block. At that moment I wished it was me that was dead.

Kirk still looked glazed, but it was nothing to the glaze that the Chardonnay and sherry had given me so I didn't pay it much attention.

'Bastard,' was all I managed to say after what seemed like several years of silence.

'Oh no.'

What sort of reply was that? I thought. The arrogant git was really playing with me now.

'Oh yes, oh yes. You ought to be thanking me, you know.' He was sounding more odd every time he spoke.

'Thanking you?'

'I've given you everything. I gave you your chicken-shit career, I even gave you one of my cast-off women to play happy families with. What more do you want? Oh Yessss.' He closed his eyes for a couple of seconds and then looked at me again. 'Oh Nooo. I was always the clever one, the one with the talent, not you. You were just a small-minded, small-thinking nobody. Now fuck off and leave us . . . oh my God.'

'What?'

'Jesus, oh God, oh Jesus, oh Christ, oh yes.' He was looking really flushed and despite everything I began to worry that he might be dying or something.

'Leave us alone.'

'Us?' I asked. He moved his hands to his lap. That was when I noticed it. It had been there all the time but in the gloom, concentrating on the face of the one I hated so much, I'd missed it. In his lap was a head. A blonde head. A blonde female head and it was moving. Up and down. To be more precise it was Princess Tonya's head and, unless I was very much mistaken, she was just finishing off giving him a blow job. I exploded with anger and frustration at about the same moment that Kirk exploded with passion and lust. I turned away from the bizarre scene in front of me and left the office, the building, the remainder of the VIP Charity Gala Open Day and my job. I could still hear Kirk's voice echoing all around me as I left, taunting me, haunting me, killing me. I thought about Kirk and Tonya. A blow job by royal appointment. He would probably end up as King Kirk. I couldn't bear it.

What I didn't know was that I wasn't the only one who was being taunted by Kirk's voice. I didn't know that Frank Lardis had left his personal address system switched on after the fanfare for Dolly Watkin's cake walk. I should have known, because although he loved to surround himself with executive toys, Frank would have had difficulty understanding how a wooden brick worked. I'd seen the red light blinking when I'd confronted Kirk in the gloom, but as Frank's office was full of blinking lights on a multitude of useless gadgets I'd paid no attention to it. I'd wanted everyone to know much I hated Kirk and thanks to the personal address system they now did. Not that the assembled press and honoured guests gave a shit about me or about how my life had been unfair and how Kirk had been personally responsible for most of that unfairness. They all knew life was unfair and that was why they didn't intend to end up in a shitty hole like Crowe House. But what they did give a shit about was the sound of Princess Tonya swallowing throatily, Kirk saying she gave better head than a pint of Guinness, and their intimate little chat over a post-oral-sex joint, before Kirk said 'Ciao, Babe', zipped up his fly and left out the back door for his next pressing engagement at the supermarket.

As Kirk and Tonya's indiscretion unfolded on the state-of-the-art high-tech personal address system, fifty-seven journalists heard it and imagined their grateful editors shaking their hands and whispering promises of promotion in their ears. Ralph Crowe heard it and saw his fortune going down a big hole marked DRAIN. Frank Lardis heard it and was pleased to note that the digitally produced sound quality had a crispness that practically put the listener in the room with the lovers. Maurice Marlowe heard it and thought it was the voice of Jesus. Prince Ijaz heard it and thought of medieval torture instruments, and on which parts of Kirk's body he would particularly like to deploy them.

Oblivious to all this, I walked aimlessly around the outskirts of Bradworth for a couple of hours and then, completely and utterly pissed off with everything, not least myself, I decided to do something useful and go shopping. With a heavy heart, I set off for the safe haven of the supermarket, unaware that, for me, it was about to become an unsafe haven.

Seventeen

Physically and mentally shattered by events at the VIP Charity Gala Open Day, my trip to the supermarket didn't help, given the presence there of Kirk, the one person who was largely responsible for my poor state of health. The shock of this unexpected encounter having struck me dead at Kirk's feet in the main aisle of the supermarket, I entered the next world via an all-white room. It had white tiles from floor to ceiling and they shone in an ethereal way. The room was chilly, which I took to be a good sign. A man was leaning over me. He was also dressed in white. He wore a white snood on his head, a white suit, and white boots, but he smiled at me with brown teeth.

'Are you all right?' It seemed a stupid question to ask a dead man.

'Who are you?'

'I'm Mr Jordan.'

It was just like in the film, and the remake of the film. It was all happening exactly how I'd always imagined it would.

'You're an angel, Mr Jordan.'

'Thanks very much, but I'm just doing my job.'

'So this is heaven.' I looked around at the neutral, sterile whiteness. It was very traditional but not very interesting.

'No, this is cold store. We brought you in here because you were embarrassing the customers and disrupting Mr St John's signing session. This is Mr Armstrong.' He pointed to a figure of a man who was so large he could do nothing else except loom. Permanently typecast, he accepted his role and loomed over me in what was an award-winning performance.

'He's in security. When you feel a bit better he wants to talk to you about the attempted shoplifting of a frozen chicken.'

'You mean, I'm not dead?' I asked, genuinely disappointed. 'One little thing and I can't even get that right.'

The doctor arrived and gave me a thorough examination, listened to my tales of distress and paused for thought. After a while he decided on a diagnosis.

'You're obviously suffering from severe anxiety, and you've also witnessed some terribly stressful events recently, such as the death of your close friend and also your father.'

I tried to think who he meant by my close friend and then I realised he meant Chopper. I smiled for the first time in weeks.

'This cocktail of despair would be enough to knock most people sideways. However, if you combine that with the effects of having a frozen chicken inside your jacket for twenty minutes, as you did, then I think we may have the complete explanation for your collapse.'

'The bastards are still threatening to press charges for the chicken, you know,' I said, able to bristle with indignation despite my poor state of health.

'Well, anyway, go home, relax and try not to worry.'

'How does one become a doctor?' I asked, with enough sarcasm to cut through a cheap steak. Released from his care

242   Jon Wright

with undue haste, I went out into the car park to admire the glory of a March evening so drab and grey it could have been the influence for men's suit design for generations. Inside the supermarket, Kirk was still writing his name for fun and profit, all memory of my demise forgotten as he basked in the adoration of his rapturous fans.

On the way home, still unsettled by the day's incidents but feeling a little peckish, I pulled into the 'Merry Pig Out' family restaurant and service station and saw a maroon Range Rover which had the registration plate K1RKY. In it sat Gina and Hen. They were engaged in a kiss which had more tongue in it than my mum's Sunday tea. As I stopped, so Gina and Hen drove away and rejoined the main road without breaking off from the kiss. Several cars swerved to avoid them – it was the kind of kiss that no one dared interrupt. To see such unexpected passion didn't make me feel unhappy, and the more I thought about it and the more things fitted into place, the less unexpected it became.

I got home late. Trish was watching television.

'How was it? How was that bastard cook?' Trish asked, sipping her eighth glass of Cabernet Sauvignon. I told her all about my nightmare of a day. Then I told her all about my nightmare of a life, as revealed by Kirk.

'All I want is to make him a little bit sorry for the way he's behaved. That's all.'

'Bollocks,' Trish said sharply. 'You want to bury the fucker so deep he'll need an Australian passport.'

She was right of course, as usual. That was exactly what I wanted, what I'd always wanted. 'I hate him. He's got success, money, fame. And he's shagged most of the women on the planet.'

'Including me,' she said, faking wistfulness.

'Thanks for reminding me.'

'Well, there're lots of things about you he could be jealous of.'

'Jealous of me? Like what?'

Trish's right hook caught me on the chin. I'd never forgotten that she and Kirk had once been lovers, but I had managed to hide it away at the back of the dusty spare room of my mind.

'I'm the woman he lost, remember?'

'Yes, but apart from you, why else would he envy me?'

'Your creativity, your personality, the length of your dick. Lots of things.'

'The length of my dick?' I didn't even bother to disguise my glee at hearing this information.

'Oh God, I'd forgotten about male penis envy. I suppose this means you'll be strutting around like a cockerel for days,' she said wearily.

We looked at each other with something approaching lust. It was a look that parental responsibilities had ensured we hadn't shared for some time.

'Upstairs?' Trish asked.

'If we can make it that far.'

We made it as far as the landing. At which point Charlie woke up and demanded a glass of 'fecking' water. He got the water without much delay. We were both so pent up with months of sexual denial that a swift mutual climax was more certain than a hose-pipe ban in August.

'Some things never change,' I said shamefaced.

'We all need a constant in our lives,' Trish said, and winked, 'and premature ejaculation is as good as any.' She pulled up her tights and went off in search of a glass of water.

'Hey, super stud. Come down here. You've got to see this,' Trish bellowed upstairs. 'You're on the news.'

'The usual fawning over our local hero, I suppose?'

'No, something amazing has happened.'

'Is Kirk dead?'

'It's even more amazing than that.'

We watched the late-news bulletin together. They ran a piece on the VIP Charity Gala Open Day, showing shots of Princess Tonya's legs while Kirk could be heard saying that he cared deeply about the frail and vulnerable and that he wanted to put his money where his mouth was.

'Let's hope that isn't where Tonya's mouth was,' Trish said.

The bulletin made a vague reference to an international incident that was brewing as a result of Kirk's behaviour. We cheered and did oral sex mimes. It has to be said that Trish did a much more convincing one than me.

We sat up through the night drinking Russian vodka and thrilling to the bulletins as they grew in size and importance. By three a.m. the incident, still without any further details being given, had become a news special and replaced the advertised movie that had been waiting thirty-two years for the honour of being watched by a few thousand insomniacs. It was hinted that the as yet unspecified incident had proved deeply offensive for Prince Ijaz and the people of Q'wmcuat. There had already been a massive demonstration in Quassia, the capital of Q'wmcuat, led by the fundamentalist religious leaders who for years had been critical of the western lifestyle of the oldest son of their leader. This was their chance to rise up, ostensibly in support of Ijaz, while actually mounting a serious challenge to the decadent ways of the ruling family and so establish a true Islamic republic. It also gave them the chance to burn a few effigies of the British Foreign Secretary which they had kept in readiness for just this occasion. Unfortunately, the wait for an Islamic republic had been a long one and the Foreign Secretary they burned was Jim Callaghan, but the point was well made anyway. Rumours of death threats against unnamed individuals were spreading and as the breakfast news came on at seven a.m. the rumour was confirmed.

'The leading Mullahs of Q'wmcuat have issued a Fatwa

against Kirk St John for blasphemous and indecent behaviour with Princess Tonya that amounts to an act of apostasy. They urge the sons of the revolution to seek out the sinners and make them bow down and offer their blood to the one true God. The British Government has reacted swiftly and issued a counter statement.' The tired-looking news reader was replaced on the screen by a blotchy-faced minister in a dinner suit, who read a statement from what looked like the back of a napkin.

'The actions of the Q'wmcuat religious leaders are unfortunate, given our long and warm relationship with that country. This is particularly true given our recent agreement to supply the Q'wmcuat Airforce with military equipment and ground crews. We hope that this agreement will not be affected by this little local difficulty.'

'Fuck. A Fatwa. That's Kirk, only the best will do for him,' I said, whistling through my teeth.

'Do you think they'll send a crack death squad over to do him in?' Trish asked.

'If they do, they'll probably have been trained by British ground crews.'

'And firing British weapons.'

'Of course.' I warmed with pride at the thought of our boys and their equipment playing such an important role in world events.

The next morning, despite no sleep at all and an unhealthy amount of alcohol still in my veins, I went out and bought all the daily papers.

'There's nothing in this,' Trish said, holding up what Charlie had left of one front page after trying to make a boat out of it.

'That's the *Guardian*, it won't be in there.'

I pulled out the *Sun* from the pile on the kitchen table. Kirk and Tonya were front page news. 'Stop Oral Shoot!' it said.

The *Mirror* also had it on the front page. 'Star Chef – A Life in Taters?'

The *Star* had an old picture of Tonya holding a banana and smiling. 'Princess Gets Gobby And Kirk Islam Chop,' the headline read.

'You were wrong about the *Guardian*,' Trish said triumphantly. 'Government chooses relationship with Q'wmcuat over celebrity's safety,' she read, yawning as she did so.

Frank Lardis rang me later that day to enquire whether I had gone mad. I said that, on the contrary I felt well for the first time in months, years even, and that any madness I had suffered had now passed. Happy that I was fully fit, he then sacked me. I slammed down the phone. It immediately rang back at me.

'Two thoughts, Frank. Wanker and dead. You already are the first and if you ring me again you will be the second,' I said calmly into the receiver.

'Is that Mr Wrose?' It wasn't who I thought it was.

'It might be. Who is this?'

'Sorry. It's Dennis Emmanus, remember? Your friend Churchill gave me your number.'

'I told you to speak to Kirk.'

'No, I want you, we've had a change of heart.'

Dennis had gone back to the old scratched copy of 'That Was Zen But This Is Nous' that he'd been given by his recording engineer, who had always rated the band. Instead of 'Probably The Last Song I'll Write About Gina', he'd thought 'Sulphate Sex' was the one that had a rhythmic quality that would transpose best to a classical treatment. It was also one of the few songs on the album that was credited to me, even though I'd actually written them all.

'Did you mention royalties?' I asked, rudely interrupting his explanation of how the creative thought processes of a record producer worked.

'Oh, not a fortune, I'm afraid. There's twelve other tunes so you'll only get approximately 9.7 pence per copy.'

'Oh, is that all?'

'And there'll be a small one-off payment for giving us the idea. Mind you, the last one I did, "Seventies Bubblegum Goes Operatic" – you may have seen it, it had a naked woman covered in pink gum on the cover – that sold five hundred K.'

'What's five hundred K times 9.7 pence?' I asked Trish, as we drove towards Norfolk, where I was taking her and Charlie on a sentimental tour of the United States Air Force bases I had once nearly died in.

'Forty-eight thousand, five hundred pounds,' she answered without hesitation, showing the mathematical ability of one whose fingers had dipped into tills with the expertise of a Canadian Goose on a salt marsh.

'Fuck a duck,' I said.

'Fuck a duck,' Trish said.

'Feck a deck and shite a lite,' Charlie said, waking up from his nap.

A curious incident happened as we left Bronte Bridge. In a lay-by we passed Kirk. He was sitting in his cobalt-blue McLaren F1, the registration plates of which read NVY 1T. At that moment neither Trish nor I envied it. Kirk had just discovered that there was something wrong with his car, but had not yet discovered that the computer-controlled petrol cap had been wrenched off in the car park of the supermarket the night before, and person or persons unknown had pissed pure oak-aged Chardonnay and medium-sweet sherry into the petrol tank. Overnight, the petrol, fine wines and urine had separated but the sudden acceleration out of Bronte Bridge had stirred the mixture up and brought the car to a juddering and final halt. Kirk wasn't alone in the car. Four children, who were all in the early stages of hyperactivity, were clambering like manic mountaineers in the confined space of the expensive sports car. The fifth child was having a pre-teenage 'no one understands me' sort of sulk while sitting on the bonnet and kicking in the front lights. There were no signs of any swarthy middle-eastern hit squads in the vicinity, which at that moment Kirk might possibly have welcomed.

'From Billy Petrol to William Pistol,' I said, nodding at the helpless car.

'It has a nice symmetry to it,' Trish agreed. I told her about Gina and Hen and the kiss that stopped traffic that I'd seen the previous night.

'It makes you feel almost sorry for him. Kirk, I mean,' Trish said, without a trace of sympathy in her voice.

'Yes,' I agreed, pausing for a micro-second before going on. 'Well, that's enough feeling sorry for Kirk, let's turn our compassion to another form of amoebic dysentery.'

Later, as we sat watching a Stealth bomber land pretty unstealthily, Trish looked at me lovingly.

'You great hairy hole, tell me what you're thinking.'

'I was thinking, we're not rich but we could do something, I mean really do something with our lives.'

'Like what?'

'I don't know. Pay off the mortgage?'

'Or go around the world in a clinker-built yacht,' Trish suggested with a faraway look in her eyes.

'Do you want to do that?'

'Not really, I'm scared of drowning. And salt water really fucks up my hair.'

'Well, what then?'

'We could start by paying off the mortgage and then buy something totally wild and insane with what's left.'

'I'd say our mortgage is pretty wild and insane.'

We watched the planes take off and land for another hour or so while Charlie, exhausted after an intensive bout of baby-talk cussing, slept quietly in the back. Trish gave me one of those looks that usually ended up with us sweating under a duvet somewhere.

'You're a nice bloke, William Wrose.'

'And is that it? Is that what they'll say about me when I'm dead? William Wrose, he was a nice bloke. Bit dull but nice.'

'You'll always be my little punk rocker.'

'I suppose it could be worse.'

'I can think of much, much worse.'

'I'm sure you can,' I said, 'but not in front of our child, please . . . It's just weird.'

'What is?' she asked.

'Getting even. It's as if nothing has changed, not really changed.'

'Really, nothing?'

'Well, not unless you count . . .'

'Yes?'

'The fact that I feel fucking marvellous!'

We both laughed so hard I nearly drove the car into an ancient Norfolk ditch.

'Maybe what's happened in your life has happened because you chose it to happen. Maybe you'd be here with me, jobless and hairless, even if you'd never met Kirk.'

'Maybe,' I said, not convinced by the argument but grateful for her confidence in me.

She ran her long fingers through my unashamedly thinning hair.

'Today, not tomorrow. What do you say?' she asked. I looked at her and smiled at the memory of her wedding-day speech. She had the same dark-brown eyes, the same crooked teeth and lopsided smile, the same soothing effect on my body and soul. Only her hair showed any signs of the passage of time, having moved from coal-black to a more subtle shade of grey-black.

'Today,' I replied with feeling. 'As a reason for being it's as good as any. Today, and fuck yesterday and fuck tomorrow.'

We watched the sun sink in a glorious blaze behind the

badly camouflaged fuel silos which had FUEL SILOS written on them in bright orange letters. Our sense of romance fully sated, we drove towards the east coast in search of a fish and chip shop that would do the same for our stomachs.